Also by Joanna Scott

DE POTTER'S GRAND TOUR

"I'LL PUT A GIRDLE ROUND THE EARTH"

PUCK ESQ

De Potter's GRAND TOUR

Joanna Scott

FARRAR, STRAUS AND GIROUX   NEW YORK

Farrar, Straus and Giroux
18 West 18th Street, New York 10011

Printed in the United States of America
First edition, 2014

Library of Congress Cataloging-in-Publication Data
Scott, Joanna, 1960–
    De Potter's grand tour / Joanna Scott. — First edition.
        pages   cm
    ISBN 978-0-374-16233-7 (hardcover) — ISBN 978-0-374-71046-0 (ebook)
    1. Voyages around the world—Fiction.   I. Title.

    PS3569. C636D43 2014
    813'.54—dc23

                                                                2013048998

Designed by Abby Kagan

Farrar, Straus and Giroux books may be purchased for educational, business, or
promotional use. For information on bulk purchases, please contact the Macmillan
Corporate and Premium Sales Department at 1-800-221-7945, extension 5442,
or write to specialmarkets@macmillan.com.

www.fsgbooks.com
www.twitter.com/fsgbooks • www.facebook.com/fsgbooks

1   3   5   7   9   10   8   6   4   2

For Geri Thoma

To the Public

A JOURNEY AROUND THE WORLD is an important matter, involving considerable time and expense, and should therefore be carefully planned. In judging of a tour and its cost, one must consider the following points: comfort and luxury provided, the manner in which the trip is scheduled, what countries are included, whether each country is visited during the most desirable season, and finally, the length of the tour—whether too short or too long, or of agreeable duration.

My Grand Tour Around the World will be not only *first-class* in every particular but the best which that term, in its widest sense, implies. I have been preparing this tour for some time past, wishing to have all my plans fully matured so as to offer *the most enjoyable trip* ever made around the Globe. The appointments, travel, hotels, carriages, and sightseeing will be unsurpassed. Plan of travel throughout the tour will be such as to make it perfectly comfortable for ladies as well as gentlemen. In short, it will be a *voyage de luxe*, and in the conductorship of the party and the character of our arrangements, the best traditions of the De Potter Tours will be fully realized.

—A. DE POTTER

❈ PART ONE ❈

Constantinople

H E LEAVES EARLY on the morning of June 10, descending the carpeted stairs to the lobby of the Pera Palace Hotel. He rings the bell at the front desk. He is about to ring again when a clerk appears from the dark interior of a back office, looking freshly scrubbed, smelling of soap. The bill is settled swiftly, and the clerk is most obliging, despite his limited French, when Armand hands him two last letters addressed to Madame de Potter, care of the Hotel Royal in Toblach. The letters are to be held and posted, he specifies, on the twelfth. Does the clerk understand the instructions? "Oui, monsieur," the clerk says, setting aside the letters and motioning to a porter. He hopes Monsieur de Potter's most recent stay has been pleasant. The coach, he adds, is already in the drive.

Outside, Armand notices that the gas lamp above the entrance to the public garden is still lit, though the sky is already beginning to glow with dawn. He removes his spectacles and rubs the lenses with his handkerchief. After the porter has returned with his trunk and hoisted it onto the baggage rack, Armand tips him a handful of piastres and climbs into his seat. The driver slaps the reins to rouse his horses, and the carriage lurches forward.

Down they go from the summit of Pera, the wheels clattering over the uneven paving stones, the chassis rising and plunging, the horses moving so fast that a small dog doesn't have time to get out of their path. The yelp the dog lets out has a chillingly human ring, and Armand thinks it must have been crushed, yet when he turns, he is relieved to see it scramble out from between the rear wheels and run off, disappearing around a corner. The horses trot briskly on, undeterred.

He resists calling out to the driver to order him to slow down. Pulling his hat on tighter, he sits back and observes the scenery, contemplating the familiar landmarks as if from a great distance— the banks and restaurants he knows so well, and the convent where, two days earlier, the members of his party were delighted to come upon the dervishes right when they were beginning to whirl.

As they pass one of the white mansions housing an embassy, he is reminded of his father, who had been stationed abroad for nearly a decade—first in Paris, then Dakar, and lastly Constantinople. He supposedly worked as a manager for a Belgian trading company, but Armand, who was stuck back in East Flanders with his brother and stepmother, believed that his father was a spy, appointed by King Leopold to pry into the secret affairs of foreign governments. He used to tell himself that he, too, would be a spy someday and travel around the world.

You could say that he did become a spy of sorts, on a self-appointed mission to gather antiquities instead of secrets, with his travel bureau providing an excuse to visit places that were out of reach for other collectors. De Potter Tours is in the business of leading wealthy tourists around the world, and the De Potter Collection is on display at the University Museum in Philadelphia. It has been an honorable arrangement, he believes. It worked for more than a quarter of a century and would have gone on working if he hadn't grown so careless.

At least he managed to keep the Americans on his tour sufficiently entertained. They never guessed that he had anything else on his mind but their well-being as he shepherded them around the city. Even when he put them on the train and sent them off to Broussa without him, they were persuaded that he was sparing them a worse inconvenience. As far as they could tell, Professor de Potter was his usual amiable self, as reliable a guide as they'd been promised in the testimonials he included in his advertisements.

From Mrs. P. A. Saunders of Cincinnati: "It was a trip I shall ever remember with pleasure. Could I go abroad every year, my choice would be to go under the care of Prof. de Potter and with his party."

From the late Henry W. Bellows, D.D., of Albany: "I have great pleasure in saying that I am acquainted with Prof. A. de Potter. I do not doubt his trustworthiness and competency to conduct foreign tours in the interest of education, and I can heartily recommend him."

From HHW of Rome, New York: "There are various ways of traveling, many, as we do, independently and at the mercy of sharks, or in parties with a courier, or with a tourist agent. The only party that we have envied was that of Prof. Armand de Potter of New York, an unassuming gentleman, speaking nine different languages. To him we shall commend any friends in the future who wish to make a tour of the Old World."

The friends of HHW would have to find another guide, since Professor de Potter won't be conducting any more parties. Never again will he have to worry about making arrangements for packs of inexperienced tourists, keeping track of their tickets and explaining the sights. On this trip, he is traveling alone.

Down, down, down rolls the coach, past buildings fronted by broken terraces and wilted gardens, to the boulevard skirting the inlet of the Golden Horn. The low angle of the sun catches the top of a minaret on the opposite hill and turns the white to rose. On the surface of the water beside the road, the reflections of the plane trees look as though they are frozen in ice.

They reach the lot beside the customhouse, where Armand pays the driver and hires a handler for his trunk. The official greets him with a yawn, waving him through without asking him to open his satchel. On the quay, he takes out the gold-plated pocket watch his wife gave him on his thirty-ninth birthday and checks the time. It will be an hour or more until the ship is ready to receive passengers. There is nothing to do but wait.

Summit to Cannes

THREE YEARS BEFORE her husband disappeared at sea off the coast of Greece, Aimée de Potter sat at the dressing table in her stateroom on board the *Noordland*, fished her pencil from her purse, and opened her diary.

"May 17, 1902," she wrote.

She paused to reflect for a moment, then added, "Left Summit by 7:35 a.m. train." And paused again.

Odd moments from the day came to mind. She thought about blinking awake in the darkness of her bedroom of their rented house at 78 New England Avenue, stirring a sugar cube into her cup of tea at the station in Summit, walking with Victor and Armand up the gangway of the *Noordland*, and turning just as the porter behind her stumbled and nearly dropped the huge birdcage he was carrying into the water. She had caught sight of a white bird with a frothy plume inside the cage, and she'd almost mistaken its loud squawking for someone calling her name. In fact, she had heard her name right then—"Amy!"—being called out by an old family friend, Mrs. Murray, who stood on the pier wafting a lavender handkerchief above the crowd, pronouncing her name the way all her friends and family insisted on pronouncing it, no matter how often she had tried to correct them.

"Amy—here I am, over here!"

Hello, Mrs. Murray! Goodbye, Mrs. Murray! The de Potters were going abroad. There was nothing unusual in this—they went abroad every year. As far as Mrs. Murray knew, the de Potters were leading another of their famous High-End Excursions, this one a four-month jaunt through Northern Europe. And because she lived a short train ride away from the Hoboken pier, she had come to see them off.

"Bon voyage to you all! I'll meet you here in September!"

No, Mrs. Murray had better not plan on meeting them there in September, for this trip abroad wouldn't be like all the others. After they were done with this tour, they intended to stay on and look for property in the south of France, in the cosmopolitan town of Cannes, where there were plenty of English churches and a variety of clubs to join, roses bloomed year round, and the refreshing, salty wind was known to have a beneficial effect for men like Armand, who suffered from nervous headaches.

Aimée thought of her sister Leila, recently widowed and living alone with her youngest daughter up in Poughkeepsie. She hadn't been able to bring herself to tell Leila that she wouldn't be back anytime soon. And since she'd kept their plans a secret from her favorite sister, she couldn't tell the rest of her family and friends. Not even Victor knew what to expect. She was hoping he'd be happily surprised when he learned that they would be staying behind in France while the rest of the party returned to America. He associated France with bonbons, carousels, and seaside vacations. He might not be pleased to hear that he'd be starting at a French school in the fall, but he was a resilient boy and would settle in soon enough.

She didn't bother to include any of this in her diary. Nor did she take up space complaining that the corned beef at her first dinner on board tasted as if it had been boiled in seawater. She didn't describe Victor's squeal of delight at a hooded gull that caught a piece of bread he tossed in the air as the *Noordland* passed Sandy Hook. She didn't report that as she sat at the table deciding what else to write, Armand and Victor were across the stateroom paging through a book of nautical maps they'd found in the ship's library. She simply wrote, "Mrs. Murray came to see us off. Sailed at 10 a.m. on *Noordland* for Boulogne," then put the diary aside, retrieved her silver comb, and unwound her braid from its bun.

"To travel is to live," Armand declared in advertisements in his tourist magazine, and Aimée liked to recite the motto to herself as a reminder that the difficulties of traveling were far outweighed by the rewards. To travel is to live, indeed—and off they raced after landing on May 27, the Americans rushing to keep up with Armand while Aimée brought up the rear, lingering for an extra moment to make a hasty note in her diary so she would always know where she'd been in the world on every day of her life.

From Boulogne they went to Amsterdam. By June 10 Armand was leading the party through the streets of Copenhagen to see "the resplendent assembly of Apostles" at the Vor Frue Kirke, Aimée wrote in her entry for the day, quoting the short lecture her husband had given on the steps of the church. The next day they made the brisk passage across the sound from Helsingør to Helsingborg. In Christiania, Armand arranged a private tour of the Viking Ship, which pleased everyone, from Victor to Samuel Worthington, Esq., of Delaware, an irritable traveler whose mood steadily improved as they headed farther north. Ever since a passing storm had caused him to roll out of his bed on board the *Noordland* and sprain his wrist, Aimée was prepared to make an extra effort to placate him. But when they rode in carriages through the Valdersdal, between rows of weeping birch, Mr. Worthington didn't complain about the hard wooden seats. On the steamer up to the North Cape, he stood beside Aimée at the rail and blew a kiss at the glittering Svartisen Glacier. And he was the one who delivered the speech that night at dinner, thanking the de Potters for treating the members of the party to the unforgettable experience of seeing the midnight sun.

All in all it was a successful tour, thanks in large part to Mr. Worthington, who proved such an indomitable optimist that no other member of the party dared complain—not when their train traveling from Cracow to Kieff broke down and they were stuck for five hours in the sultry heat, or when they discovered that the Hôtel des Bergues in Geneva had lost their reservation, and they had to gather up all their luggage and move to the Hôtel Métropole, or even when Armand rose during their banquet in Lyon and announced a substitution in the program: *"Mesdames et messieurs*, ladies and gentlemen, Madame de Potter and I thank you for permitting us to share the delights of Northern Europe with you. Now it is my pleasure to inform you that the esteemed Monsieur Gastineau, assistant *directeur* of the Paris branch of the American Bureau of Foreign Travel, will be accompanying you back to the United States while my wife and son and I remain . . . *en France!"*

To Aimée's relief, no one in the party objected to the change. They all understood why the de Potters would want to stay in France and agreed that they would have done the same if they, too, had been free to start their lives over again.

But the de Potters weren't starting over, not exactly. Rather, they were nearing the culmination of the project they'd begun more than twenty years earlier and were ready to enjoy the prosperity that was the result of their hard work. They wanted what all their customers already had—a permanent abode for their child, a place to leave and to return to at the end of each trip. And if they were particular in their preferences—if a well-appointed residence in Albany or New York, Los Angeles, Pasadena, or even Summit, New Jersey, wouldn't do—it was because experience had taught them that they would thrive best in an environment that matched the sensibilities they'd been cultivating through, in Armand's words, "continuous exposure to the accomplishments of diverse civilizations." More simply, as Aimée wrote to Mrs. Murray to explain why they wouldn't be disembarking with the rest of their party at the pier in Hoboken, even those in the tourist profession deserve a home to call their own.

They moved to Cannes on October 5, 1902, into a rented villa on the chemin Prince de Galles. Aimée was woken early the next morning by doves roosting in the palm trees. She peeked into the adjacent bedroom and saw that Armand was still asleep, then she checked on Victor, who was curled like a cat on top of his bedspread in his own room.

Picking out her clothes from her closet, she enjoyed the awareness that she could take her time getting ready for the day. She moved slowly, as if she were testing her strength in the aftermath of a long fever. When she looked in the mirror, she saw a woman she would have envied if she'd been a stranger. True, her hair was dusted with a powdery gray, her forehead threaded with fine wrinkles. The skin beneath her chin had begun to sag. But her cheeks were still round and youthful, her lips were smooth, and the blue of her eyes was as bright as ever. As she fastened a string of pearls around her neck, she couldn't help feeling impressed by the obvious evidence of her poise. She was proud of her privileges even while she remained attentive to the needs of others. Admiring the reflection of a woman who had reached a station she hadn't known enough to aspire to when she was young, she felt as if she'd come to the end of a tour that had lasted for years and years, and she could finally relax and enjoy herself.

When they took Victor to his boarding school in Mandelieu the following week, Aimée assured him that he could come back at any time and attend the neighborhood school if he preferred. But he was so quick to make friends that it didn't occur to him to be unhappy. In his first letter he reported that he had a new best friend named Simon, who slept in the bed next to his, and a new pet, a lizard named Pegasus, who lived in a jar. In his second letter, he announced that he was the only boy in the class who had been inside a pyramid. Also, he'd caught another lizard, and now Pegasus had a companion.

Aimée wrote back on a postcard with a picture of the seaside boulevard de la Croisette on the front: "Dearest Victor, You make Papa and I very cheerful with your letters. Let us know if you need extra blankets. Our days have been quiet now that Papa isn't traveling so often. We take long walks and go to the flower markets. Papa will come on Friday at five o'clock promptly to bring you home for dinner. We send bundles of love, Maman."

She included a note at the bottom of the card: "PS—we like our villa so well that we have extended the lease another three months."

They celebrated Christmas with roast goose and plum pudding. In the early spring they began visiting properties for sale in the area. On Easter of 1903, wearing a spring costume made by a dressmaker in Nice, a pink, lacy affair with a tulle skirt and silk jacket and a hat crowned by a magnificent white feather that might have been plucked from the same bird the porter on the *Noordland* had almost dropped into the water, Aimée announced to the friends who had gathered for dinner that the de Potters would finally have a permanent home. After looking all across Cannes, they had purchased a seventeen-room villa on the avenue de Vallauris.

The Villa du Grand Bois had a swooping marble staircase leading to the front entrance, a white stucco façade crowned by a bracketed cornice, and two flanking towers, one encircled with three tiers of wrought-iron balconies. It had been closed up for two years and would need a good airing out. The garden was overgrown with borage and nettles. The basin of the fountain had cracked in half, and a stone nymph had fallen from its pedestal. But the top floor had a view of the sea, the perfume from the thick wisteria vines hung in the air, and when the de Potters first came through the front gate, the splash of afternoon light gave the villa the sheen of fine marble. They knew at once that they had to make this magnificent estate their own. They thought themselves especially lucky when the owner agreed to lower the price.

They moved in September, and by their anniversary in October they had the help of a full-time staff that included a cook, a maid, and a gardener. On November 20, the furniture and boxes they'd left in storage back in New Jersey arrived, and Aimée and Armand devoted themselves to unpacking. They set out the crystal, sorted through clothes, and repacked their woolens in their steamer trunks. While Armand organized his curios on the shelves of the fine gilt cabinet that had traveled with them from France to America and back to France, Aimée put their books and photograph albums in order in the library.

On November 26, Armand had a meeting at the bank all morning. As planned, Aimée met him for lunch at La Réserve in the center of Cannes. He was uncharacteristically late and arrived disheveled, with his coat open and his hat in his hands, as if he'd run all the way from the bank. But he said grandly, "*Ma chérie*, one day I shall prove myself worthy of your affection," kissing her gloved hand in his courtliest fashion. And later, when they were at Galleotti's furniture shop, he sprang out from behind a set of bureaus on display, swinging her into his arms. They'd come to look over the Stevens cane-mesh reclining chairs that were for sale, and they had a laugh trying them out, kicking their feet up and testing the levers.

It was a pleasant day all in all, though not until evening, when she was writing a note in her diary, did Aimée remember that it was a holiday. Back in America, friends were sitting down to their Thanksgiving feasts. Here in Cannes, the de Potters were quite too busy to celebrate.

Aimée was a farmer's daughter and used to waking early. She didn't think it strange to work right alongside the servants. She would go after a clogged drain with a plunger while Felicie prepared dinner, or she'd follow Ernestine from room to room with a second feather duster, chattering about anything in an effort to practice her French.

After finding a drawing of the original plan in the cellar, she turned her attention to the garden. She hired a local mason to repair the broken fountain and bought huge terra-cotta pots to place around the perimeter of the grass terrace. She planted clumps of lavender around the fountain and filled the pots with carnation plants. She had François spread gravel and repair the steps of the paths that curved out from the terrace, and she helped him thin brush from a little orchard of apricot and cherry trees on the west side of the garden. Once he'd trimmed the box hedge, she filled the flower beds with rosebushes and geraniums and more carnations. She bought a stone bench to set beneath the gnarly branches of a grand old magnolia. For the boundary just inside the back wall, already partly established with tall cypresses, she brought in a dozen saplings. For the final touch, she had a plumber lay a new pipe to the fountain, and soon water was spilling from the pitcher being tipped by the nymph.

With so much rewarding work to be done at Grand Bois, she was grateful to be free from the demands of set itineraries. The de Potters could travel when they wished and stay at home for as long as they pleased. Armand took a short trip to Cairo in April, and in May he and Aimée joined the Old World Tour in northern Italy. With Victor they spent a week in June at Baden-Baden and the rest of the summer in Cannes. Time passed too quickly. In the long letters Aimée wrote to her friends back in America, she liked to say that the only thing she lacked was a means to slow the hours so she could fully savor the pleasures of life in the south of France.

On the twenty-first of October 1904, the eve of their twenty-fifth wedding anniversary, they hired a car, picked up Victor from his school in Mandelieu, and drove to the mountain village of Auribeau-sur-Siagne, coming as close to the top as the narrow street permitted. They had lunch at a café and lit a candle in the chapel. On their way down, the chauffeur drove so fast that Aimée's scarf blew right off her head.

Lightning and thunder kept them awake that night. Armand joined Aimée in her room, his feigned fear of the storm his pretext for diving under the covers. Oh, she'd let the whole household know what a clown he was if she couldn't stifle her giggles. "Stop, please stop," she begged, but of course he knew she meant *don't stop*, and he didn't.

By the time they came downstairs the next day, Felicie had already prepared a lamb stew. After the meal, they walked with Victor into town, where they treated themselves to chocolate ice cream topped with marshmallow parfait. Back inside the front hall of Grand Bois, they found the servants waiting with a basket of flowers. Armand opened a bottle of champagne to share with everyone—even Victor was given a thimbleful. Armand presented Aimée with a silver bread basket and platter, along with a Limoges ceramic head of a peasant girl. Aimée gave Armand a silver coffeepot.

"Is it possible to be *too* happy?" she murmured later, when they found themselves alone for a moment. She interpreted the short laugh he offered in response as fondly conspiratorial. She playfully straightened his bow tie before giving him a kiss.

Such a perfect day deserved a record, and that evening, after Armand had left to take Victor back to school, Aimée headed out to the garden to write in her diary. Stopping in her husband's study to find a pencil, she noticed an envelope on the desk. It was from the University Museum in Philadelphia, where her husband had his collection of Egyptian treasures on loan. She felt curious. Since the letter had already been opened, Armand surely wouldn't mind if it was opened again.

The letter turned out to be nothing more remarkable than a handwritten note from Mrs. Stevenson, the curator in Philadelphia, who was writing in response to Professor de Potter's recent inquiry to tell him that she would not have time to compose a comprehensive catalog of the De Potter Collection in the near future—news that Armand would hardly have felt compelled to share with his wife. She did not expect him to report to her on every piece of business related to his collection. The only surprising element was that he had so successfully hidden his disappointment.

She couldn't remember the last time he'd spoken of his collection at the museum in Philadelphia. Why hadn't she thought to ask? She knew he was as sensitive about his antiquities as if he'd made them himself. He might as well have made them. It had taken him nearly thirty years and dozens of trips to North Africa to acquire treasures that included not just rare jewels and sepulchral bronzes but also a painted sarcophagus that contained a mummified high priest of Thebes. And though he could have sold his antiquities long ago, he had chosen instead to deliver them at his own expense to the University Museum, where they were on display in the Egyptian Section—the same section overseen by Mrs. Stevenson, who had failed to keep the promise she made years ago to write a catalog that would confirm the importance of the De Potter Collection.

Aimée turned the envelope over and examined the postmark. The letter must have arrived that morning. Her husband had been nursing the wound all day, and she'd been oblivious.

Unless, she considered, he hadn't been wounded at all—a far likelier possibility, she decided. He hadn't told her about the letter from Mrs. Stevenson because it wasn't important to him. What did a catalog matter when they could fly in an auto down the hill from Auribeau-sur-Siagne? Here in the south of France,

Armand had grown newly carefree. Disappointment belonged to the past, along with the headaches that used to plague him during a crisis. He didn't need recognition from distant universities. It was impossible not to be content now that they were comfortably settled at Grand Bois.

She brought her diary out to the garden and sat on the stone bench beneath the magnolia. Small, cream-colored moths flitted about in the weak light of a kerosene lamp. A cart clattered by up the road. A nightingale started to sing. As she waited for the gate to open and her husband to return, she made an entry in her diary. She didn't mention the letter she'd found in the study. Instead, she wrote about walking into town for ice cream, listed the gifts they'd exchanged, and noted that the carnations were still in bloom.

New York to Tivoli

IN THE BEGINNING, the day he stepped from the gangway onto the Battery embankment in New York, he was tongue-tied in his conversation with the immigration official, and when the official wrote his name as Pierce L. A. Depotter Elsegern, he didn't dare to correct him. Nor did he object when, in the customs line, he was asked to step aside and make room for a Polish count, the same count, he recalled, who had refused to return his greeting early in the voyage, when they'd found themselves alone together in the ship's saloon.

It was dreadfully warm, and the air was thick with the stink of manure and steam and tar. He felt self-conscious in his old-fashioned waist-jacket and his rough cotton cravat. Yet the Polish count's fine black cape was wool. Wool on a hot summer's day! Which was worse, Armand asked himself as he followed the count toward the street—to be dressed humbly or to be unprepared for the local climate? He had his answer soon enough. If you were a count, it didn't matter if you were wearing a winter cape on a late summer's day, for there would be an official to meet you and direct you to a nearby carriage, and there would be servants to save you from the trouble of having to locate your trunk in the jumble of luggage that had been dumped by the stevedores.

Someday, Pierre Louis Armand de Potter d'Elseghem would have his own coach with red velvet seats waiting for him when he arrived in New York. His name would be recorded correctly, and he wouldn't have to use the forename *Pierce* on official documents for the next twenty years. Someday, he would have plenty of money to spend on amenities and wouldn't have to heave the trunk into the cab himself while the driver finished sealing the roll of his cigarette, drawing his tongue along the edge of the paper with a long lick and then facing his passenger with a wink that Armand thought obscene.

As he rode in the cab along Broadway, he dreamed of the day when he would be the guest of honor at a dinner and would find himself sitting next to the same Polish count who had snubbed him on their transatlantic voyage. It would be one of those rare moments of comeuppance, and Armand would relish it in private while politely chuckling at the count's tasteless jokes. The future, he was sure, would make up for all the humiliations of the past. He promised himself that he would be *heureux au jeu et heureux en amour*: lucky at cards *and* lucky in love.

He would tell his wife that he'd come to America to teach French at a private school, though no position was waiting for him when he arrived in New York. He would describe himself as a knight of the Order of Melusine, never admitting that he had to pay a considerable sum for the privilege. He would claim to be the grandson of a renowned Belgian writer and political leader named Louis de Potter, eliding that his grandmother had been the mistress of Louis and worked as a cook. He would speak of his relatives who owned the Castle of Loppem in Belgium without revealing that the de Potters of Loppem refused to recognize the illegitimate de Potters of the hamlet of Melle. At Loppem, he said, he had fallen down a spiral staircase and had to have a silver plate put in his skull. But the truth was, he had never set foot inside the Castle of Loppem.

Truth was a worthy goal, yet it was as swift as time itself, and one had to hurry to keep up with it. He was always in a hurry, even on that first day at the Gilsey Hotel, when he had no appointments on his calendar, nothing but blank days ahead. After finishing his steak and draining, against his better judgment, the watery liquid the waiter called coffee, he procured a local newspaper. He skimmed it from front to back, paying special attention to the notices of new businesses and real estate transactions. Then he set out walking.

He walked down Water Street to Fulton and across to Wall Street. He rested in Trinity Church and listened to a choir rehearsing. In the late afternoon he took the ferry to Brooklyn, where he heard a lecture at the Brooklyn Institute. Titled "Dullness and Viciousness in the Home and School," it was delivered by an ancient clergyman who, despite his decrepit appearance, was so inspired by moral indignation that whenever he roared out his favorite phrase, "a blessed paragon of virtue," he'd spray a shower of spittle over the ledge of the podium.

Armand was impressed by the man's vigor, as well as by the variety of topics listed in the institute's weekly schedule. He decided to make the long trip to Brooklyn the following day for a lecture titled "The Clam—a Study in the Survival of the Fittest." The lecture was scheduled to begin at five. By half past the hour the speaker still hadn't appeared, and most of the audience left. But a small group stayed behind to talk among themselves. After Armand overheard one of the men claiming that Darwin's ideas were considered blasphemous in Europe, he intervened to offer a gentle correction. He announced that he was from Belgium, and he could say with certainty that Professor Darwin's influence was widespread among his countrymen—as evidence he cited a popular new book about parasites by Professor van Beneden of Louvain. The Americans were pleased to hear it and wanted to hear more. Introductions were exchanged. Armand learned that the men were all members of the Dredging Club—an organization dedicated to dragging New York Harbor in search of, as they explained, "rare fish, zoophytes, and odd crustaceans previously unknown to man." Finding the foreigner to their liking, they invited him to join them for an excursion the following Saturday.

He kept busy during the week, and by Wednesday he had leased a small furnished apartment at 5 Barclay Street. He found a framer to mount a portrait print of Louis de Potter that he'd brought from Belgium. On a whim, he purchased a pair of authentic-deerskin moccasins to wear as bedroom slippers. In Central Park, he ate his first popcorn ball covered in caramel.

On Saturday he woke before dawn and made his way by train and ferry to a trawler at a Brooklyn pier. The other members of the club were already on board, and as he hurried to join them, he slipped and almost tumbled into the water but managed to throw himself forward onto the deck. For this he was immediately labeled "the flying Belgian," a name that stuck through the following Saturdays when he and his fellow club members crisscrossed the New York Harbor.

Armand had been looking forward to the social aspects of the jaunt and forging new ties. He believed that to prosper he needed good, loyal, well-connected friends. The more people he knew in America the better. But that first morning he spent with the other members of the Brooklyn Institute's Dredging Club, he found himself so riveted by the muddy haul in the net that he stopped listening to the conversations going on around him. He was startled by the intensity of the suspense as the dripping net was being lifted from the water. He felt as though he were watching an image sharpen inside a crystal ball. What was there to find in the putrid scrapings from the bottom of the New York Harbor? Why, nothing less than relics from the forgotten history of the world.

Everything that came up in the net was potentially interesting. But while the club members were most excited at finding natural curiosities, the flying Belgian was fascinated by the items the others preferred to discard: the waterlogged handbags and boots and pieces of timber from shipwrecks.

He stood off to the side of the deck, studying a square piece of ashwood that had broken from a mast and was so soggy from its decades underwater that the splinters bent like rubber. With the tip of his knife he scraped away the slime and revealed the mark where the boom had been ripped off during what must have been a terrible storm. Where was the ship coming from? he wondered. What was its cargo? Who perished in the wreck and who survived?

The following Saturday he brought a knapsack and was allowed to take away whatever he could carry. After a month he had enough to constitute the beginnings of a collection: pieces of driftwood and sea glass, a woman's leather pump, the speared tip of a wrought-iron curtain rod, and, the greatest treasure of all, a pair of rusted handcuffs that Armand liked to imagine had once pinned a murderer to a bailiff.

To his collection of refuse from the New York Harbor he added glassware he bought at flea markets. Soon he graduated to broadswords and rapiers he found in antiques shops around the city. But he was forced to admit to himself that a collector can't live on air.

After having little success trying to resell a sword with a cracked handle, he became convinced that a fortune could be made in real estate, and he began collecting buildings. He came across an advertisement announcing the auction of a warehouse in Orange, New Jersey. With the letter of credit an uncle on his mother's side secured for him in Brussels, he convinced the Island City Bank to loan him two hundred dollars, and he bought the warehouse, then resold it three months later for a small profit. He used the money to purchase another property in nearby Montrose, though this one turned out to be his albatross. Of the four families living in the building, only three paid their rent on time. A couple with several small children didn't bother to pay rent at all.

In the three years after he landed in New York, Armand made money, lost it, and made more. He joined academic organizations and social clubs. He published a weekly journal about French grammar and became a senior officer of the Dredging Club. He let it be known that he was available to give lectures on French language and European history. He was invited to speak at a meeting of the American Oriental Society and at Union College in Schenectady.

Just a few months earlier he'd been an obscure French tutor in New York City. Now he was becoming known as a reputable scholar. He showed his American audiences that there were few subjects he couldn't hold forth on. He had influential friends. Yet his debts were growing.

He continued to spend his afternoons at the library. After reading John Henry Parker's book about excavating Rome, he decided that he wanted nothing more than to be an archaeologist and create a collection with artifacts he dug up from the earth. But he had neither the appropriate training nor the affiliation to become an archaeologist, and he was having difficulty securing another loan. He gave up investing in real estate for a time and concentrated on smaller items. At an estate sale on Long Island he paid two dollars for an alabaster bowl that would years later join his antiquities on the shelf of his gilt cabinet.

Though he had a collector's instinct from the start, he couldn't afford to be a collector. He was barely able to pay his bills. He decided he needed a change. What he needed, he finally had to admit, was a reliable salary, so in the spring of 1874 he responded to an advertisement for a French instructor at the Montrose Military Academy. He was hired to begin the following fall.

In Montrose he met a girl named Miranda outside the library late on a crisp October afternoon. She was the daughter of the school's headmaster. Her black hair looked streaked with veins of copper when the sun shone on it. Unbraided, her hair hung to the middle of her back; piled in a bun, it exposed the curve of her ears; when strands came loose after she'd been running, they'd stick to her moist lips.

If he'd had true athletic ability, Armand would have ended up marrying the daughter of the Montrose Military Academy's headmaster. But at a gymnastics exhibition, while attempting a difficult routine on the parallel bars in front of a large audience that included Miranda and her father, he lost his grip and fell, landing half off the mat and smacking his head on the floor with an awful crack that he would hear in his dreams for the rest of his life.

He didn't remember much beyond the sound of that crack. He didn't remember being taken away in an ambulance or drifting in and out of consciousness for three days, or being wheeled into surgery, where the doctors inserted a silver plate to mend his fractured skull. He didn't even know he had a plate in his head until a nurse told him. He would have a vague memory of being bothered by a tingling in his scalp and trying to pick at the metal beneath the bandages. Long after the bandages had been removed, the plate would remind him of its presence by giving him an occasional piercing headache, or, more rarely, making him feel as if the ground were tilting beneath his feet.

His recovery prevented him from saying goodbye to Miranda when she went off to her boarding school in Massachusetts. Though he couldn't remember if he'd ever actually loved her, he thought it appropriate to write a poem in her honor. In "Hymn du Soleil," he compared her beauty to a sunrise. He sent the poem to her in an envelope sealed with red wax. She never wrote back.

He'd been raised a Catholic, but after his accident he decided he preferred the looser rules and the social status enjoyed by his Episcopalian friends. In the spring of 1875, he left the Montrose Military Academy and moved to New York, intending to enroll in the General Seminary. His plans changed, however, after he was contacted by the headmistress, Miss Lucy Plympton, of St. Agnes's School in Albany, who had heard of his skills as a lecturer. She offered him a job teaching French at her school. He accepted. And when St. Agnes's closed and Miss Lucy Plympton took over the Albany Academy for Girls, she appointed Armand a member of the faculty.

Among the students studying French at the Albany Academy was one Amy Sutherland Beckwith, eighteen years old, with silky light-brown hair that she wore in a braided topknot, alert blue eyes, and lips pressed together in a determined line, as if she were forcing herself to suppress a squeal of joy. From the start of class, Armand was aware of her staring at him from a desk at the back of the room. Later, he let himself imagine her relief to hear that he wasn't yet married. He wasn't at all surprised to find that she had engineered an opportunity that would let Professor de Potter take closer notice of his devoted student. In December 1877, he received an invitation to perform his skit about Napoléon at a meeting of the Tivoli Literary Society, hosted by Mr. and Mrs. William Beckwith. He cordially accepted.

Tivoli to Brussels

AMY BECKWITH had never met anyone as worldly as her new French professor at the Albany Academy for Girls. His ears were especially finely formed and fit snugly against his greased brown hair. His deep-set eyes seemed lit by an interior flame. The bump on the slope of his nose gave him a hint of ruggedness. She wondered if he had lost his temper and broken his nose in a fist-fight. But from his dignified bearing, Amy judged him to be slow to anger. In other ways, though, he was boyishly jittery and could hardly sit still while her father was introducing his performance. She watched as he interlaced his fingers and twiddled his thumbs, a nervous habit that she understood to be an expression of an energy he could barely contain. He gave the impression that he was sure he was destined for great things, yet instead of appearing conceited, he seemed modestly attuned to the responsibility of his fate. He *would* do great things, she was convinced. He was admirable in all respects. He had the signature of nobility that was most evident in the area between his mustache and his beard, where the tip of his pink tongue would occasionally appear to moisten the perfect bud of lips. From the moment she first saw him at the front of the class, she wanted to kiss those lips and, in doing so, give her simple life new meaning. Professor de Potter made everything fresh and interesting. He had stepped out of history, landing on the doorstep of the Beckwith farmhouse and looking strikingly like a young Napoléon Bonaparte.

He was elusive in the beginning. Some said he was French by birth, others Dutch. He called himself Pierce in public, Armand in private. Sometimes he used Elseghem as his last name, other times de Potter. On the nameplate on his office at school, he was Professor P. L. de Potter.

After his performance for the Tivoli Literary Society, Professor P. L. de Potter offered to take questions.

"Professor, how do you know so much about Napoléon?" one man called out from the back of the living room.

"My mother's father served as a general under Napoléon," Armand replied. "He told my mother, who told me, that when the emperor was deep in thought, he would twist his forefinger inside his ear to loosen the wax, *comme ça*."

The laughter faded, and someone else called, "Did your mother ever meet Napoléon?"

"As an infant, she once sat on his lap!"

The audience murmured in appreciation.

"What did your father do, Professor?" Mr. Beckwith asked in a voice that was mostly jovial but contained a touch of suspicion.

"My father . . . ?"

"Your father's line of work."

"My father was a diplomat."

"And your father's father?"

"My father's . . . ?"

"Your paternal grandfather."

Armand raised his eyebrows, as if surprised at being asked a question when the answer should have been obvious. "Why, he was Louis de Potter."

Those present that day pretended to be amazed. They didn't admit that they'd never heard of Louis de Potter. It took Amy a trip to the library in Albany to learn that Louis de Potter was one of the leaders of the Belgian independence—that brave little country's own Thomas Jefferson—and, as she reported back to her family, the citizens of Dutchess County were probably the only educated people in the world who didn't know who he was.

To think that the grandson of Louis de Potter had come to Tivoli, New York, to play the worn-out Napoléon in exile and pace the living room of the Beckwiths' farmhouse as though it were the garden of a crumbling villa on St. Helena. Who wasn't enthralled?

They didn't consider that there was no way to verify the claims their guest made. He was perceived to be impeccably distinguished, with a connection to history that couldn't be matched in America. "The sketch of Napoléon, as performed by Prof. P. L. de Potter, was well worthy of praise," according to the Red Hook reporter who wrote about the meeting. The applause was vigorous and prolonged, and the audience asked the performer for an encore, for which he recited Macbeth's "tomorrow" soliloquy. The reporter concluded that the Tivoli Literary Society had never before had such a successful gathering. He didn't bother to mention that the Beckwiths' dog, Lulu, wouldn't stop barking and had to be banished to the cellar, or that after his performance Prof. P. L. de Potter invited Miss Amy Beckwith to join him for tea.

In the spring of 1879, Professor de Potter took a leave of absence from the Albany Academy and went abroad for three months, ostensibly to visit his family in Belgium. When he returned, he was thinner and brisker in his manner. He carried a new walking stick topped with an ivory handle. He had a pale patch on the bridge of his nose where his skin had been blistered by the sun one day when he'd forgotten his hat. He'd brought back a box full of old coins and knickknacks made of brass, onyx, and alabaster—purchased, he said, for next to nothing at open markets and antiques shops.

He was clear and purposeful as he laid out his plans for the future. He announced that he had decided to start his own tourist business. He claimed that a fortune was to be made offering luxury excursions to Americans, and with his fluency in multiple languages and his background in Europe, he was confident that he could avoid the aggravations suffered by inexperienced guides.

He set the cost of his first Long Summer Tour, including all tickets and fees, at a competitive $235. He hired an accountant, Fletcher Vosburg, to balance the books.

On the day the American Bureau of Foreign Travel advertised its first tour to the public, the man known to his colleagues as Pierce asked his student Amy Beckwith to be his wife. They were married at 11:00 a.m. on Wednesday, October 22, 1879, at St. John's Reformed Church in Upper Red Hook. The bride agreed to change the spelling of her name to *Aimée* when she became Madame de Potter, and though the groom signed *Pierce L. A. de Potter d'Elseghem* in the church registry, he would go by *Armand*, the name Aimée preferred.

They spent their wedding night at the Beekman Arms in Rhinebeck, where they ordered eggs Benedict and a bottle of champagne for their dinner. Aimée came out from the suite's small dressing room wearing an ankle-length, pink satin nightgown. Even as she closed the curtains and reached for the knob to turn down the lamp, extinguishing the flame completely, she felt that she was about to begin the most important task of her life.

As she understood the contract of marriage, she was obligated to follow the usual course and produce a child. Her mother had done the job neatly five times, giving birth to three girls and two boys. She nearly succumbed on the fifth round from milk fever after Tom was born, but she pulled through. Amy—rather, Ai-mée, she mustn't forget her own name!—had confidence that she herself would pull through. And if she privately associated inter-course with barnyard antics, she was ready to sacrifice herself to fulfill her duty.

She had sprayed herself with the eau de toilette Armand had given her for her last birthday, and as she made her way cautiously across the dark room, she worried that she hadn't used enough perfume—or had she used too much? She slipped beside her hus-band into the bed, ran her tongue across her lips to dampen them, and waited to be kissed.

But Armand didn't kiss her, not right away. He just stroked the side of her neck, a gesture that she found too puzzling to enjoy. She wondered if he was waiting for her to kiss him—but would that seem too brazen for a young bride? Would he prefer her to be coy or timid or saucy, or maybe to stretch out like a cat under the gentle pressure of his hand? How could she not know the desires of the man she had aligned herself with for a lifetime? She wasn't used to such uncertainty. To be lying in bed with a husband whose thoughts were shielded by his silence, while her own thoughts were in turmoil . . . what had she gotten herself into, falling in love with a mystery!

His fingertips were icy, his palms warm, his beard wiry against her cheek. Driven only by the need to pin down the man she had married that morning, she found his mouth in the dark-ness and raised herself on her elbows, clamping her lips on his so hard that their teeth knocked together with a little clattering sound.

She tasted pipe tobacco and a tangy, salty flavor she couldn't identify. She wondered if she had surprised him with her kiss. Then, as she felt his hand slip beneath the hem of her nightgown, she forgot whatever impression she hoped to make and turned her attention within herself, experiencing the heightened awareness achieved by closing her eyes in a room that was already lightless.

The next day they set off on a steamer bound for Liverpool. Following an itinerary Armand had mapped out in his office in Albany, they traveled from London to Paris, down to Italy, and back north across Europe to Belgium on a dry run of what would be the first De Potter Old World Tour.

Every place they visited, Armand recorded information, writing across the columns of the only notebook he had on hand, a thin Brown Brothers & Co. savings-account passbook, bound in soft lambskin. At the National Gallery in London, he made a note that twenty-three paintings by Reynolds were on display. At the Louvre, he wrote that a panel by Uccello "contains heads of Giotto, Donatello, Brunelleschi, Manetti & himself, representatives of Painting. Sculpture. Architecture. Mathematics & Perspective." He described three paintings by Morales as "sublime, refined, delicate." At the Pitti Palace in Florence, he listed paintings by Allori and Giorgione and Botticelli. Looking at a small triptych in the Uffizi, he described Montagna's "delicacy of touch."

Everything was beautiful. Everything was interesting. Watching her husband make his notes, Aimée experienced curiosity as a delicious hunger and was proud of her increasing sophistication. The knowledge she gained with Armand's help gave her a feeling of uncanny authority. She felt her transformation almost physically, as if her self-assurance were making her lighter on her feet.

The only time the newlyweds came close to arguing was when

they were sitting at a café in the piazza outside the Pantheon in Rome, sipping lemon soda and idly watching a beggar woman in rags, bent over her cane, moving among the crowd. They watched for a long time, long enough to see dozens of tourists give her money. As the hunchbacked old woman limped past their table, Aimée gave her a lira. They continued to watch her as she wandered back through the crowd. They were still watching when the church bells began to ring for vespers, and the woman stood straight, pushed back her hood to reveal her dark eyes and smooth, pale skin, and marched off, her cane tucked under her arm.

Aimée was appalled. Armand, in contrast, made no secret of his amusement. He was impressed by the performance and insisted that the girl had earned her wages fairly.

"You approve of her duplicity?" Aimée asked sharply.

"*Ma belle*," he said, fixing his gaze on his wife, "I mean no harm, but you must recognize that the poor girl is protecting herself against a worse fate."

She appreciated her husband's eagerness to sympathize with such a creature. She would have sympathized, too, if only she hadn't so easily been fooled.

From Italy they took a train north through Switzerland. They spent two nights in Geneva, then continued on to Belgium, arriving in Brussels at midnight, in the midst of a storm so severe that the water streamed over their shoes as they crossed the street. But by the next morning the rain had passed, and they woke to a sky lit a pale blue that Armand swore could only be seen in Belgium.

They were staying in a suite at the Grand Hôtel Mengelle, a first-class hotel on the rue Royale. They had a leisurely breakfast and then hired an open carriage to take them to the Cathedral of St. Gudula, where Armand wanted to show Aimée the pulpit's florid carving of Adam and Eve creeping from paradise. They spent the rest of the morning in the Royal Museum of Fine Art and ate their midday meal at a small café across the street, where Armand remembered being served chocolate cake on his seventh birthday. Afterward, they walked through the Grand Place and fed the pigeons with crumbs from a roll Aimée had stashed in her purse.

She was surprised that they couldn't find the time to visit the de Potter relatives who lived at the castle in Loppem. They did meet his brother, Victor, for dinner on their last night in Brussels. When Aimée asked in her best French for stories about their grandfather Louis de Potter, Victor, who was nearly a foot taller than his brother, spilled the soup from his spoon back into the bowl and exchanged a glance with Armand. "I was telling you about the skirmish at Yelalla, along the Congo River," Victor said. He hadn't been telling them any such thing, but Armand chimed in, "Yelalla, yes, you were saying?"

"I want to show you . . ."—Victor pulled a heavy copper crucifix from his satchel—"this Katanga beauty I took off the corpse of a native."

Victor had been educated at a school in Brussels, and after serving for two years in the Belgian military he came home to East Flanders. By then their father was dead, and Victor lived in the family home with his stepmother. All Armand had said about his father's second wife was that she'd been born on a farm outside the village of Waterloo five years after the defeat of Napoléon, and she preferred to speak only Dutch. He resisted complaining outright about her, but Aimée guessed that the stepmother was one of the reasons her husband had moved to America.

They took the train to Antwerp the next day, and as they traveled through the countryside, Armand puffed on his pipe and gazed silently out the rain-streaked window at the fields. What was he thinking about? Aimée remembered the intimacy of her wedding night. Now she longed for a concurrent intimacy that would enable her to read her husband's expression. He was so distant from her right then, as much a foreigner as when he'd arrived in the classroom for the first time in Albany. He had rarely spoken about his brother, Victor, and she thought she understood why—he was far coarser than she would have expected for a member of the European aristocracy. She wondered about his father, who had died when Armand was seventeen. Had he really been a diplomat, as Armand claimed? She wondered what the family house in Elseghem was like, and if her husband had misrepresented his past. Even if she went ahead and asked him to clarify, she couldn't be sure that he would tell the truth.

What a horrible tangle of fears. She might as well come right out and call him a liar. She had no evidence that he had lied to her. If his brother lacked manners, it wasn't Armand's fault. Even if Armand had exaggerated his family's wealth and importance, he couldn't have invented the basic facts. What cause did she have to be suspicious? He was merely looking out the train window at the countryside of Belgium. The truth was not that the person Aimée loved most in the world was guilty of misrepresenting his past, but that she didn't know everything about him.

She was proud of her nimble intuition and had a reputation among her schoolmates for being an astute judge of character. But she remembered that she'd been wrong about the beggar woman in Rome. Could she have been wrong about her own husband, too? As she watched him looking out through the rain, she told herself that if nothing else, her experiences over the past three months had made her keener, more confident in her ability to see the truth. The inconsistencies she'd discerned in his account of his past added color to the picture, and color added depth. That there was more to him than she had initially perceived would only make the marriage more thrilling. Already she had come to know him in a new way in bed. Now she could look forward to another kind of knowing that would develop gradually, through the accumulation of experiences over days and years and decades. She was ready to be surprised by him. She had no doubt that the more he revealed himself to her, the more there would be of him for her to love.

❄ PART TWO ❄

The Regele Carol

INSTEAD OF GOING DIRECTLY TO HIS STATEROOM, he climbs to the upper deck of the *Regele Carol* to take in the view of Constantinople. From the rail, he watches the two sailors who brought him to the ship row back to shore. A felucca glides past them toward the mouth of the Bosporus. On an ironclad frigate anchored nearby, a red flag slowly rises on a pole.

He decides to walk to the other side of the deck, where he can look out at the black walls and towers on the nearest hillside. He tries to orient himself, tracking from the palace to the Hagia Sofia dome and across the jumble of rooftops of the Seraglio. He wonders if he's right in identifying the roof of the shop where, on a whim two days earlier, he'd bought a small bronze statue in the shape of the youthful Bacchus.

The water has the glassy stillness of a pond, and his attention is caught by his own shadow on the surface. He bends and straightens his arm. The elongated shadow bends and straightens. He curls his arms over his head and presses his chin against his chest, making a ram with his shadow—an image he remembers showing his son just a few weeks earlier, using the light from his magic lantern.

The breeze grows warmer and the harbor busier. Ripples spreading from the wake of a passing barge slap against the hull of the ship. New passengers keep arriving, and in the time since Armand has been standing at the rail of the upper deck, two Russian women and a girl have claimed their chairs. One of the women opens a book; the other woman and the girl share segments of an orange. The citrus fragrance reaches Armand, and it makes him sharply aware of his longing to be back at Grand Bois, sharing an orange with his wife and son.

He imagines what he'd say if his wife were standing with him on the upper deck of the *Regele Carol*. Maybe he would have confessed everything right then. No, he wouldn't. He would continue his efforts to postpone revealing his plan to her by drawing her attention to the domes crowning the mosque of Suleiman the Magnificent.

Right then the whistle sounds the ship's imminent departure. Armand plugs his ears with his knuckles and watches the Russian woman, who keeps right on talking to her daughter, trying to make her words understood above the noise.

There is more activity on deck as several boatloads of passengers disembark. He wonders how long he has been standing there and takes out his watch. Two days earlier at the Yeni Valideh Jami' he had made a show of setting it to Turkish time. Here in the land of the sultan, where the clock follows the sun, it is just past three in the morning.

He signals to a steward and speaks to him in German, expressing his desire to be directed to his cabin. He is met with puzzlement. He guesses that the steward is Romanian like most of the crew. But Armand doesn't speak Romanian. He tries Greek, then English, and finally, in French, succeeds in communicating his meaning.

The steward is slender with bowed legs and burly arms. His

green eyes would have been piercing, but it seems he can't help but fix his gaze slightly below eye level, a habit that makes his manner, otherwise plain, seem obsequious, or even furtively judgmental, as if he were the kind who mocked his superiors behind their backs. Armand's response is to run his fingers through his beard in case he has crumbs there, though he's sure he doesn't, since he had no breakfast that morning.

The steward leads the way down the stairs to the first-class section, moving along the corridor so quickly that Armand has to take a couple of running strides to keep up. When they reach the room, they find the door already ajar, which concerns him, though he can't come up with a good reason to complain. The room is more spacious than he'd expected for such a small steamer, and his trunk is stored securely beneath the bunk.

He dismisses the steward and begins arranging his room. Whenever he travels on a ship, he goes through the same routine: He sets out his reading glasses and opens his notebook to one of his lectures, in this case about the mythological sea kings of the Aegean. He folds down a corner of the blanket and fluffs the pillow. He wipes his spectacles with his handkerchief. He lays out a fresh shirt and runs a damp cloth across his vest and jacket, though lunch is still several hours away. Then he starts reading: *Here where the magical past is astonishingly real, and, if real, supremely interesting to us . . .*

Cannes to Lausanne

BY THE SPRING OF 1905, two months before Armand disappeared at sea, Aimée had written so many letters about the advantages of life in France that her friends and relatives back in America began to be persuaded. Miss Plympton, former headmistress of the Albany Academy for Girls, decided to retire in Cannes. Mr. and Mrs. Tamour, who had been their neighbors in Albany, came to visit the de Potters and ended up buying a villa down the hill from them. And Aimée's sister Leila sent her daughter Gertrude to Cannes to study French.

The American Bureau of Foreign Travel had full-time staff in offices in New York, Detroit, and Paris. The business, in its twenty-sixth year, published a thick brochure titled "De Potter Tours for Pleasure and Study Abroad," with "well-matured and leisurely itineraries," "intelligent sightseeing under expert guidance," and "veritable voyages de luxe at reasonable cost." Each tour had been repeated dozens of times by the same guides, and each guide made his own arrangements for interpreters. Armand was hardly needed. Although he liked to join the tours in Europe and Egypt for short intervals, he was home more often than not and frequently gave personal tours around the region to whoever happened to be visiting.

On the day they planned to take Gertrude to see the Rothschild gardens in Grasse, they were still at breakfast when the morning mail arrived. Among the letters were several from members of a De Potter traveling party and one from a guide named Gustav Turgel.

Monsieur Turgel regretted to inform Professor de Potter that an accident involving the DOT party—shorthand for the De Potter Oriental Tour—had occurred in the harbor of Jaffa. He explained that a boat transporting the party from a khedival steamer to shore had been capsized by a rogue wave, and the passengers and crew had been thrown into the water. Everyone had made it to shore alive, but all the luggage was lost. The travelers were recuperating in their rooms in the Grand New Hotel. Monsieur Turgel assumed he could borrow off the bureau's credit to replace essential items. He was sorry to say that the current accommodations were shockingly inadequate and only added to the party's general displeasure. He asked if he could have permission to move the group to the Hôtel du Parc. He added that several members of the party had promised to write to Professor de Potter directly.

In their own letters, some travelers threatened to take legal action against the American Bureau of Foreign Travel; others demanded immediate compensation. One man promised to publicize the news of the accident so that anyone back in America who was planning to join a De Potter tour would know exactly what to expect. The losses claimed were considerable—purses and wallets stuffed with cash, a set of diamond cuff links, two pearl necklaces, an emerald brooch.

Armand's pallor had turned a grayish hue by the time he

finished reading through the letters, and Aimée worried that he was about to suffer one of his dizzy spells. She pressed him back into his seat when he started to stand. No, he said with irritation, he was fine. She mumbled something about the distressing news from Jaffa. He announced that nothing could be done about an accident that had already occurred. Putting the letters aside, he insisted on going ahead with their trip to the Rothschild villa.

In Grasse, they spent nearly two hours strolling paths that wound between massive yuccas and blue palms. The skies had cleared, and Gertrude claimed to be intoxicated from the perfume of the blossoms. To prove it she staggered ahead, weaving from side to side, plucking the flower of a geranium and tucking it into her hair.

Aimée hardly noticed. She was preoccupied with the news they'd received that morning, even though she respected her husband's wish not to speak of it. In Alice Rothschild's gardens they spoke only about the plants that were in bloom, and over lunch at the Hôtel de la Porte they wondered whether the dressing on the salad was excessively sweet, and if the rain would return.

Back in Cannes they busied themselves with chores in the hour left before supper and made arrangements to take a carriage ride to the seaside village of Théoule with friends the following day. Alone in her room that evening, Aimée thought further about the letters they'd received that morning. She opened her diary and wrote, "Can see trouble ahead." Then she stared at the words, not entirely certain what they meant.

The next day, after Armand didn't appear at breakfast, Aimée went to his room and found him in bed with the shutters still closed. She sat beside him and touched the back of her hand against his forehead. She assured him that he didn't have a fever.

Still, he felt too seedy to go to Théoule, he said. He hadn't slept at all the night before, and now his head was throbbing.

She asked him stupidly if he was worrying over the accident at Jaffa. He waved away her question and announced that there was nothing more to be said about Jaffa. But there had to be more to say about Jaffa. She wished they could have talked at length about it. She wanted to persuade him that they were lucky, no one had been killed, and they were fortunate to have the resources to satisfy the injured parties. Yes, the public would hear about the accident, and there might be a temporary drop in applications for upcoming tours, but the business would survive. Her husband would take charge, as he always did, and make the necessary restitutions.

First, though, he had to suffer one of his nervous headaches. If she hadn't loved him as she did, she might have blamed him for letting himself be dominated by misery. She was irritated by her own helplessness. She could do no more than encourage him to try to sleep and leave him alone for a few hours.

She set out on errands, stopping first at the apothecary to purchase menthol for her husband, then continuing on to the post office. She spent another hour walking the length of the beach below la Croisette before returning home.

Entering through the kitchen, she stopped to taste the soup Felicie had left simmering on the stove. In the front hall, she slowly unwrapped her scarf. She felt inexplicably self-conscious, as if she had just discovered that she was being watched by her husband. It was especially strange, then, that she should find herself watching him, his body framed by the salon's pocket doors, his back to her as he tinkered with the curios in the gilt cabinet.

She was glad to see that he'd gotten out of bed and he wouldn't need the menthol after all. His absorption in his work impressed her. He was like a clockmaker tinkering with pins and gears.

She heard a clatter and saw him reach for the ivory elephant from the chess set and stand it upright on the shelf. She hoped nothing had been broken, then told herself it wouldn't much matter. The curios relegated to the gilt cabinet had been bought from street vendors for a franc or two, and most of the pieces were too damaged or too poorly made to be of interest to Egyptologists. Some, such as the chess set, or the strange flat-headed iron figure with untextured hair that fell to its shoulders, didn't even come from Egypt but were caprices bought on his journeys around the world. Together it was a motley group, "my assemblage of misfits," Armand had once said.

Still, he could occupy himself sorting and arranging the collection in the cabinet for hours at a time, in the hope that he'd one day discover something of value among his misfits. Aimée thought it an unrealistic hope, but she knew that it calmed him to handle the pieces. And after his efforts to put his finest treasures on display for the public to enjoy, he was allowed to indulge himself in private, especially at a time when he'd been shaken by the news from Jaffa. The least she could do was allow him a moment of peace and slip away before he realized she was standing there.

Victor came home for the Easter holiday, and when Felicie saw him, she exclaimed at how much he'd grown in just a few weeks. He was nearly as tall as his mother and kept stumbling over his feet. He'd outgrown his suits, so Aimée brought him to Nice to buy a new one. Gertrude came along, and they met friends for tea at Rumpelmeyer's. Back in Cannes, Aimée took Gertrude and Victor to hear vespers at St. George's. They met Armand at Grand Bois and had dinner on the terrace, the table positioned just far enough from the fountain that they wouldn't get wet if the breeze sent the spray in their direction.

All these activities Aimée diligently listed in her diary. She chose not to mention that when she'd returned from Nice, she'd found Armand in his study rereading the letters from Jaffa. She didn't bother to say that when she reached for the letters, he tossed them to the floor and demanded, as if she were one of his accusers, "Explain to me why this accident is my responsibility!"—then left the room abruptly. His anger was best forgotten. And though she was right to predict that before the day was over he would express remorse, taking her into his arms and apologizing for his outburst, she saw no need to include this in her chronicle. All she wrote that evening was "Lovely day, but letters from members of Party distress us and our hearts are heavy. Sat in garden in p.m."

The following Sunday, neighbors dropped by and ended up staying for tea. Just as they were leaving, the de Potters were surprised to see Gustav Turgel, the conductor of the De Potter Oriental Tour, walking up the hill toward their front gate. He had sailed from Jaffa to Marseille and then taken the train to Cannes instead of continuing directly on to Paris.

A young man, Alsatian by birth, he had the demeanor of someone much older, with a polished bald head and lips that turned down at the corners. Aimée took an immediate dislike to him. Over the dinner that Felicie hastily prepared, he launched into a more graphic version of the accident. He said that Mr. Leroy, a stout merchant from Scranton, Pennsylvania, had been inconsolable after the sailors decided he was too heavy to lift onto the rescue boat and instead dragged him through the water to shore. He said that the right arm of the elderly Mrs. Cunningham from Boston had nearly been twisted out of its socket, and that Mrs. Cunningham's niece had vomited into her hat during the carriage ride to the hotel.

How much Armand would have to pay in penalty, they didn't yet know. They didn't want to know. He might have been an adventurer, but he was poorly equipped to engage in a drawn-out legal battle he was sure to lose. The whole affair was proving increasingly threatening, though perhaps Monsieur Turgel was exaggerating some of the details for the sake of drama. At the very least, Aimée thought it rude of him to visit without sending word ahead. She was glad when he left Grand Bois after supper to catch the night train for Paris.

At the beginning of May they drove Victor back to school. As they bounced along between fields of new sunflowers and lavender, Gertrude—giddy at being young and lovely and riding in a motorcar in the south of France—started singing "Always Leave Them Laughing," and they all joined in on the chorus, even Armand. Then they ate sandwiches and passed around a box of bonbons to share. For the first time in many days, Aimée allowed herself to hope that their hard-earned serenity would soon return.

Back at home, she picked pink and white carnations from the garden and arranged the bouquets in vases around the salon. In the evening, she and Armand read aloud to each other from the copy of Tennyson's poems he'd given her when they were engaged.

Armand was due to lead a tour in early May, and on the Sunday before he left to sail to Naples, Aimée celebrated his upcoming birthday by waking him with kisses. They had breakfast together, and while he finished preparing for his trip, she and Gertrude went to the service at St. Paul's and then to admire the view from the top of the clock tower at the Villa Fiorentina, across the street from Grand Bois.

After they'd climbed back down, she rested in the shade while Gertrude wandered off to explore the garden. She listened to the squeaking of a child's violin coming from inside the villa and watched a black cat that had planted itself on the bottom step of the tower and was picking grit from its paw.

When Gertrude returned, she wore a halo she'd woven with daisies. She announced that if she could find a way to do it, she, too, would settle permanently in Cannes. "How lucky you are, Auntie," she declared.

The girl was right: Aimée was lucky to have found Armand de Potter and to have escaped the provincialism of her friends back home. Because of Armand she had the chance to collect armfuls of carnations, to ride in automobiles through the countryside of Provence, and to preside over Grand Bois. Armand had introduced her to the world across the ocean and made it possible for her to structure her days in such a way that she was continually enthralled. As Madame de Potter, life was never boring. She was reminded of this as she watched Gertrude in her daisy halo trying to catch one of the lizards scurrying up the wall of the Villa Fiorentina clock tower.

The next morning, Armand left to lead the Classic, Oriental, and Alpine Tour. He prepared for the trip in the usual way, packing his trunk and putting his tickets and passport in order, reviewing his itinerary, reading up on the archaeological sites he planned to visit. Aimée saw him off at the station in Cannes instead of accompanying him to Marseille, since she had a meeting at noon with the architect who was designing the gardener's cottage. She wrote in her diary that night, propped up in her bed by a pair of tasseled pillows, "A. left today for Naples." She considered writing a line about the fine coq au vin Felicie had prepared for dinner. Instead she just added, "Cloudy & damp."

She kept herself busy visiting and receiving friends, running errands in town, going to the dentist and to church. The weather remained unseasonably cool and rainy, and a flare-up of rheumatism made her fingers stiff. On some days she and Gertrude declined to join friends on excursions and instead stayed home, reading or playing cards by the fire. The builders started digging the cellar for the gardener's cottage. Several times, often in fog and drizzle, Aimée invited her niece and Miss Plympton to accompany her on a carriage ride down to la Croisette to see the waves crashing against the jetty.

The weather began to improve toward the end of May. On the first of June Aimée hired a car and took Gertrude and Miss Plympton to Mandelieu to pick up Victor at his school. A few days later they set out on a trip together, traveling through the Vars Valley to Grenoble and Lausanne on a new itinerary Aimée had agreed to test out for De Potter Tours.

She expected to enjoy herself, but things started to go wrong. The first hotel they stayed at was a musty place, with a nest of scorpions in the closet. Not only did Victor develop a cough and have to spend a day in bed, but poor Miss Plympton didn't fare well either. In Puget-Théniers she was nearly prostrated by the heat and humidity, and by the time they reached Grenoble she was, as Aimée reported in her diary, "entirely used up."

The group arrived in Lausanne on June 10. After suffering the heat on the slow train from Grenoble, Aimée shared Miss Plympton's exhaustion. She left Victor in Gertrude's charge and retired to her room right after dinner. She pushed open the shutters that the maid had latched, then sat on the window seat and took out a book. She lost herself in this absorbing fantasy about time travel for several hours, reading straight to the end. Not until several months later, when she was finally returning the book to the shelf at Grand Bois, would she consider the coincidence: while she'd been following the time traveler up to the point when he enters his machine and disappears forever, Armand de Potter had gone missing.

El Kef to Tunis

YOU CAN BE SURE that if he were telling this story, he wouldn't begin in Constantinople. He wouldn't begin with his arrival in New York, or even with his introduction to the Dredging Club of the Brooklyn Institute. He would begin in the outpost of El Kef, in that godforsaken dirt alley where he lost his way in 1879 after making the mistake of smoking a rare hashish offered to him by a proprietor of a tea shop.

But it could hardly be called *smoking* when all he'd done was take one quick puff, the bamboo stem still moist from the lips of the old Berber who had offered him the pipe. He hadn't felt any change in the quality of his consciousness after that single puff, but he eventually felt something . . . was it three days, or three hours, later? The hashish had followed him and spun its web, snaring his thoughts, so he couldn't remember how he'd come to this place, or where he was supposed to be.

Back then he was still a naive traveler and hadn't learned the importance of always mapping out his route. He knew, at least, that he was in an outpost called El Kef, in the northwest corner of Tunisia. But in his muddled state that day he could not posit a self capable of remembering why he had come here in the first place. He remembered that once as a sublieutenant for the French military he had visited El Kef. He wasn't a sublieutenant anymore, so why was he back? He had the vague impression that he'd returned to the village to search for something he'd misplaced, but he couldn't remember what it was.

He stumbled along a path bordered by polished black stones. For no good reason, he tried to catch up with a goat that was trotting urgently, as though fleeing the slaughterhouse. At the juncture of the path and the hard-packed road leading out of the palm grove, he lost sight of the goat and wasn't sure which way to turn. He turned left, crossed between beds of dense, spiky aloe, and passed through a low archway, entering a corridor that curved endlessly into the darkness and promised to lead nowhere.

As he moved forward, he was reminded of walking down a beach into the water. The ground was soft-packed sand like a beach, and the walls were a lemony, dimpled limestone. Moving farther along the corridor, he expected the darkness to be impenetrable. But as he rounded a bend, he saw a glow trickling in from a distant opening.

For a man who didn't know where he was going or how he had ended up in his current location, light was a more appealing destination than darkness, and he quickened his pace. Now at least he was a man with a sense of direction. With each step his purpose intensified. He was not just a man walking forward toward the source of light. He was a man who for a reason he couldn't yet articulate was hopeful that soon his whereabouts would be clarified. Hope, then, was a welcome attribute, and as a hopeful man whose boots crunched the top layer of sand he proceeded along the corridor.

He was increasingly hopeful as his senses had more to identify. There was the faint, greasy smell of his own sweat, the bitter taste of lime dust in his mouth, the occasional crumbling when his hand rubbed along the wall. Eventually he heard what he thought was the rustling of palm leaves in the breeze. But the source of the sound wasn't the wind moving through the palms, he realized as he drew closer. It was human breath moving from the lungs and emitted through pursed lips as murmurs.

Murmurs signaled that he had reason to be wary. He was hopeful and wary as he approached the source of the light and the murmuring. New questions came to mind. Should he be silent and observe the scene ahead of him without revealing his presence, or should he arrive with a bellow of a greeting?

He didn't have a chance to decide, for he was suddenly there, where the corridor opened up to a doorless entrance and the white light of the sun created a cube amid the shadows occupied by three white-robed, turbaned men. Two were squatting on the sand, knotting fine threads, and the third was standing, looking down at their work. All three offered the intruder no more than an indifferent glance before they resumed their conversation, trading hushed sounds with an intensity suggesting that whatever rug they intended to weave would be the product of reluctant compromise.

He stood for a long while observing them, envying even more than their concentrated absorption in the work of weaving their facility with a language he did not yet understand. He wished he were a man who spoke the language of these weavers. He could be that man if he set his mind to it. He must have been drawn to this place for a reason.

He was jealous of the Arabs' secrets and yet oddly comfortable with his exclusion, for now he knew where he was. He was in a place where time couldn't penetrate and nothing would ever change, in the presence of men who had been singled out and blessed with immortality. But it wasn't God they had to thank. It was the ingenious machine mounted on a tripod in the corner of the workroom: a Phoebus mahogany box camera, its lens like a pig's snout inhaling the light.

When he was nineteen, Armand spent five months in Algiers as a sublieutenant for the French army, under the leadership of Crémieux, a government minister appointed to assimilate Algeria into France. Armand's duties at the time involved supervising the transportation and settlement of Alsatian refugees fleeing the Franco-Prussian War. He took one long expedition with his regiment, traveling by train to Biskra, then on horseback across the Algerian desert from Biskra to Constantine. From Constantine they traveled by diligence to the outpost of El Kef in Tunisia. A week later they returned to Algiers.

Constantine was in the midst of a devastating drought, and with French speculators buying up all the grain and emptying the silos, famine was spreading. By 1871, 20 percent of the region's Muslim population had died of starvation. As a nineteen-year-old sublieutenant surrounded by fellow soldiers, Armand did not witness the full scope of the suffering, and he heard only faint rumors of the simmering unrest among the local tribes. Then, on the road between Constantine and El Kef, the regiment passed the desiccated corpse of what Armand thought was a dog but turned out to be a child—a boy of about six or seven. The officer in command ordered his regiment to dig a grave, and Armand was one of the men who helped bury the child.

After that, he wanted to leave the desert and never return. Not until he moved to America were his memories stirred in a different way. It was as if he'd carried sand in his pocket, and he found the sand again, took out a handful, and felt it sift through his fingers. He thought about the corpse of a child, left out for the vultures. He thought about the sleepless night he spent with his regiment on the edge of a bedouin camp, when he'd stayed up listening to the bedouins make a strange music by rubbing stones together. He thought about the way the brilliant constellations seemed to flash and spin.

Six months before he married Amy Beckwith, he used a portion of the money he'd saved to sail back across the Atlantic. He went first to visit his brother in Belgium, though he spent only a day with him before leaving for North Africa. He was longing to hear the music of the bedouins and see the stars dancing in the sky again. He couldn't shake the feeling that he'd missed something on his last visit.

On the outskirts of El Kef, he met a young photographer named Alexandre Bougault. He learned that Bougault had come from Algeria, where he'd been serving in the French military, and had recently bought himself the Phoebus box camera with the rack-and-pinion focuser. Bougault had the notion that he could have a profitable career selling albumen prints of desert scenes to tourists. So far in his brief search for marketable images of North Africa, the reality of dust and poverty had disappointed him; he preferred arranging scenes with a theatrical flourish, posing his subjects and manipulating the light in ways that enhanced the impression of hazily exotic beauty. His ambition was to sell as many prints as possible rather than to represent the truth. What did European tourists care about the truth?

Bougault was delighted to hear his visitor greet him in French. Armand himself felt an uncharacteristic relief at meeting a Frenchman so far from home. While the photographer continued with his work, the two men traded stories about their military service and discovered that they had mutual friends. In the time it took for Bougault to use up his supply of negative plates, Armand regained sufficient clarity of mind to accept when the photographer invited him to have a drink.

Instead of staying in the one hotel thought to be suitable for foreigners in El Kef, the industrious Bougault had arranged a deal with a rug merchant. In return for buying rugs to resell in Paris, he was given a room in the merchant's house and two meals a day. He and Armand sat in the garden behind the house until it was dark, drinking a syrupy tea that made the ends of their mustaches sticky. Bougault showed Armand a photograph of a girl he'd left behind in Paris. Armand showed Bougault a photograph of the girl waiting for him in Tivoli. They boasted of their wealth and their family connections and were at a point when the tenor of their conversation could have gone toward either suspicion or agreeable curiosity when Bougault exclaimed and pointed to the ground. A huge beetle, as brown and round as an overripe plum, was scuttling in the shadows close to the house. The beetle disappeared into a crevice before either man could grab a rock to crush it. They fell into a long silence, and when their eyes met, they burst into merry laughter, like boys who had broken a tiresome rule without getting caught.

From this initial meeting, they struck up such an easy friendship that the rug merchant assumed they were brothers. Armand kept Bougault company while he designed the scenes for his photographs; Bougault helped Armand sharpen his sense of purpose in his life. He came to think of the arid landscape as a place exempt from modern corruption—the version of the desert as illustrated in Bougault's photographs was the true version, and the reality visible without the camera's aid was just a lie.

He saw two weavers in brilliant white robes sitting near the sun-washed entrance of an ancient catacomb, delicate threads stretched between them, while a third weaver leaned against the archway and observed their effort with impatience.

He saw a donkey carrying two huge bundles of broom, being led by an Arab along a narrow dirt street. He saw a boy watching from the shadow cast by the front wall of a house. He saw the Arab bend his head, at Bougault's direction, so that his face was hidden by the white hood of his immaculate robes.

He saw two beautiful girls dressed in silk gowns and gauzy headscarves lent to them by Bougault, sitting in their dirt yard grinding spices. He saw the girls combing the dirt with their bare toes. He saw one of the girls extend her hand languorously for a turbaned visitor to kiss. He saw that the turbaned man who had been hired by Bougault to play the part of the courtier was actually the Maltese gardener at the hotel where Armand was staying.

He saw the same gardener wearing traditional bedouin robes sitting on a camel on a rocky hilltop behind the ruins of the Roman baths beyond the gates of El Kef. Armand thought it was a fine, suggestive scene, but Bougault disagreed. He wanted an infinity of sand in the background, not ugly rocks and ruins.

They left the Maltese worker and the camel in El Kef and traveled by diligence to Souk-el-Arba and from there by train to Tunis, arriving shortly before midnight. They were given rooms in the house of Monsieur Alapetite, the French resident-general, who was a friend of Bougault's. They spent the evening drinking a tarry anise liquor and arguing about the future of Tunisia, which the resident-general thought a hopeless place and Armand and Bougault believed was a gold mine for the French.

The next day the two men left for Constantine by train. From Constantine they took the diligence to Biskra, where they hired horses and a guide and rode into the desert, reaching Mraier, an oasis famous in the region for its thousands of date palms, in the late afternoon. They were given bed and board at the French military barracks.

In the morning they found an Arab with his own herd of camels. The Arab was a clever bargainer and demanded forty francs for the use of his camel and an additional ten francs to lead the two men a short way into the desert, to the top of a dune.

Armand stood at the photographer's side and watched as the Arab, dressed in bedouin robes, mounted the camel. The camel pushed itself up to standing. The Arab rocked perilously on the wood-and-rawhide saddle and then, following Bougault's order, shaded his eyes with his hands and searched the infinite emptiness of the desert for some sign of life.

On their way back to Mraier, they met a group of Sudanese slaves waiting outside the gates of the village, their faces and robes streaked with dust. Bougault spoke with them and learned that the slaves had been left in charge of the camels while their master finished his business in the village. Bougault spent nearly an hour trying out different arrangements. At the end, he created a tableau with two of the camels sitting on folded legs, the other two camels standing with two of the Sudanese men holding their reins while the third man sat in the foreground with his back to the camera, draped in the spotless white robes Bougault had given him to wear.

The group's master appeared and demanded payment for the service provided by his slaves. Bougault obliged, giving him five francs, and the group set out to continue their trade in the next village. Armand watched them trek as if in slow motion across the sand, the figures shrinking with the distance and finally disappearing over the rise of a dune.

Where the Sudanese men and their camels had been, Armand saw sand seas and salt terraces blistered by heat. He saw a beautiful, vast, windblown nothingness that hid the secrets of its ancient history. And thanks to Bougault, he saw the potential for making a fortune from this land.

On the road to Constantine, Armand asked for copies of the finished photographs. Bougault peered at him strangely without answering, his lips turned up in a half smile, his silence awkward at first, then unnerving. Armand shifted in his seat to move away from him and make the boundaries clear. Bougault's response was to set an exorbitant price for each print, which Armand refused to pay. The two men argued so violently that the diligence they were riding in shook from their fury. By the time they'd reached Constantine, they had agreed that they wanted nothing more to do with each other, and Armand was left to fend for himself.

In his own dream of the desert, Armand was never thirstier than his bedouin guides. He drank only when they drank. He knew thirst to be a sign of weakness. Only foreigners admitted to thirst. Rather than complaining, he sucked whatever moisture was left from his tongue, his gums, the raw lining of his cheeks, before he ever let himself beg for more than his fair share of water. He swallowed the gravel in his throat, squeezed his dry lips together to seal them. He would rather collapse than speak of his thirst. He was willing to lie there, forgotten, while the rest of the caravan moved on, the jingle of the bells on the camels' collars grew fainter, night settled over the dunes, and the river of stars flooded the sky and poured down to earth.

He opened his mouth to catch the jewels released by the sky. When he was finally satiated he sat up and looked at the endless space around him, marveling at his aloneness even as he felt confident that when the sun rose the next morning, another caravan would arrive and offer him a ride.

At some place deep in the core of his being he believed that he wasn't destined to die in the desert. He hadn't been afraid on that first long expedition to El Kef when he was in the military. He hadn't been afraid on his explorations with Bougault. And he wasn't afraid now, lying on his back in the sand.

In Armand's unreal version of North Africa, a brave man could make a fortune. He didn't have to persuade the reticent natives to pose for his camera. All he had to do was lie there under the stars, open his mouth, and drink in the night's treasures.

Days later, or just hours, he woke in his bed at the hotel in El Kef. Before his thoughts clarified, he had the impression of being someone important, as though he'd been charged by some high government official with a crucial diplomatic mission. He imagined speaking fluently in front of a large group of Arabs, explaining to them that he had been authorized to usher in a new period of prosperity and friendship between the French and the people of North Africa.

But on the streets of El Kef there was no prosperity. There were low-slung mud houses and dirty children who followed him everywhere, begging for money. They followed him as he crossed the plaza where the fountain sent its huge spray into the air. They followed him to the ruins of Kasr-er-Roula, an ancient basilica that was said to have been the repository of great treasures. When he started to dig in the dust with his walking stick, the children did the same.

They dug for hours, until the sun was low in the sky, but they found nothing more than shards from broken columns. Armand returned to his hotel, but he was back at the ruins early the next morning. Word spread through El Kef that the white man was digging again, and the children gathered to help. They kept digging through the day and returned the next day to dig some more. They dug and dug and dug until, at last, their labor was rewarded.

"M'sheer, m'sheer," one boy called, and ran toward Armand holding what looked like a dead fish he had unearthed. A fish in the desert! But it couldn't be dead because it had never been alive. It had rubies for eyes, papery brass scales, and a hinge in its center so it could be made to wiggle. As Armand examined the fish, he discovered that the head was detachable. When he pulled it off, the children who had gathered around him hooted Arabic words that sounded to Armand like mockery. He emptied the sand from the fish and replaced the head. Then he jerked the hinged fish in a savage motion toward the nearest boy and growled. The children shrieked and ran away, and Armand put the fish in the pocket of his linen jacket. It was the first of many treasures he would take from the desert.

Under Bougault's influence, Armand formed a confused impression of North Africa, which stood, at least as he wanted to perceive it, as the one place in the world where time did not progress in its usual relentless fashion. Change was unwelcome here. The past had been given permanent shape in relics that were of great value to the future. The present was full of danger yet ripe with possibility. The same monotonous landscape that made it easy for foreigners to lose their bearings kept its treasures snugly stored below its surface. A man just needed to know where to look.

On a train from Tunis to Cairo, he met a Dutchman who had retired from his work at the embassy and lived in a private residence in Alexandria. Hearing of Armand's interest in antiquities, the man showed him a pure-gold Ptolemaic coin that he'd recently purchased from a dealer in Luxor.

"I sense that you are an inexperienced collector," the man said. "Allow me to give you a short lesson." As the law stood in Egypt, he explained, the national museums had the right to acquire all antiquities found during excavations, but at a price fixed below what could be obtained elsewhere. For this reason, the dealers preferred to offer their wares to foreign collectors. But these transactions had to be conducted in utmost secret, and collectors needed to prove that they could be trusted not to disclose the source of their acquisitions to the Egyptian authorities.

"My advice to you, sir, is to offer my name as a reference," the Dutchman said, handing him the card of the dealer who had sold him the gold coin. He added that he'd heard about some Arab brothers who had dug up a cache of treasures in the Valley of the Kings. If Armand was interested, he'd better hurry to Luxor, the man advised, for the treasures would surely be gone within the week.

A Trip up the Nile

IN THE HILLS outside Luxor, in the early morning before the sun rose and before the tourists disembarked from their steamers and the donkeys were saddled and guides assigned, the four Abd-er-Rasoul brothers climbed the cliff behind the Ramesseum, cleared the rocks they'd used to hide the cave they'd made, and resumed their digging.

The government called them criminals, the representatives of museums called them vermin. They were the inheritors of a tradition that was as old as the first mastaba of Saqqâra. Seal the entrance of a tomb with a three-ton slab of granite, and they would break that slab apart. Hide a secret chamber behind a false one, and they would find it. In the land of the living, even a withered finger was worth enough piastres to buy food for the day. What did the dead need with fingers anyway? The less weight carried into the afterlife the better, and industrious thieves were ready to help lighten the load. Besides, any treasure they dug out of the earth was rightfully theirs, since the land belonged to their father. In a just world, it would be so, but in the unjust world of Luxor in the 1870s they were whipped with a bastinado on their bare soles and thrown into jail if they were caught peddling their wares to tourists.

The trick was to not get caught. So they dug in the predawn darkness, when the night sky was just beginning to lighten and the first whisper of the sun's torrid presence was carried by the breeze. Deep inside the cave, with the stones re-piled behind them to camouflage the entrance, the four brothers felt no breeze. Instead, they felt the heat of the torch carried by the youngest brother and smelled the limestone dust that mixed with their sweat, staining their faces with a thick gray paste.

These skilled grave robbers had learned the craft from their father and uncles, who'd learned from their father, who'd discovered that plundering the old tombs was a good way to supplement the income from his small farm. How strange that foreigners were willing to pay—even pay handsomely—for a mummified head or pieces of broken crockery. But the grandfather of the four Abder-Rasoul brothers had understood that the law of supply and demand will always prevail. For years, the family had been meeting the foreigners' demand for relics with a steady if trickling supply, passing along the secret maps of the tunnels from one generation to the next.

Beneath the peak of el-Qurn, the trickle was about to erupt in a flood. One of the brothers widened a gouge in the wall, the rock crumbled from the impact, and the flickering light of the torch revealed the engravings of the cartouche above the entrance of a subterranean passage. The passage was six feet square, and the fearless brothers followed it westward for twenty-four feet and then turned northward, continuing deep into the mountain before the passage terminated in a stairway. One after another, they descended the stairs. At the bottom, the youngest brother raised the torch he was carrying, casting enough light for the brothers to see that this forgotten mortuary chamber contained a dragon's hoard of treasure, there for the taking.

Armand made no secret that he owned some of the jewels that had been looted by the Abd-er-Rasoul brothers from Deir-el-Bahari—including feldspar colonettes and faience mystic eyes, an alabaster ring, an amethyst amulet, and dozens of scarabaei in porcelain, lapis lazuli, jade, amethyst, silver, and gold. He also convinced the brothers to sell him the object that would prove the most important of his early acquisitions, though it was only in wood: a shabty, or "sepulchral statuette," as Armand would describe it in his *Old World Guide*, that "shows the *uraeus*, emblem of royalty on the forehead; and it bears the *cartouche* of Ramses II."

To this day, this shabty is one of only three wooden examples known. The cartouche links it to Ramses II, whose tomb was plundered during the XX Dynasty. The contents of the tombs were then reconsecrated in the XXI Dynasty and sealed inside the chamber that the Abd-er-Rasoul brothers discovered. Until Ahmed Abd-er-Rasoul was arrested in 1881, the brothers were busily selling their goods to foreigners, and Armand, with thrilling ease, was eagerly adding to his collection, convinced that he was playing an important part in bringing the treasures to light.

Three years after he lost contact with the Abd-er-Rasoul brothers, Armand expanded the offerings of the American Bureau of Foreign Travel. The new itinerary included stops in Jerusalem, Samaria, Nazareth, Damascus, Constantinople, Athens, and Patras. But the bulk of the tour—the entire month of February—was dedicated to Egypt. While he made sure to give the impression that his main concern was the comfort of the members of his party, he also let it be known that he was looking to establish himself as one of the world's premier collectors of antiquities. He always offered the local traders a higher price for their goods than what the government would have paid and avoided asking the kinds of questions that would have caused them to put away their wares and make a hasty retreat. The trips proved so fruitful that he repeated them on a dozen separate occasions, either on regional tours or as part of De Potter's Grand Tour Around the World.

Following an itinerary that never varied, the party left Marseille on a Messageries steamer bound for Alexandria. They stayed at the Grand New-Hotel in Cairo and spent the first four days visiting museums and mosques and bazaars. On the fifth day they set out early for Ghizeh, traveling by carriage through the Ismaileeyah quarter of Cairo, over the Kobri el Gezira Bridge, along an avenue bordered by acacias and palms, and across a broad embankment to the edge of the desert, where they would mount camels and trek the last half mile to the base of the First Pyramid.

After Armand paid the entrance fee, the party would march in a file into the pyramid, stumbling through the dark tunnels and expressing disappointment at finding the burial chambers empty except for a single unlidded granite coffer. Back outside again, they fed their apples to the camels and assumed that every Arab peddler spoke English. They each paid twenty piastres to the Sheikh of the Pyramids for permission to ascend the First Pyramid. Groups of Arabs were usually milling about, and for a few piastres they could be called upon to pull and push the visitors up the side. Some young boy would always try to impress the tourists by running up one side of the pyramid and down the other, as quick as a lizard. And a photographer was sure to be on hand to provide them with a record of their adventures.

Satisfied that they'd "done the Pyramids," as they would say

in their letters home, the group embarked up the Nile aboard a Cook's steamer. They sat on a deck shaded by a large awning and spread with rugs, and while a dragoman in attendance poured filtered Nile water for those who were thirsty, Armand described the sights they passed: the white-winged dahabeahs moored under a bridge, the wooded island of Rhoda and its ancient Nilometer, clusters of mud huts, sugar factories, and white-domed mosques. They watched fellahin scoop water from the river and empty the buckets into tiny canals that laced the fields. Sometimes the villagers stood on the shore saluting them. At night, a stake was driven into the riverbank to moor the boat. The silence of the desert was unbroken, except when the captain chose to tie up the steamer near a sakiyeh, a wooden irrigation wheel turned by oxen. Then the passengers would have to try to fall asleep to the sound of the slimy wheel creaking for hours.

On each stop—in Bedreshayn, Bellianah, Assioot, Denderah—they were met by a crowd of shouting, barefoot boys and braying donkeys. Using saddles Armand had rented in Cairo, the men and women of the De Potter party would mount the donkeys, the boys would brandish sticks, and the party would set off at a gallop, passing through palm groves and mud villages, along the edge of the desert marked by a stark line of yellow sand that bordered the green fields, between deep pits lined with shreds of mummy cloth, all in order to see the ruins of ancient temples, broken pieces of colossal statues, and tombs half-buried in the sand.

Always at the Coptic monastery at Gebel-el-Ter, a naked monk would swim out to the steamer, begging for alms, and the passengers would make a game of dropping coins over the rail into his bucket. At Beni-Hassan, farther up the river, there would be more donkey boys waiting for the steamer, along with an especially large group of villagers. As they rode through the village, naked children would run alongside their caravan, offering dusty little bundles for sale that Armand explained were the mummies of cats dug up from an ancient cemetery in the neighborhood. He liked to surprise the Americans, who were easily disgusted, by purchasing a bundle for five piastres. Over the years he'd collected more mummified cats than he could count.

But the tourists had to hurry if they wanted to keep up with their guide, especially once they'd disembarked at Luxor. Even Aimée was left behind when her husband dashed off through the maze of halls and chambers dug out of the solid rock of the mountains. Up the stone steps, down the sloping corridor, across enclosed terraces, and into the temple that had supplied Armand with the bulk of his collection: Deir-el-Bahari.

Wait for your party, Prof. de Potter! But he couldn't wait. He had to go ahead of the group to allow himself a minute alone. Since 1881, when the Abd-er-Rasoul brothers had finally been caught, archaeologists appointed by the Egyptian authorities had been hard at work. The first time Armand had visited Deir-el-Bahari, the one chamber that was open to the public still had a floor of rubble. Through the years, the ancient cenotaph became increasingly tidy, until Armand hardly recognized it. But each time he arrived there, he would stand in calculating silence, wondering if any new treasures had been found.

The travelers never suspected that their guide was concerned with something more important than their interests as he led them through Deir-el-Bahari. Only Aimée knew the extent of his appetite for antiquities. And the next day, while they picnicked among the ruins of the Temple of Isis on the sacred island of Philae, only Aimée knew where he was going when he disappeared.

On the rooftop terrace of the Temple of Isis was a small temple dedicated to Osiris, where Armand would retreat, leaving his wife to preside over the picnic and make up excuses for her husband while he indulged in a rare spell of solitude. Standing on the terrace admiring the view—the waste of sand and rock stretching south, the foaming waters of the cataract to the north, the white houses of Assouan in the distance, veiled by the palms—he would see it all as if for the first time, and he would reflect on the combination of luck and ingenuity that had brought him to this lovely place. Lost in reverie, he would go so far as to imagine the past alive again, seeing in the glint of far-off quartz the jewels of a crown balanced on a pharaoh's head, hearing in the cataract the rumble of stones being dragged by slaves to a temple.

What an enterprising civilization once reigned here, producing beautiful objects for the sole purpose of sealing them for eternity in tombs. Yet Armand couldn't help but wonder: Did it ever cross the minds of the artists that their work would be unearthed one day in the distant future? Did they secretly hope that the tombs would be plundered and their creations acquired by men who would appreciate their beauty and tend them accordingly?

On their journey back to Cairo, Armand would periodically leave his touring party in Aimée's care while he went to meet with his Arab friends who dealt in antiquities. But though he returned to the ship with sealed packages of varying sizes, from ring boxes to shipping crates, the travelers either didn't notice or didn't care. All they wanted to do was collapse on the nearest surface—a flat rock, the ground, even the side of a dozing camel, and think about nothing. They were too worn-out from their expedition to listen to Professor de Potter go on about the history of his latest acquisition.

❧ PART THREE ❧

At Sea

HE EMERGES FROM HIS CABIN on the *Regele Carol* at midday, as the ship steams toward the open sea. He claims an empty deck chair for himself and unfolds a copy of a week-old *Le Temps*, the only newspaper he can find. He reads the paper slowly, front to back. Between pages he looks up and watches passengers stroll past. For no special reason he spends a long time observing a gray-bearded man as he struggles to secure his cigarette in a slender ivory holder.

When the bell sounds for lunch, he makes his way to the dining room and finds the seat he's been assigned among a group of English and American tourists. He is surprised to feel a rare desire to speak candidly with the strangers at his table. He would like to talk about death and eternity, to measure their beliefs against his own. Instead, they begin with the usual greetings, trading names and professions. Armand introduces himself as "Professor de Potter." No one bothers to ask about his field of expertise. The introductions continue. There is a banker from Virginia and a retired vicar and his wife from the village of Swindon in England. The banker announces that he has been to England twice, to Liverpool and London. The vicar is pleased to hear it and invites the banker and everyone else at the table to come visit his parish if they are ever in the vicinity.

When the waiter arrives to fill water glasses, Armand recognizes him as the steward who showed him to his cabin earlier in the day. Now he is wearing thick spectacles that magnify his lazy eye and give him a strangely artificial appearance, as though he were staring out from behind a mask.

Armand sits quietly through the remainder of the meal, listening politely to the vicar's wife complaining about her sore tooth and the banker from Virginia complaining about the plumbing on the ship. The first officer comes over to say hello, and the banker asks if he can send a cable. The officer apologizes and explains that they plan to have a telegraph installed on board next month.

After the officer moves on to another group of passengers, the vicar's wife looks at the remnants of the roast chicken on her plate and declares that she is ready for dessert. Her husband signals to a stewardess, who clears the plates and then returns with the dessert cart. The conversation turns toward the potential merits of the various cakes and pies on display. Speaking in faltering English, the stewardess recommends the chocolate cake. The vicar's wife, having noticed the same surnames on their name tags, asks the girl if she is related to the steward who has just taken their orders. The girl seems slightly nervous about admitting it, but yes, she says, Nico is her brother, confirming the woman's suspicions that the whole Romanian crew belongs to the same family. "Did you notice that they all have brown eyes and black hair," she says, smiling at the girl, who clearly doesn't understand.

Armand resists pointing out that the steward, Nico, has green eyes. He declines dessert, and while the others make their choices, he sets his napkin on his plate and excuses himself, explaining that he must find the captain to speak with him about a business matter.

It isn't exactly a lie: he usually makes a point of introducing himself to the captain, though he won't on this voyage. Anyway, the captain has already left the dining room, and Armand feels no urge to seek him out. Instead, while most of the passengers are still finishing their meal, he goes up to the deck to enjoy the fresh air.

The wind, blowing from the west, is brisk and warm, and as he turns his face to it, he has the impression that the air is liquid, flowing with enough force to blow away memories and disperse the past to make room for the present. Backlit by the bright sun, the body of a gull flying alongside the *Regele Carol* is a dark silhouette, and its wings seem to move in slow motion, as though tied to strings.

It is pleasant on the upper deck, and Armand remains there until other passengers emerge from the dining room and settle into their chairs. He sees the vicar's wife and decides to avoid her. Heading toward the stairs, he passes the Russian women he'd seen earlier in the day. They exchange polite nods, as though they were actually acquainted, and as Armand moves on, he finds himself thinking about how readily people assume a familiarity when they are away from home. Travel puts people at risk of losing their sense of identity, which is part of the thrill of it, in Armand's mind. He welcomes the experience of being separated from the usual markers of familiar surroundings. He is known for his joke of pretending to be lost and threatening to keep the members of his party wandering the streets for hours. Really, though, they understand it to be a ruse. The travelers will only pretend to be worried, and he will only pretend to be lost. Ever since El Kef, he makes sure to have a map in his pocket and a plan in mind.

He is so obviously committed to his current plan that he feels as if he's already rehearsed it. First of all, to return to his cabin he needs to descend one level to the first-class berths, as simple as that, so why he continues descending another flight, and another, until he finds himself on the narrow corridor outside the ship's boiler room, he can't explain. But there he is, and across from him, tucked against the wall, their mouths latched, their bodies melting together, are the Romanian steward with the lazy eye and the stewardess who had identified herself as his sister.

The boilers make such noise behind the closed metal door that the lovers don't hear him and continue their fondling. They look innocent enough, but Armand is so instinctually appalled that he barges forward and pushes the two apart.

The young siblings are flustered. They have reason to be flustered! They have been caught in their deceit. The steward begs in French for the monsieur to excuse him, while the girl pleads in Romanian. Armand rises to the drama: *"Mon Dieu,"* he says in his most theatrical, booming voice, "didn't you tell me he was your brother?"

"Non, non, monsieur—" are the only words the girl can muster right then.

The steward, in his furtive, hushed manner, communicates the truth to Armand: in French he explains that she isn't really his sister, she is his fiancée, and they are going to get married, though it is a secret, it has to be a secret, for her family has already chosen her a husband, a hateful man who will kill her if he finds her. He mustn't be allowed to find her, and the steward and stewardess would be forever grateful to Monsieur if he refrained from revealing their secret to anyone.

He is preparing to reply when a sudden banging of metal against metal erupts in the boiler room. The three of them watch the closed door, waiting for it to swing open. But it doesn't open, and they remain alone in the corridor long enough for Armand to explain that he can help.

Helping, he surmises, should involve money. These two innocents will need more than each other. Yes, he will help the young lovers begin a new life together. Although they hadn't been part of his original plan, the steward and stewardess seem to have been put there to test him. There is only one right thing for him to do. He unfolds his wallet and lifts out several five-franc notes, gesturing with the money toward the steward, who balks and withdraws a step.

"Take it," Armand urges him in French. "You must take it."

"Please keep your money, monsieur."

"Take it, I insist!" He counts, showing them the bills. "Forty! Sixty! And more and more and more! How much do you want? I know what it feels like to be in love. I want to help you begin your new life!"

The steward and stewardess look on, their suspicion growing. Armand guesses that these youngsters think of themselves as familiar enough with the ways of the world to know better than to accept money for nothing. *Nothing* always comes with hidden strings attached. And here is a gentleman attempting to pay them for work they didn't do. Surely he wants a favor in return; everyone wants something, if not now then later, which is why, after finally accepting the money, the steward addresses him coldly, explaining to Monsieur that they have to return to their posts immediately or their absence will draw notice, and the lovers hurry back up the stairs without even taking the trouble to thank him.

Cannes to Piraeus

THE FIRST LETTER from Armand, posted a week earlier in Constantinople, arrived two days after he disappeared at sea, though at that point Aimée was still unaware of his fate. She read it while sitting at the dining room table with Gertrude and Miss Plympton.

"*Ma chérie*, I regret to convey bothersome news, but yesterday I ran into difficulties in Constantinople and now am in need of your assistance. I left my satchel in my hotel room and the door unlocked for a few minutes while I met the Lidfords for tea, and the lovely pouch belt you gave me last Christmas was stolen. The maid has been questioned, to no avail. The thief could have been anyone in the vicinity. Unfortunately, besides two hundred francs that were in the wallet, the belt contained my passport and visa. As you know, without the documents I am not permitted to travel internally in Turkey and therefore am unable to accompany the party to Broussa.

"I have put Mr. Lidford in charge of the tickets and sent the party ahead without me. From Broussa they sail to Costanza and on the 14th will board the train to Bucharest. They are scheduled to arrive in Budapest on the 17th. I need you, dearest, to meet them there, at the Hotel Royal, and conduct the party through the Alpine portion of the tour. At your convenience you may secure a special passport for me from the consulate in Budapest and send it by messenger to Constantinople. I will leave directly upon receiving the passport and meet you at the Hotel Toblach in Toblach no later than Wednesday the 21st.

"I am sorry for the inconvenience, my beloved. I invite Gertie and Miss P. to join you for the excursion, at my expense. Your devoted husband, Armand."

This was not at all what Aimée had been expecting to hear from her husband, and she sat staring at the open letter in silence while Miss Plympton and Gertrude watched her. Finally, she said that she had some business to take care of in Budapest and she would leave in a day or two. She insisted that Gertrude remain in Cannes to attend her French classes, but Miss Plympton—ever eager for adventure, though she'd barely survived their most recent trip—was welcome to accompany her.

Aimée waited nervously that day for the afternoon mail, but there was no additional letter from Armand. She wondered why one of the agency's European associates couldn't have handled the affair, but she went ahead and bought the tickets for their journey and set out the next day with Lucy Plympton.

The first leg of the train ride was uneventful, and they stayed over and rested in Zurich. On the sixteenth they traveled to Innsbruck, where Miss Plympton decided to remain for a few days while Aimée continued on the night train by herself. She reached Vienna early the next morning. She waited at the station and took the first train to Budapest, arriving in the heat of a muggy afternoon.

She pushed through numbing fatigue to meet with one of the members of the party, a young woman from Albany named Miss Maxwell. Aimée pretended to want to hear about Miss Maxwell's experiences up to that point in the tour, asking her about her impressions of Naples and Athens and Constantinople even as she hoped for reassurance about her husband. But all Miss Maxwell said in reference to him was that Professor de Potter was the most learned man she'd ever met.

Aimée was able to resolve the issue of the passport and sent a courier to Armand in Constantinople. She remained anxious and stayed in her hotel room all day, trying to press on in the book she'd brought along but reading the same page over and over.

As Armand had requested, she took charge of the De Potter party, and the next day she led them from Budapest to the Austrian city of Klagenfurt. The following day she continued on with the group to the village of Toblach in the mountains of northern Italy. At times she convinced herself that she was comforted by the scenery, but she couldn't stop thinking about Armand's last letter. He'd said he had lost the proper documentation. Yet he had many friends in Turkey—why hadn't he asked them for help in securing permission to travel through the country?

At the hotel in Toblach, she found several telegrams waiting for her. They weren't from Armand, but they were about him. She saw that they were from the American consulate in Athens and the Piraeus police and had been sent to Aimée in Cannes. Gertrude must have forwarded them to Budapest, then they followed Aimée's trail to Toblach.

Standing in the lobby of the hotel, she was so confused that she had to reread the set of telegrams three times before she grasped the central facts: her husband had boarded a ship named the *Regele Carol* in Constantinople; he had been the single occupant of Stateroom 17; when the passengers disembarked in Piraeus, he wasn't among them; his current whereabouts were not known; his belongings were found in his room.

She clutched the counter to steady herself. One of the women in her party who was in a nearby chair looked up from her newspaper and asked her if she was ill. Moments later she would have no recollection of what she said in response. When she followed the group into the dining room, she felt a strange numbness that spared her temporarily from contemplating the import of the telegrams. She was no more capable of solving a simple math problem than processing the news of her husband's disappearance. An intense weariness came over her, and she longed to sleep. Yet her years of experience showing tourists what they wanted to see served her well. She was able to appear calm and confident when she was dining with the group and even participated in a long conversation about the health benefits of mountain air.

No one in the party minded when she excused herself early from dinner. By then they were absorbed in a good-natured debate about the differences between the Italian waiters and the waiters they'd left behind in Budapest. They paused only to agree to meet the next morning for a hike, and to wish Madame de Potter good-night.

Back in her hotel room she reread the telegrams until she had memorized the details: the name of the ship, the name of its captain, the time of arrival in Piraeus. What was her husband doing on a ship bound for Piraeus? He was supposed to wait in Constantinople for the messenger to bring the copy of his passport and then to meet his wife in Toblach. But here she was in Toblach, reading the notice that he'd gone missing.

She tried to persuade herself that the Greek officials were misinformed. Wasn't it possible that Armand had never boarded the SS *Regele Carol* for Piraeus? Where was he, then? It could be that he was still in Constantinople. But what about the trunk with his belongings that had been left behind in Room 17? Oh, the trunk must have been put on the wrong ship in the confusion at the port—mix-ups like that weren't uncommon. Then how to explain that Armand had been listed on the manifest? That wasn't Armand—it was the thief who had stolen Armand's passport. Armand had received the duplicate passport and was on his way to meet his wife in Toblach. Or he was already back in Cannes, sound asleep in his comfortable new bed. Everything would be all right once the truth was sorted out. Or else a nightmare had begun that would last for the rest of Aimée's life, and Armand de Potter was to blame.

She couldn't help it; she was overcome by fury. Her husband was missing at sea. He had gone missing on purpose. She knew him too well and didn't have to wait for more information to fill in the blanks. Her husband had always been a weak man, too easily hurt by snubs and gossip. His fate was as obvious as if she'd been there to witness it. But he had made sure she wasn't there: the whole story of his missing passport had been a ruse to distract her. Everything about his life had been a ruse. The truth of his deception was as sharply outlined as the towering outcrops of the Dolomites outside her window, jagged silhouettes in the moonlight. He had married her to make her a widow. He who had authored his own impeccable reputation—he'd known all along that he wouldn't be able to keep up the pretense forever, yet she would be required to do just that in his absence. Oh, how she hated him right then. She hated him for being as weak as he was clever. She hated him for tricking her into marrying him, for letting her get used to her happiness and then abandoning her and their child. She had never hated anyone before, and now she hated the man she loved most in the world.

She hated her husband until the next day, when two letters from Armand arrived with the afternoon mail. Aimée's hand trembled as she accepted her mail from the desk clerk, but she had enough sense to return to her room rather than open the envelopes in the lobby.

The letters had been written on stationery of the Pera Palace Hotel and posted in Constantinople. One extended over several pages and the other was just half a page.

In the shorter of the two letters, Armand gave instructions on financial matters Aimée would need to attend to in his absence. The details were clear. She would find the key to his safe-deposit box in the upper right-hand drawer of his desk. Inside the box was his life insurance policy from Mutual Life, paid in full.

The longer letter confused her, and though she read it slowly, she was unable to comprehend its meaning.

"*Ma chérie*," her husband wrote. "By the time you read this letter I will be gone to the Field of Amenti." What was he saying—where was the Field of Amenti? Then came a declaration about the beauty of truth and an invocation to "Almighty, Everlasting God." The letter was written in pencil. The words *I beg you* were crossed out, the sentence left unfinished. "Do not forget," he wrote, "there is something to learn from every civilization." For reasons he would never understand, he was never invited to join the Grand Loge. He hoped his son would have more success. He declared that he was a good Christian who believed in the transmigration of the soul. He listed evils he had *not* committed in his life: adultery, betrayal, the murder of another human being. He had never pointed a gun at anything other than a painted bull's-eye, even during his military service. He had never knowingly sowed discord. He wanted to make sure he said the appropriate prayers when the time came. He was writing to say goodbye to his sweet chérie. Oh, yes, she knew the meaning of goodbye. But what did palm wine, cinnamon, and myrrh have to do with anything? And who was "Prof. HH," and what right did he have to call Armand a fraud? There had been a meeting in Constantinople.

Armand didn't say what had gone wrong. It didn't matter, he insisted. He told her never to doubt his love for her and Victor. His conclusion made little sense and yet was presented as if it were a verdict reached through careful deliberation. He wrote, "Now that you have read to the end, you will understand why you must destroy this letter. You must destroy both letters immediately, for your own sake, and for the sake of our dear son."

She would do anything for the sake of their son—but what was she supposed to understand? That Armand was never coming home? He loved her, that much was clear, and she loved him. Love was something she understood. She also understood that she was supposed to destroy the letters, and she would, as soon as she located the box of wooden matches she always carried in her purse. Where was that box? Here was her drawstring coin bag, her packet of calling cards, a pencil, her opera glasses, her train ticket and passport, and, at last, the matchbox. But the first match broke when she struck it, and though the second match lit, the flame sputtered out along the edge of the letter, and she needed a third match. Three matches it took to set the paper aflame, and then it took the second page to feed the flame, and then the second letter to keep it burning—three pages separated into smoke and a fine ash that smoldered in the basin of her sink and kept her mesmerized for just long enough that by the time she realized that she shouldn't have burned the letters without rereading them one more time, it was too late.

A moment later she could hardly remember what he'd written to her and still didn't understand why he'd wanted her to destroy the letters. Maybe there were no letters. Had she even read them?

There was a knock on her door—the hotel maid was in the hall, she must have smelled the smoke, quick, open the window, Madame was terribly sorry, she had lit a candle, no, she had lit a cigarette, yes, it was true, Madame was a smoker, that was one of her secrets among many, yes, Madame had more secrets than the world would ever know.

But the maid hadn't smelled smoke. She was just checking to see if Madame needed anything.

Madame needed only to make time go backward, to the day before her husband set out on his last tour, so she could keep him with her and prevent him from ever leaving home again.

The following morning she hired a hotel guide to lead the De Potter party on their hike while she stayed behind to send a telegram to the American consul in Athens. By the afternoon she had a response confirming that Armand de Potter had disappeared at sea, and his body had not been recovered.

She asked for a glass of water from the agent but couldn't drink, her hand was shaking so. Yet somehow she managed not to faint. Somehow she managed to get herself back to the hotel and listen to the members of the party tell her all about the scenery she'd missed on their hike, the wild goats perched on rocky precipices, the tiny blue flowers poking out of the snow. What a wonderful time they were having on their Classic, Oriental, and Alpine Tour. Thank you, Madame de Potter, for being such a considerate hostess.

She traveled to the Italian city of Feltre in the Veneto with the touring party, then back north to Zurich and Lausanne. For three days, she played her part expertly—and why shouldn't she? All her marriage had been training for this most demanding of roles. She was refined, cultivated, admirable in all respects. Her surface was impenetrable. No one in the party even caught a glimpse of her turmoil, and when another guide from the agency finally arrived to take her place, the travelers could only say that they were sorry to see her go, and that, as Miss Maxwell put it, Madame de Potter was the most gracious woman she'd ever met.

She took the train from Lausanne to Paris, arriving at ten thirty in the evening. She was met by the director of Armand's Paris office, Edmond Gastineau, who helped her check in at the Hotel St. James on the avenue Bugeaud. She ate a sandwich alone in her room, then soaked for hours in the marble tub.

The next morning she discovered that she couldn't withdraw money from their account at the Crédit Lyonnais Bank. She demanded to see the manager. She waited nearly an hour, and when the manager finally came out from his office, he had an oversize file, which he set on the table in front of Aimée without opening. Pinching and smoothing the tips of his long mustache, he explained that the de Potter account had been closed by Monsieur de Potter nearly a year ago.

She was beginning to understand what Armand had been trying to communicate in the letters that she'd burned. She returned immediately to her room at the St. James, packed her suitcase, and moved to the Hotel Oxford & Cambridge. From there she met Edmond Gastineau at the agency's office. She told him about the closed account. And though she hardly knew the man and had never conferred with him on anything more pressing than what he would like in his tea, she said, "I need your help, Monsieur Gastineau. I need you to help me borrow from the agency's account."

He was honest with her: the agency couldn't pay its bills, and Brown Brothers refused to extend more credit. She touched her fingers to her ears to remind herself which earrings she was wearing—the Venetian pearls Armand had given her for her fortieth birthday. Her mind whirled with calculations—what would the pawnbroker give her for her earrings, and how did that sum compare with their true value?—even as Edmond Gastineau offered to transfer money from his personal account into hers. She refused. He kept insisting, until she finally accepted his charity.

She sent telegrams to officials in Athens and Piraeus begging for news, but she didn't wait for a reply. She bought a ticket for Greece, and on the fifth of July, at nine thirty in the evening, she left on the *rapide*, enduring a hot, tiring journey through the night to Marseille.

She spent the day waiting at the port on a bench. To people passing by she must have seemed a cold, arrogant woman, rigid in her posture, her mouth frozen in a severe line, the panic in her eyes hidden by the shadow of her hat. To Aimée, the world itself was cold and arrogant, and she cringed at everything: the smoke belching from the steamliners, the harsh sunlight reflecting off the water, the stevedores going about their work with brutal indifference, as if they'd heard the news but didn't care that Armand de Potter was missing at sea.

She boarded the SS *Yangtze* for Piraeus at five in the afternoon. It took the steamer two days to reach Naples, and Aimée spent most of her time in her room, reading and sleeping. In Naples she stayed on board, watching the activity on the quay from the deck. Her husband had passed through Naples not much more than a month earlier. What did he experience when he stood on the deck of the steamer? Were there those same little boys, both of them shirtless, in short overalls, climbing up a stack of fishing nets on the pier? Did he feel faint from the heat? Did it occur to him that he might never return home?

She reached Piraeus on Monday at four in the afternoon. With an American woman, a missionary's wife she'd met on the *Yangtze*, she hired a cab for the long ride into Athens. She checked in at the hotel where Armand had stayed one month earlier—the Hôtel d'Angleterre.

The next morning she met the local dragoman, Chorafas, and together they went to all the local hospitals to look over the lists of patients. Their last visit was to the city morgue, where Aimée waited on the street, sweltering in her long dress, while Chorafas went inside to make inquiries. He kept her waiting for so long that she began to grow light-headed. She became sure that he had found her husband and was postponing his announcement of the discovery while the corpse was prepared for viewing. She rehearsed her response to Chorafas when he finally came out: she would collapse in the dusty street, a crowd would gather round, they would carry her into the morgue, flutter fans around her and open a jar of smelling salts, and when she had sufficiently recovered, Chorafas would be speaking gently, telling Madame de Potter how sorry he was to have to inform her that . . .

". . . no gentleman matching your husband has been delivered to the morgue."

"What?"

"The coroner is certain."

A dazed "Oh, then . . ." was all she could muster, though she wanted to ask Chorafas if he was surprised. She wanted to say how strange it was for a man to disappear without a trace.

He led her back to the hotel and offered to accompany her to dinner. She thanked him but declined—she would have dinner alone in her room.

The next day she moved to Mrs. McTaggert's Pension and then took the train on her own to Piraeus. She went first to the police station, where she interviewed the police chief, who spoke limited French. He assured her that his officers had conducted a thorough investigation. Monsieur de Potter had been seen on the deck of the *Regele Carol* late at night by a steward and a stewardess. His room was empty the next morning, and he never appeared for breakfast. His last reported interaction with a fellow passenger was in the evening of the first day of the voyage. A clergyman who had shared his table at dinner said that he'd met Professor de Potter on deck later, and they'd had a friendly exchange. Evidence pointed to an accidental drowning as the cause of death, the police chief said. But he added that two details were suspicious: First, an empty belted wallet had been found in Monsieur de Potter's trunk. She was confused, until she realized that he was referring to Armand's pouch belt. Yet Armand's pouch belt had been stolen from his hotel room in Constantinople—he'd written Aimée to tell her. She refrained from objecting and asked about the second detail. This involved another passenger, an American, on the *Regele Carol*. The American had testified that he'd seen two peddlers in Piraeus trying to sell a small, antique bronze that he was sure had belonged to Monsieur de Potter. But the peddlers had left the area before they could be questioned, taking the bronze with them.

They were gone for good? Aimée asked tensely. The police chief regretted to inform Madame that the two peddlers would be impossible to track down. And the American who had given the testimony had already sailed for home.

She thanked the man for his thorough work. She was emphatic in agreeing with him that her husband had been the victim of an accident. No better explanation was available than that Professor de Potter had suffered a dizzy spell.

After leaving the police station, she went to the office of the Romanian Steamship Company. The manager repeated what the police chief had told her, then invited her on board the *Regele Carol*, which had returned from its most recent voyage to Constantinople that morning. He introduced her to the captain, who was just finishing the lunch that had been delivered to him on the bridge. He untucked his napkin from his collar, dismissed the officers at his table, and invited Madame de Potter to take a seat across from him.

The captain, who spoke English with admirable fluency, launched into an account that was so similar in phrasing to the previous reports that Aimée began to wonder if all the officials of Piraeus had been given a script. But the captain could do better than the others and support his story with witnesses. Before Aimée could think to ask to meet with them, he called in the steward who had seen Armand standing at the rail, along with the stewardess who had been with the steward at the time. He invited Madame de Potter to interview them.

She addressed the stewardess first, asking her in English if she, too, had seen Professor de Potter on deck late at night. The stewardess looked toward the captain in bewilderment. The captain motioned to her to answer the question.

"Yes, madame."

"Do you mean to say you saw him?"

"We see him on top the rail."

Aimée was confused. "On top?"

"I mean I see nothing, madame . . ."

The captain came to the aid of the stewardess, declaring that she had been conversing with the steward and was turned away from the foredeck at the time that the professor was at the rail. And on the steward's behalf he explained in French that if the professor had been seen falling overboard, the alarm would have been sounded and a rescue attempted. It was unfortunate that no one discovered he was missing until the next morning.

The steward, a tall, thin Romanian with thick bottle glasses, burst into tears. He had done nothing wrong, he insisted. He'd seen Monsieur de Potter standing at the rail, looking out at the sea. Monsieur had tipped his hat to him in a friendly greeting. The steward naturally assumed that Monsieur would return to his stateroom after he'd finished smoking his pipe.

Aimée reassured the young man that he wasn't to blame. She

explained that her husband had a silver plate in his head from an old injury and was prone to dizzy spells—he must have lost his balance and fallen over the rail. It was no one's fault, she said. She needed to emphasize the likelihood of an accident and prevent a lengthy investigation. She wouldn't be able to stand by if innocent men—either the peddlers with the bronze or the steward—were wrongly accused of causing her husband's death.

She asked if she could be shown the room Armand had occupied, Room 17, and then asked to be left alone. As she sat there, she tried to imagine how he had spent his last hours on the ship. It would have been preferable to believe, as the steward had suggested, that he'd gone outside to smoke his pipe. But she knew from his letters that after leaving Constantinople, he'd needed more than his pipe.

She sat on the bed until the captain came and gently urged her to leave. She didn't want to leave. This was the last place her husband had slept. The mattress was thin, with uneven creases. His comfortable new bed had been carried into Grand Bois just a few months earlier. He had slept in it for the last time in his own house on the night of May 7. He had kissed her goodbye on May 8 and gone off without telling her that they were on the brink of financial ruin. He had launched himself into the sea for the sake of an insurance indemnity. Now, when she reached out her hand, he wasn't there to hold it.

If only she had been there with him on the deck of the *Regele Carol*—she would have grabbed him by his shoulders and turned him away from the sea. She would have reminded him that they'd lived modestly in a rented one-bedroom apartment in Albany when they were young; they could do it again. She didn't care about money. Armand was mistaken in his belief that she needed luxury to be satisfied. Yet she was filled with regret at the recognition of her own mistake. She hadn't just been happy since they'd moved into Grand Bois—she'd been *too* happy, thus inviting a disaster to even the score.

Back at Mrs. McTaggert's Pension at the end of the day, she opened Armand's steamer trunk, which she had claimed from customs in Piraeus. Lying on top was his pocket watch, stopped at 12:23. She wound the stem and held it against her ear for a moment. Then she picked up the pouch belt, the same belt she had given him as a present last Christmas, which he was supposed to wear cinched over his shirt whenever he was traveling in foreign lands. This was the belt that had supposedly been stolen from his room in Constantinople. He must have decided to leave it on top of his clothes as his apology for his lie about the theft—concocted in desperation as an excuse to abandon his touring party.

She checked the pockets for contents, hoping there might be a letter to her. There was no letter, but the belt wasn't empty, as the police chief in Piraeus had said it was. It contained Armand's passport, now one of two copies, since she'd procured a duplicate for him in Budapest. Tucked in one of the side slots was his calling card with his name: Mr. P. L. Armand de Potter. And there was a card for Valentin's Parfumerie on the avenue de la Gare in Nice.

The card from Valentin's perplexed her the most. Why had he emptied the wallet of money but left the card? Had he forgotten it was there? Or had he left it behind for a reason? Could it be his final message to her? It was just a card for her favorite *parfumerie*. If he had enclosed the card in a letter to her, it would have been an invitation to buy the finest perfume Valentin's sold. Instead of sending the card to her directly, he left it in his trunk, for no other reason, she decided, than to encourage her to indulge herself. It was a small token offered as his last gift to his wife: he wanted to assure her that he had outmaneuvered his creditors and preserved the remnants of his fortune for his survivors.

She couldn't bear going through the rest of the trunk and prepared to lower the lid, though not before catching sight of her husband's notebook. She opened it and ran her finger over the title of the first lecture, "The Sea Kings of the Aegean." She couldn't read the rest of it through the blur of her tears, but she could guess the stories it contained, the ones Armand loved to tell about monsters, labyrinths, jealous gods, and treasures buried for thousands of years.

This was a region where legends persisted and impossibilities became real. Why, then, couldn't she tell a new story herself, one about a husband who was pulled from the sea by fishermen, but because of his ordeal he was suffering from amnesia and couldn't remember his name? Or this: After throwing himself overboard, Armand de Potter swam for miles, reaching the shore of a distant island, where he was nursed back to health by a deaf, old woman who lived alone with her goats. Did the stories need to be credible? What about the *in*credible ones that offered miracles as facts? Wasn't anything possible in this land of ruined temples and broken statues?

She opened her diary and recorded the events of the day. She wrote that she had gone on board the "Regele Carlo," muddling the name in her grief. She reported that she'd spoken with the captain and the stewardess and sat in the room where her husband had slept. She wrote, "There is no longer any doubt—he is dead, Room 17!"

She meant it as a definitive conclusion. But the ink blotted as she drew the exclamation mark, and the more she tried to sharpen the line, the more it looked like the curve of a question mark.

The Long Summer Tour

ONCE HE OPENED HIS OFFICE at 645 Broadway in Albany in the summer of 1879, everything seemed to fall easily into place. When he wasn't teaching the girls at the Albany Academy to say "Regardez cette jolie oiseau dans le ciel," he was at his desk reading his Baedekers, designing itineraries, and composing advertisements. He listed all foreseeable expenses and rehearsed train and steamer schedules. Soon he was making notes for a practical tourist guide to offer by mail order, writing essays about tourist sights for local newspapers, and giving lectures to community organizations about the joys of travel.

The American Bureau of Foreign Travel—sole agency for De Potter's European Tours—was one of many similar businesses in the region, and it could easily have been one of the casualties of the growing competition. But he distinguished his enterprise in two ways: he put the emphasis on luxury travel, and he gave his tours a more pronounced educational component than his rivals did, even going so far as to include with his offerings a three-week program of courses in language and culture at De Potter's Language Institute in Paris, which he billed as a finishing school for American girls.

He identified himself as a doctor of letters, born and raised in Europe, with degrees from universities in France and Italy. By the age of twenty-six, he could claim fluency in nine languages. He had already traveled widely and knew how to flatter the managers of the world's finest hotels. He had extensive reference books on more subjects than he could count. Knowledge was his form of magic, and he aimed to awe his customers by putting his erudition on display.

As the agency grew, Aimée began helping Armand with arrangements. Soon she was planning menus, proofreading the itineraries Armand had drawn up, and writing flattering letters to prospective customers. She taught her own beginning-French classes at the institute in Paris in September and then again in January. She accompanied her husband whenever he went abroad.

The de Potters, bolstered by each other, presented a unified front. Arm in arm, they led their parties across Europe, wading fearlessly through mud when it was raining, oblivious to the dust coating their faces as they wandered through the Forum in Rome. When the restaurant owner in Dijon complained that the Americans weren't drinking enough wine, Aimée and Armand went off together to confer with him, and they agreed to pay an extra franc for each guest. On a hot day in Lausanne, they treated the entire party to ice cream. They were always the first at the breakfast table and the last to go to bed at night. They never complained about fatigue or stumbled as they walked along the broken cobbles of some narrow street, and if they ever got indigestion from the *choucroute* served in Alsace, they never admitted it. They were always in good spirits, glued to each other's side. They were praised as a single entity for their patience and consideration. When they were thanked, they were always thanked together.

The Language Institute turned out to be short-lived, but only because the American Bureau of Foreign Travel was so successful.

The Long Summer Tour was followed by a second Long Summer Tour the next year. In winter, the de Potters led a tour through Greece and Italy. The Winter Tour was followed by an expanded version of the Long Summer Tour, with additional stops in Italy and Ireland. Soon the de Potters were spending more time in Europe than in America, and their tours were proving so popular that they had to turn applicants away.

One applicant they were happy to include on the Long Summer Tour of 1886 was Mrs. Bessie McLaughlin, a librarian and amateur journalist from Massachusetts. After sending in her deposit, she wrote to Armand requesting permission to write a chronicle of the tour, to be published serially in her hometown newspaper. It was welcome publicity, and Armand wrote back to say that he was at her service, ready to offer whatever help she might need in her efforts to document her travels through the months ahead.

Mrs. McLaughlin made it clear that she prided herself on her independence. She would be leaving her husband at home, and she didn't need Professor de Potter or anyone else to influence her opinions. She would decide on the pleasantries to list in her articles, as well as the shortcomings of the tour. If she was uncomfortable, she would let her readers know.

Luckily, the steamship surpassed her expectations, and in her first article she reported that the staterooms were large and light, with new patent toilets and electric pneumatic bells connecting to the steward's department. Two saloons and a smoking room were midship. Steamer chairs graced with woolen rugs and goose-down cushions were plentiful.

The ship hadn't yet passed Montauk Point when Mrs. McLaughlin began sizing up the other travelers. The tally in her first article included "the dignified but kindly Judge Griswold of

Catskill, New York" and a doctor in attendance, with the unlucky name of Paine. There were elderly aunts who preferred the shelter of the cabins, along with their charges—college girls wearing "literary spectacles," who stayed up half the night wandering about on deck. A Massachusetts schoolmistress was described by Mrs. McLaughlin as "ubiquitous, interrogative, and enthusiastic." And there was Madame de Potter, who quickly distinguished herself for being "unassuming in her manners." Before the end of the first day, she had delighted her companions with her "choice conversations" and had "already won their hearts by her gentle womanliness."

But gentle womanliness was not enough to defend the inexperienced travelers against seasickness. On the second morning, the waves were high, the foghorns blowing, and a raw drizzle stung the faces of the passengers, who wondered what they'd gotten themselves into as they groaned and rushed to the rail and then stretched out in steamer chairs in a long row under the shelter of the midship overhang, "giving the once cheerful deck the appearance of a hospital ward," wrote Mrs. McLaughlin, trying to steady her own shaking hand, sucking miserably on one of the sour balls Madame de Potter had given out.

The weather improved by the third day. Mrs. McLaughlin roamed the ship, jotting down her observations. She noted that Judge Griswold won the shuffleboard tournament, Miss Morgan of Wellesley College was pleased to wake up every morning to a fresh box of roses, which her fiancé waiting for her in New York had entrusted with the stewardess, Miss Filer of Detroit played her banjo at night, and Professor de Potter took promenades with the young ladies and entertained them with animated descriptions of the places they'd soon be visiting.

They arrived on the moonlit night of the fifteenth at the entrance of the English Channel. By Wednesday afternoon the "gray, long-armed windmills" of Holland were in sight. The *Noordland* anchored at the mouth of the shallow river Scheldt, waiting for the tide to rise before continuing upriver to Antwerp. Though they were within a stone's throw of land, the travelers had to spend one more night in their staterooms, passing the time playing euchre or reading, or, in Mrs. McLaughlin's case, translating her notes into legible prose.

"Surely it must be a dream—this lovely panorama of quaint old cities, with their treasures of art and historical glories," wrote Mrs. McLaughlin about their arrival in Holland, and then corrected herself: "IT IS NO DREAM," she announced, but rather "a blessed reality that we look with our own eyes upon the country of William the Silent."

From Amsterdam they traveled south by train to Italy and spent three weeks on a grueling tour from Milan to Naples. "The brain whirls before the accumulated treasures of the ages," Mrs. McLaughlin wrote about Italy. It was all too much for the De Potter party to take in, and for an amateur journalist to recount in any detail. "Ears weary of the names of Roman emperors and even Michael Angelo," she wrote in relief when they left Italy behind, "we move on to Switzerland, the land of the gods, where nobody has to burden his or her mind with information for two blessed weeks."

They crossed the Brunig Pass in the Alps and rode in carriages along the Tête-Noire to a village in the shadow of Mont Blanc. "We will not attempt to describe the scenery," Mrs. McLaughlin announced, then went on to describe the scenery: "snowy summits wreathed in clouds that are tinted early and late with the delicate rose and pearl of an opal tower."

From Switzerland they went up to Cologne and traveled by

boat up the Rhine to the village of Coblenz. They continued on to Frankfurt and from there took the night train to Paris.

They spent a week in Paris touring the parks and museums. On the last night, Armand hosted a banquet at the Hotel Chatham and presented each member of the party with a souvenir menu. Toasts were made, songs were sung, and Mrs. McLaughlin recited a ballad she'd written titled "Invasion of Europe by De Potter," which began with the group's disembarkation from the *Noordland* ("The fifty umbrellas were spread in the breeze, / The fifty portmanteau courageously seized") and moved through a lengthy catalog of her impressions of her fellow travelers. By the time she'd covered Mrs. de Long, "who always looked pleasant whatever went wrong," Mr. McClure, who "once seated, could not bear to stir," and Miss Sarah Potts from Glens Falls, New York, who "ran a whole temperance meeting at home / But whisper it not! Fell a victim at Rome, / To the humming decanter, and sad to relate, / Was observed to be slightly unstable in gait," Mrs. McLaughlin had fortified herself with so much champagne that she, too, was slightly unstable in gait, and she slurred her words as she read her tribute to "our leader, that ablest of men / Long, long may he live, and with Madame de Potter, / Lead crowds of Americans over the water."

The Americans stumbled drunkenly up to bed and slept so late the next morning that they missed the train to Calais. Armand had to pay extra to get them on the next train in time to catch the ferry to Dover. But they sailed through the night as planned and arrived in London in time for a performance of *Fidelio* at Covent Garden, which everyone in the party thought splendid.

The tour, in Mrs. McLaughlin's opinion, had gone smoothly. The party's general satisfaction was reflected in the reports she sent to her editor. A few members may have expressed annoyance that they had to finish a European tour with a five-day visit to the unremarkable country of Ireland, but the rest shared Mrs. McLaughlin's pleasure. She wrote about how they all "popped like corn on a shovel" as they rode in a jaunting car along a country road in Killarney. They admired Muckross Abbey, which Mrs. McLaughlin declared more lovely than any ruin along the Rhine. And after recrossing the Irish channel to Holyhead, they took a pleasant ride through Wales to Chester.

Mrs. McLaughlin described the last portion of the trip as "PERFECTLY MARVELOUS." Not until the party set out from Liverpool on August 31, on a three-year-old steamer named *The City of Chicago*, did everything begin to go wrong.

In retrospect, Armand would note earlier signs that the trip was unraveling. The Shelbourne Hotel was crowded, and the staff treated the De Potter party as an inconvenience. The bread at dinner was stale, the chops were overcooked, and the waiters didn't come around to refill the water glasses. One of the ladies in Armand's group wondered too loudly if Dubliners were all suffering from a mental disorder. This same woman discovered the next morning that her purse was missing, and Armand spent half the day trying and failing to recover it.

Shortly after they set out from Liverpool, the ship called *The City of Rome* passed them, running at the full steam generated by her huge boilers, which burned three hundred tons of coal per day and seemed to be traveling at nearly double the speed of the *Chicago*. The travelers were disappointed to hear that the rival ship would arrive in New York ahead of them and demanded to know why their conductor had booked them on such a slow steamer.

In the evening a dense fog overtook them, and shortly after 2:00 a.m. on the morning of the sixth, the *Chicago* sideswiped a fishing schooner. Many passengers slept through the crash. Others heard nothing more than a mild thud. But the rumor that they'd hit an iceberg began circulating, sleeping passengers were roused by panicked friends, and several members of the De Potter party rushed to board the lifeboats.

While the *Chicago* suffered no measurable damage, the schooner had a section of its rigging torn off. The schooner's captain and first mate met with Captain Watkins of the *Chicago*, and after they'd returned to their vessel, Captain Watkins announced that the damage was determined to be minimal and the schooner remained fully seaworthy.

They were still four days from Sandy Hook. As the ship sailed on through the darkness, the de Potters reassured the nervous ladies in their party that the *Chicago* wasn't taking on water. Aimée set the example by returning to her room. But by then, Armand had already given up on sleep, and he spent the rest of the night settled on deck in his chair, wrapped in a cocoon of blankets, feeling the rise and dip of the deck as a lulling buoyancy, giving him the impression that he was weightless.

Toward 4:00 a.m., he became aware of a clanging sound that he thought was the familiar shipboard sound made by a metal ring blowing against the flagpole on the upper deck. But then he began to perceive that it had an unfamiliar rhythm, with a drawn-out, high-pitched ringing.

He realized that the steward's department was on the other side of the wall behind his head, and he was hearing the sound of one of the pneumatic bells being rung from a stateroom. While he couldn't hear the stewards responding, he sensed that deep inside the ship, the night's stillness was being disturbed for a second time.

He waited for some sign of the activity to emerge on deck. His intention was to get up and investigate the matter if no one appeared, but he waited too long and fell asleep. When he woke several hours later, his blankets were soaked through from the fog, and Judge Griswold of Catskill was standing over him, grumbling his name, with a stern, pitying look on his face, as though he were sentencing a prisoner to execution.

He informed Armand that Mrs. Lilian Martel, an elderly woman who had been accompanying her niece on the De Potter tour, was ill with fever, and Dr. Paine had been attending to her through the night. Shortly after 4:00 a.m., Dr. Paine had sent a steward to fetch Armand in his cabin. But Armand hadn't been in his cabin. He had spent the night in his steamer chair, and when he finally arrived at Mrs. Lilian Martel's bedside, he was too late.

Dr. Paine had already returned to his quarters, leaving behind two stewardesses, along with Mrs. Martel's niece. One of the stewardesses sloshed a wet mop over the floor while the other collected towels that had been scattered about in the room. The girl sat in pale, stunned silence beside the blanket-covered mound on the bed. She seemed unaware of Armand's presence at first, but when he cleared his throat, she looked up at him with a puzzled expression, as though she expected him to explain what had happened to her aunt.

He could explain, all right. Though it seemed not to have occurred to the girl, Armand knew that he alone was responsible for her aunt's death. He was the Pied Piper who had persuaded this innocent American woman to risk thieves and accidents and disease. He had led her across the ocean just so she could view in person scenery and cathedrals and works of art she could very well have admired in reproductions in a catalog, in the safety of her home. Yes, it was his fault that Mrs. Lilian Martel was dead, at the age of sixty-three. She'd been in good health up until the previous evening and should have lived at least another decade.

But she had made the mistake of going on a De Potter European Tour. Armand had seduced her with his advertisements. Based on his claims about the benefits of travel, Mrs. Lilian Martel had decided that she wanted to give her niece a chance to see the Old World.

Throughout the journey she'd been a quiet, congenial traveler, easily pleased. She had eaten heartily and made a point of sampling all the available desserts. She had laughed at Dr. Paine's jokes. She kept track of her purse and never complained about her accommodations. She had listened attentively to Armand's lectures. Because she had no special needs, he kept forgetting she was there.

Dr. Paine had misjudged the seriousness of her condition. But how could he have known she was in danger when she gently complained that she felt "out of sorts" at dinner? He prescribed milk of magnesia and sent her to bed. She slept through the collision with the schooner and the panic that followed. Her niece couldn't rouse her. Dr. Paine was summoned, but his smelling salts had no effect. By sunrise, Mrs. Lilian Martel was barely breathing. By breakfast time, she was dead.

A coffin was constructed by the crew that afternoon. The chaplain scheduled the service for the dark hour of 5:00 a.m. the following morning. The plank was hung from the lower aft deck, as far away from the midship staterooms as possible so as not to disturb the passengers who wanted to sleep. Only the de Potters, Dr. Paine, Judge Griswold, and Mrs. Martel's niece were on hand.

Goodbye, goodbye. What else could be said when a coffin hastily built from disassembled pinewood crates was being pushed down a creaking plank into the dark sea? Stop! That's what Armand wanted to say, for he suddenly had a terrible thought: What if the old woman wasn't really dead? What if Dr. Paine, who was known to have a tin ear, hadn't registered the whisper of her heartbeat with his stethoscope? And was that knocking Armand heard as the crew prepared to tip the coffin overboard the sound of scrawny knuckles rapping against wood?

The head of the box hung out over the edge of the plank. The two crew members assigned to maneuver the plank had paused, looking to the captain for direction. The captain nodded, and the men both grunted from the exertion as they lifted the plank and sent the coffin sliding into the sea.

Poor Mrs. Martel. She had gone to the trouble of surviving for sixty-three years, and this was what she got as thanks: a handful of mourners and a watery grave. In a moment the coffin had been swallowed entirely. But those in attendance kept watching the water until the trace of foam left behind by the box had dispersed, and the only remaining proof that Mrs. Martel had ever existed was a family resemblance apparent in the features of her baffled niece.

"BURIAL AT SEA" was the heading Mrs. McLaughlin used for the last section of her final article. "At 5 o'clock in the morning of the 7th a woman was buried at sea. Those who witnessed the solemn service said the occasion was a sad and desolate one. The coffin was wrapped in the American flag and slipped down a plank into the great deep. The husband of the woman was said to be awaiting her arrival in New York."

Aimée spent the rest of the morning with Mrs. Martel's niece, keeping her company, watching over her while she rested. Armand passed the time in his stateroom reading *The Count of Monte Cristo*. Though he had read it twice before, he'd brought it along on this tour for those few occasions when he wanted a distraction. Rather than rereading from cover to cover, he would page through the book and pause at his favorite passages.

For a few minutes, he was absorbed by the scene in which the imprisoned Dantès sews himself inside the sack that had contained the corpse of Faria. When Armand came to the end of the chapter, he looked up, caught sight of the gray sky outside his portal, and shuddered, overwhelmed by an awareness of finality that was paradoxically indisputable and yet would have been impossible to translate into words. But even if he couldn't describe the perception, it was strong enough to trigger one of the headaches he feared.

He put aside his book. He tried to ignore the pain and set out arranging his clothes in his trunk, though they weren't due to reach New York for three days.

As he refolded his shirt, pressing the creases flat, he decided two things. First, in the unfortunate case that God so willed it and one day he followed poor Mrs. Martel overboard, he would add a stipulation to his will: *In the event of my body being lost at sea, that a monument in my memory be erected by my wife, in such a place as she may select but where she will also choose to be buried.* And second, he would make full use of the time he was allotted and prove once and for all that he was worth something.

He considered that the jewels he'd bought from the brothers in Egypt were worth something. He should be worth something, too, because of the metal plate in his head. As he touched his finger to his head, he remembered that the doctors had told him the plate was silver. Why hadn't they used gold? He was convinced that if the plate in his head had been made of gold, it wouldn't cause him such pain.

The pain was worsening. He thought he might vomit and reached for the basin. No, he wasn't going to vomit. He was going to faint. He was going to fall, just as he had once fallen off the parallel bars, careening backward in his stateroom, his head about to hit the floor as he braced himself against the sound, that awful crack, but first—

"Poor dear, what's wrong? Oh, you're ill, my love."

He was her love, and she was his. *Ma bien-aimée.* She had arrived in time to save him and knew exactly what to do when he had one of his spells. She would begin by helping him into bed, and the rest would follow: the cold cloth draped over his forehead to cool the molten metal in his head; the menthol cone; the soothing touch of her hand.

Dantès survived, and Armand would, too. His love had kept him from falling. He vowed that someday he would do the same for her.

Shelter Island to Nice

ANYONE WHO KNEW the de Potters when they were young saw that success came easily to them. The pieces of their material lives fell neatly into place. Aimée could point to a painting in a gallery, and it was hers. Armand was known for his talent of always being in the right place at the right time, when the rarest ancient treasures were first offered for sale. Together, the de Potters kept adding to their possessions, filling their rooms with art and antiquities gathered from around the world. As the tourist business grew, they had more money to spend on beautiful things. They were always on the lookout when they traveled, with cash in hand.

The one addition to their lives that eluded them was a child. For the first few years of their marriage they enjoyed their freedom, even as they prepared themselves for what they assumed was inevitable. But by their fourth anniversary, the inevitable hadn't happened. They launched a more concerted effort, but nothing came of it. A year passed, two years, five years. Aimée began to fear that she would never be a mother. Armand assured her that their child would come along in his own time—and he finally did, ten years into their marriage and three weeks before his due date, on June 8, when Aimée had gone to visit her brother Tom in his summer cottage on Shelter Island.

Luckily, Armand had returned to America from his most recent tour and reached the island in time for the birth of their son. And luckily for Aimée, she was vigorous enough to tolerate a labor complicated by excessive bleeding. When Victor emerged, his lips were a shade of blue that the doctor thought ominous. But he soon brightened with a good rubbing, and both his mother and he grew stronger with each passing day.

For the first six years of his life, Victor was carried around the world as if he were a porcelain doll. He was as portable as a doll, as willing a traveler. He was reasonable about sampling the foods

of different cultures, as long as he could have a sweet at the end of the meal. He spoke French fluently by the age of four. He loved steamships and the adventure of stormy transatlantic passages. But he was also fragile, always thinner than other boys his age, with weak vision and prone to fevers and respiratory ailments. After a doctor in Cairo finally warned the de Potters against taking their son on extended excursions, Aimée stayed behind to care for him.

She stayed behind with Victor in the fall of 1897, when Armand set off on his third tour around the world. They boarded at the Villa Francinelli in Nice, where Aimée experienced the unfamiliar discomfort of idleness. Victor was enrolled in the neighborhood school, and in the afternoon their nursemaid, Rachel, took him to the park. At her meals with other boarders, Aimée pretended that she had somewhere to go each day. Alone in her room, she passed the time writing long letters to her husband.

She was secretly glad when, in December, Rachel announced that she was returning to Dijon to help with the care of her aunt's new baby. With Rachel gone and the school closed for the winter vacation, Aimée had Victor all to herself. She dressed him in his trim little sailor suit and took him for strolls along the Promenade des Anglais. On warm afternoons, they spent hours on the beach, stacking smooth flat pebbles into towers.

A box arrived the day before Christmas with presents from Armand. For Aimée there was an antique ceramic bowl with a dragon crowning the lid. For Victor there was a thick leatherbound stamp album, and he immediately set out to fill it with his collection of postage stamps.

She watched her son as he sat on the floor beside his box of loose stamps. From time to time he would push away his black curls that kept falling across his glasses. He hummed softly, absorbed in his work.

She was about to pick up a book when he asked, "What's this one, Maman?"

"Let's see—why, it's from Algeria."

As she examined the stamp, she was surprised at how clearly she could remember its source. They had sailed to Algiers on the SS *Columbia* in December 1893 and bought stamps and postcards the day they arrived.

"This must be from Egypt," Victor said, separating the stamp from the others. Aimée sat on the floor beside him to see the stamp more clearly.

It was, in fact, from a shop in Ghizeh. They'd first taken Victor to see the Pyramids when he was three. She remembered clutching him as they rode together on a camel across the desert. Then, on the little steamer that carried them up the Nile, she'd tied a leash around Victor's waist so she could keep him from wandering to the foredeck, where the rail was low.

Here was a stamp from the Vatican, purchased the same day in 1894 that they'd taken Victor to mass at St. Peter's, and he'd copied the other worshippers and lowered himself to his knees when the papal procession came up the aisle.

And these were American stamps Armand had brought home from a trade show of philatelists when they were renting a furnished cottage on West Twenty-Third Street in Los Angeles. Aimée remembered New Year's Day was mild that year, and they had taken the train to Pasadena to see the Flower Tournament.

"Is this a real stamp, Maman?"

It was the souvenir stamp of the Chicago Exhibition, where they'd gone in the spring of 1893 to see Armand's collection of bronzes on display. They'd left Los Angeles on the Santa Fe route that April, and in western Kansas the train was brought to a halt by a dust storm, which turned to snow. Victor had developed a hacking cough that persisted through the night. They were all exhausted when they arrived in Chicago thirty-six hours late.

"This is just an ordinary one," Victor said, a little hurt, as if he'd been tricked. Aimée recognized it as a Duval stamp from Paris, where they'd lived for three months in an apartment at 60 avenue d'Iéna, in the sixteenth arrondissement. She remembered that she'd decorated Victor's birthday cake with roses. A few days later, she had hired Rachel to help with Victor's care. She was amused to recall that they'd brought Rachel with them when they traveled to the seaside in Brittany, discovering too late that Victor's nursemaid had a sensitivity to the sun. While Rachel stayed behind to read magazines in the cabana, Victor and Armand and Aimée splashed in the water and built sand castles. After Victor caught a crab, he carried it about in a pail with him all day. He was still small enough that when they took long walks along the beach, Armand and Aimée could hold his hands and swing him between them.

That was the same summer when Armand surprised Aimée with his announcement that he had arranged for them to go to a spa near Nevers. They'd been there twice before, and each time it had been awfully hot. It was as hot as ever in Nevers that year, but Armand was hopeful that the water treatment at the spa would provide relief from his headaches. After three weeks, he had declared himself cured, and they returned to Paris. But the cure didn't last forever.

"This one is from India, I think."

No, Victor was mistaken—it was a stamp from the bazaar in Tunis. They'd sailed to Tunis in December 1895 and celebrated Christmas in their hotel room. That was the year she'd bought curtains at the bazaar, Armand had found a cartouche bag for himself, and they'd bought the stamp for Victor.

Here was a souvenir stamp from Carthage, where they'd spent the day wandering through the ruins and peering into cisterns. And one from Oudna, where they'd gone in a carriage on New Year's Day to see the Roman ruins. She would never forget how the wind had whipped up sand spouts, and the driver stopped the horse in the shelter under an ancient aqueduct. They'd kept the blinds pulled closed and eaten their lunch inside the carriage, but still enough sand had gotten into the carriage that Victor had a coughing fit, which relented only when the windstorm had passed.

Here was a stamp from Malta, and another from Egypt that must have been bought the year they stayed for an entire month in Cairo, when Victor was five. They did not bring Rachel along to Egypt, and Aimée was frantic trying to keep up with Victor, who wanted to dart across the busy streets when he saw a flash of something interesting on a merchant's cart. She had expected it would be easier when they met up with a De Potter touring party for a trip up the Nile. But the day before they were to board the steamer, Victor developed a high fever and coughed up yellow phlegm. They'd called in a German doctor, who diagnosed pneumonia. Armand was obliged to leave his family and lead the Nile cruise on his own, while Aimée had stayed with Victor at the hotel in Cairo. She sat up with him for four nights in a row and would have collapsed from exhaustion if the hotel hadn't found her a Sudanese girl to fill in while she rested in the afternoons.

Though Victor had recovered completely, the illness marked a turning point for the family. That was their last trip together to Egypt and the last time Aimée and Victor joined Armand on any of the extended tours to the south and east. The family still traveled on trips to the United States and across France and Northern Europe. But while Armand led his tours around the world, Aimée stayed behind to keep watch over their delicate son.

Following his tradition of falling ill during the holiday season, Victor caught a cold and sneezed and coughed through the week after Christmas. On New Year's Eve, Aimée put him to bed early and then spent the evening alone in her room. She had a sore throat herself, and except for the warm crackling of the wood fire, her surroundings were unbearably dreary. Her husband was across the world, and though Aimée and Victor had been given the chance, they couldn't keep up with him. And if they couldn't keep up with him, then they would be confined to the prison of whatever place they were expected to call home. What was home but a cell with four walls and a door with a glass knob that had a spiderweb of cracks across one facet? And why hadn't any of her friends in Nice called on her that day? And what if Victor's health worsened?

Armand would have insisted that Victor was more robust than she allowed, and his frequent illnesses would make him stronger in the long run—that's what a doctor in Geneva had once told them, and Armand would have repeated it, if he'd been there to comfort her. She brooded about her husband's absence, the emptiness that seemed to rub against her skin, the pasty feeling on her tongue. It struck her as absurdly wrong that on the last day of December in the year 1897, Armand wasn't there for her to kiss. She was a spirited American woman, it was New Year's Eve, and she was alone in her room, watching the flames devour a log while her husband was off frolicking with his party in the gardens of Macao.

Her dear mother had died two years earlier, when the de Potters were in Damascus. Aimée hadn't had a chance to say goodbye. And now there was her father to worry over, a widower, sickly and confined to his farmhouse in Tivoli. He had what she liked to

117

describe as an indomitable disposition, yet it seemed the world was going to have its way and make him suffer, along with everyone else. A letter from him to Victor had arrived the previous week. He had explained that he had "pleurisy of the left side" and encouraged his grandson to obey his parents and say his prayers. He had signed the letter, "Good night."

It was all too much for her, and she began to weep. She wept silently, pressing her fist against her lips. She wept loudly, muffling the sound with her pillow. She wept with disgust at her inability to control her emotions. She wouldn't have thought it possible to feel so alone—this despite that she could have picked up her pen and written to her husband, imploring him to come home, and he would have obliged, finding a substitute to conduct his Grand Tour. Her awareness of the strength of their love should have been enough to ease her loneliness. But she couldn't ask him to come home, and it would be seven months before she and Armand were together again.

She was too absorbed in her self-pity to hear her son calling to her from the adjacent bedroom. When she didn't go to him, he came to her.

He was standing there watching her when she finally lowered the pillow from her face. She was ashamed to be seen by Victor in such a state. She smoothed her lace nightcap and tried blinking away her tears in an effort to hide the truth, all too obvious, that she who presented a front of formidable composure to the world was the weakest of women.

"I can't sleep," Victor announced, oblivious to his mother's misery, forcing a little cough to earn her sympathy. The light of the fire reflected in his glasses. His flushed cheeks were enough of a prompt for Aimée to focus all her worry: a fever might signal pneumonia. Here it was closing in on midnight on New Year's Eve, and somehow she must find a doctor. The proprietress, Madame

Vollard, lived on the ground floor and was nearly deaf. Would she hear when Aimée pounded on her door? All these thoughts were going through her mind as Victor climbed onto her lap. She felt his forehead and was reassured by the coolness of his skin. She kissed the tip of his nose.

"It's very late, darling. Why are you awake?"

"I don't know."

She could tell from his pout that he had a confession to make, but he would need coaxing. "Have you been coughing?" she asked gently.

He shook his head.

"Does your throat hurt?"

"No."

"Are you hungry?"

"No."

"Will you tell me what's wrong?"

He picked up the string of her cap and coiled it around his finger. He stared sullenly at the floor.

"I lost something," he finally admitted.

"What did you lose?"

"Nothing."

"Something isn't nothing. Tell me the truth, Victor. I won't be angry with you."

"My halfpenny Rose Red."

"Why were you looking through your album when you were supposed to be sleeping?"

"You promised you wouldn't be angry!" He burst into tears. She assured him that she wasn't angry at all and held him close, hiding her amusement at the melodrama—her dear, sweet boy was upset about losing a halfpenny postage stamp! She was glad to have the chance to comfort him, to be a source of strength, to provide a model of serenity—this made her feel like herself again.

She wasn't going to waste her time feeling sorry for herself. She was Madame de Potter inside and out. And after she and Victor had scoured his room and she had finally found the stamp, which had fallen beneath the bureau, after she'd tucked him back in bed and set his beloved album on the table close to him, after she'd listened to him talking about all the stamps he wanted to collect to fill the empty slots still left in the album, she considered how lucky she was at having two treasure hunters to love.

PART FOUR

At Sea

He only meant to rest for a few minutes and is not aware of having fallen asleep in his steamer chair. But when Armand opens his eyes, the sun is lower in the sky and the strait has widened, melting into the sea. The shoreline is barely visible in the distance. On the chair beside him, the banker from Virginia is paging through a book about Greece.

Armand realizes he could be of service. Without invitation, he advises the banker to start his tour with the Agora and avoid climbing up to the Acropolis in the heat of the midday sun. The banker thanks him for the advice and announces that he has already climbed up to the Acropolis—twice—during the previous week of his tour, before he set out for Constantinople. He is on his way home, he says, and yes, it has been a splendid trip, except that he failed to find anything to bring back to his wife. She is afraid of sea travel, the banker explains. Ever since she suffered terribly from sickness on the Chesapeake when she was a girl of ten, she won't go near any kind of boat. If the banker wants to travel overseas, he has to travel alone. But his wife always enjoys the gifts he brings back from foreign lands. And here he is returning to her empty-handed.

An idea comes to Armand as he listens to the banker's story. "If you'll excuse me, sir," he says, "I'll be right back." It takes only a minute or two for him to hurry to his stateroom and open his trunk and find the box containing his most recent acquisition—the small bronze statue of Bacchus that he'd procured in Constantinople. Back at the banker's side, he hands him the box. "Please give this to your wife, with kind regards."

The banker hesitates, as suspicious as the steward and stewardess had been in the face of Armand's generosity.

"Go on," Armand urges. "Open it."

The banker raises the lid and examines the figure, turning it over in his hand. "It's marvelous, but I expect it cost you a fortune."

"Honestly, the dealer didn't know the value of it, and I bought it for next to nothing. Really, he practically gave it away. And now I'm giving it to you to give to your wife. Take it. I insist!"

The banker is cannier than the steward and stewardess and less reluctant than they had been to close a deal he is sure to profit by. "Well, then, I accept," he says, adding, if it isn't too much trouble, that he would like a receipt, even though no money has changed hands. Armand obliges by writing out a bill of sale and signing it over to the banker. "I hope your wife enjoys it," he says kindly. "Oh, and by the way, I wouldn't declare it at customs if I were you. The Ottomans have strict rules about exporting antiquities."

Armand offers the warning as helpful advice, not expecting that it would be enough to annoy the banker, who clearly prides himself on being impeccably virtuous in his business dealings. If he can't declare it at customs, then he doesn't want it. He snaps the lid closed and hands the box back to Armand with a grunt of displeasure. "Thank you," he says, "but I prefer to find a gift for my wife on my own."

As he takes possession again of his little bronze, Armand considers how difficult it is to be magnanimous in a world that rewards suspicion. The banker goes back to reading his book about Greece, leaving Professor de Potter stuck with a treasure so lacking in interest that he can't even give it away.

Grand Bois

THE DAY SHE RETURNED from Greece—five weeks after her husband disappeared at sea—Aimée began to dream about him. In the first dream, he was in bed with her. The lamp was off, and the shutters of her window were closed tight. She couldn't see him in the darkness, but she could feel him.

In the second dream, she was standing with a group of tourists outside the front door of the château in the Touraine they'd rented for the first half of 1887, the Château Montagland. The door opened, and Armand was there, ready to welcome the party and greeting his wife as if she were a stranger.

A servant stood nearby, playing "The Star-Spangled Banner" on the piccolo. American-flag bunting was draped from the corbels. The wall alongside the stairway was decorated with circular Toledo swords from Armand's early collection. A plaque of hammered brass, with a portrait of the wife of Francis I, hung above the entranceway.

Armand led the group into the kitchen, where a servant Aimée had never seen before was arranging brioche on a plate. His expression was somber, but he had the ruddy, fat-cheeked face of a cherub. A rustic knotted-wool rug was on the floor, and a fire burned in the hearth.

Armand continued past the servant without a word, through the kitchen, down the hall, and pushed back a pair of pocket doors, revealing the room he called "the *petit salon des arts*," which was identical to the salon in Grand Bois, except that there was no gilt cabinet.

Armand gestured toward the clock on the mantel, the one given to the de Potters by members of the Long Summer Tour of 1884, made of black Egina marble, with miniature pillars in imitation of a Greek temple. As if on command, the clock began to chime, and the sound woke the white marble Venus de Milo, who bent her head from one side to the other as though to stretch her stiff neck. The bronze Italian soldier across the room caught Aimée's eye and winked at her lasciviously. The wooden Daughter of Madame Angot raised herself on her rosetted slippers and pointed first toward the miniature bronze Psyche, who was embracing her dying gladiator, and then toward the marble Moses, who thrust his fingers into the flowing billows of his white beard as if to search for something there.

It was wondrous and frightening and beautiful all at once. Even in the dream, though, Aimée was aware that some trick must be involved. Before she could ask their guide about the lights and mirrors he used to create the illusion, she woke up.

The day after this second dream, she went into her husband's study, lifted the pedestal bowl, folded the embroidered runner, and carefully opened her husband's desk, only briefly sifting through its contents before closing the lid.

"Gray day," she wrote in her diary that night. "Opened A's

desk—like uncovering the face of a corpse—& his hand placed all these things as they are. How can I go through all this & live."

Every day that week she had meetings with bankers, lawyers, and once with the Entrepreneur, as the consultant called himself. He'd been recommended by Edmond Gastineau, who knew of him only by reputation. He was famous, Gastineau said, for saving his clients unnecessary fees. But the famous Entrepreneur, who sat across from her veiled by the haze of his cigar smoke, had only one piece of advice on how to handle the debts Armand had left behind: Madame de Potter *must, must, must* avoid giving the impression that she was desperate.

She may have been desperate to find money to pay her bills; she would have no difficulty, though, disguising the reality of her finances. As Madame de Potter, she had learned to play her part with seemingly artless grace. Now as a widow, she had already developed a new confidence in her ability to hide the truth. All she had to do was tell people what she wanted them to believe.

She wanted them to believe that there was no crisis her husband hadn't been capable of handling. That's what he'd persuaded her to believe while he was still alive, successfully shielding her from the scope of his debts. Looking over the bank records, she wondered if there were investments he had made long ago that he'd forgotten to record. She doubted it, but the next day she opened her husband's desk for a second time, knowing that among the stack of his passports and visas, she would find the key to his safe-deposit box, along with a copy of his will:

"In the name of God, Amen: I, Pierre Louis de Potter d'Elseghem, commonly known and subscribing myself as Armand de Potter, being of sound and disposing mind, memory and understanding, but realizing the uncertainty of human life . . ."

He indicated that he wanted all his just and legal debts to be paid as soon as possible after his death; he bequeathed to his wife all his stocks and bonds on deposit and his Paid Up Life Insurance Policy; he bequeathed to his wife and son the total value of his Tourist Business in New York and Paris, and his collection of Egyptian Antiquities. He requested, "In the event of my body being lost at sea that a monument be erected to my memory by my wife."

She paused, rereading the stipulation he'd put in years ago. *A monument be erected to my memory . . . A monument . . .* How strange it was to read these words now. What sort of monument had he imagined for himself? A weeping angel? A pyramid?

They were supposed to grow old together and had already begun to enjoy a kind of retirement from the frenzy of the tourist business—reading, art study, travel, long walks in this beautiful country, returning to the home they called Paradise. She remembered asking her husband if it was possible to be *too* happy. How she regretted the comment.

Her regret was worsened by the mystery of his end, which made death insubstantial. A telegram or a ring at the gate in the evening would make her start. When a letter arrived containing a Kodak taken of Armand during his last weeks alive, she almost called out, as if to summon him from the next room: *Come see, my love, come look at yourself!* But her voice caught in her throat when she realized that in this photograph taken of her husband during his final tour, he had his own camera in his hand, as if he were preparing to take a picture of her as she looked at him, and he was seated on the base of a tombstone.

She tried to stay occupied in the days that followed. She went to the dressmaker's in Nice and bought hyacinth bulbs at the market. She ordered mourning cards and wrote letters. Eventually she forced herself to open her husband's desk once more.

Looking through his passports and visas, she was puzzled by certain inconsistencies. From the documents, she couldn't be sure whether her husband first arrived in New York in 1871 or 1873, whether he was born in Belgium or France and stood five feet six inches or five feet eight inches tall. She attributed such mistakes to Armand's accent. A news clipping dated September 18, 1875, announced that a man named "Mr. T. De Potter" would be in charge of the French Department at St. Agnes's School in Albany. The *T*, she guessed, was misheard when Armand pronounced the initial *P* of his first name. In a later report, Mr. T. De Potter had become "Prof. Pierce L. De Potter, the French instructor in St. Agnes's School," who was praised for giving a "particularly vivid" lecture, "The History of France from Francis II to the Present Time," with "choice selections from the poets" interspersed.

She preferred to read his own articles and lectures. He had spent so much of his time writing, even when he wasn't in his study. If he didn't have a journal with him, he wrote on the backs of envelopes. He used a pencil when traveling, a gold-banded Waterman fountain pen at home. Shortly after they'd moved to Cannes he had bought a Remington typewriter and taught himself to type. When he wasn't making notes for a lecture or writing an essay about his travels, he wrote letters and postcards. Occasionally he wrote short skits, such as the one about Napoléon for the Tivoli Literary Society. He wrote about the Ottoman Empire, the ancient Greeks, the pharaohs of Egypt. He wrote a long essay about Egyptian techniques of embalming. He wrote about Dutch, German, Flemish, Neapolitan, Lombardian, and Florentine art. He wrote at length about Fra Angelico. He wrote about land ownership in Great Britain and the guilds of Bruges.

Some things didn't fit, such as when he singled out Bacchus for special praise in his lecture on the Greek gods: "Nothing from mythology has been of more use to artists," he wrote, than the "wild night Bacchanals"—this from a man who rarely allowed himself more than a single glass of wine at dinner. In his lecture on Constantinople, his remarks about the present sultan, Abdul Hamid, remained incomplete: "Though much is said against him, he has introduced many reforms in his empire—and I believe modern history will point to him as one of Turkey's most enlightened rulers. —But!!!" And there were several pages of an unfinished story Armand had titled "The Little Corporal," about a French cavalry officer named Louis Pierre d'Elseghem, who discovers at the age of twenty that he is the illegitimate son of a Belgian nobleman.

Aimée found the story confusing, and Armand had apparently agreed, for he'd drawn a big X in red ink across every page. But he'd left unmarked a strange passage about the Belgian nobleman Antoine David Dupont, the father of Louis Pierre d'Elseghem, who after gambling away the family's fortune flees from his disgrace to a farm in the Australian outback, where he lives out the rest of his life in obscurity, raising goats and making a sour, nearly inedible cheese.

It was a pointless digression in an ill-conceived story. Mostly, though, Armand's personality was so vividly expressed in his writing that Aimée could think of no other response than to pray to God to return her husband to her. For a moment, while reading his reflections on the value of politeness in an essay he'd published shortly after they were married, she could almost be persuaded that he was there in the room, reciting for an audience: "Society is a masquerade, and with the invitation to participate comes the important responsibility of choosing a costume. Whatever may otherwise be the disguises worn by one's associates, it must be agreed that the most appealing mask is that of politeness. A well-bred man should be polite to all from the grandest to the humblest; courtesy is the seal of a perfect education."

Her darling gentleman, who fooled everyone, even his wife, with his civility. She'd assumed that together they buoyed each other enough to survive any troubles they encountered. And how insignificant their troubles seemed from inside the walls of Grand Bois. Even the threats from the travelers in the Jaffa accident lost their sting, or so Aimée thought. Weren't she and Armand enjoying the masquerade together, whirling through high society hand in hand, disguised as royalty with their invented names, convincing tourists that they had to pay for the privilege of their company? Yes, her husband was polite to all. He had even doffed his hat to the steward on the *Regele Carol*.

She called to him; he didn't reply. All she had to conjure him were these remnants: scribblings in his journals, lecture notes, unfinished essays, and the letters he had written to her over the years. It seemed there was nothing he hadn't written about or was not planning to write about. And it amounted to no more than a pile of papers that anyone other than Aimée would have thrown away.

She was slow to begin the business of settling the estate and careful about keeping the manner of his death a secret. When she finally sent Armand's will to G. A. Hereshoff Bartlett, her lawyer in Paris, she offered only the brief explanation that her husband had accidentally fallen overboard and drowned off the coast of Greece.

Bartlett's response was equally brief: "I am this moment in receipt of your letter enclosing your husband's will. If you leave the will with us, it will be for the purpose of our preparing all the papers." He wanted to be sure that he had full charge of the probate work, for "this is no easy matter," he wrote, "but on the contrary a most delicate undertaking." He warned Aimée that he couldn't predict what the legal costs would be. "They may be 1,000 francs and they may be 5,000 francs," he declared. "It frequently happens that an apparently trifling and simple matter may involve very intricate questions of law and necessitate the most delicate and skillful handling." As an example, he returned the copy of the most recent will, which included an addendum declaring that "such deposits" as his accounts at the Société Générale were all *joint* deposits with his wife, and requesting that the property due to his son be held in trust until Victor was twenty-five, "he to enjoy the income with his mother until that time."

Armand had dated the addendum "Cannes, January 28, 1904" and signed it, but according to Bartlett, it was invalid because it hadn't been witnessed. Yet even if it had been witnessed, it wouldn't have made a difference in the settlement, Bartlett said, since there already were equivalent stipulations in the older will.

Aimée was left wondering why Armand had gone to the trouble of inserting the addendum without telling her. As she reread the paragraph, she lingered over the phrase *such deposits*. Why hadn't he mentioned that he'd closed their account at the Crédit Lyonnais? Had her husband meant to put a portion of his wealth out of his wife's reach so he could draw on it without her knowledge?

In the next moment she felt disgusted with herself for her suspicion. Armand had kept his debts secret to spare her from financial worries. Clearly, she saw now, Grand Bois had been beyond their means. Her husband had also been borrowing money to cover the debts associated with his antiquities. He had paid more for the treasures than he could afford. The addendum was evidence that as early as January 1904, he was trying to protect his estate from creditors.

Over the next two weeks, new questions arose. Bartlett wrote to say that the insurance company demanded additional proof of the death of Mr. de Potter before they would agree to pay the indemnity. They wanted bond in the form of collateral evidence, such as an affidavit by the captain of the vessel stating that Mr. de Potter went on board but did not leave the vessel. After receiving written testimony from Chorafas, the dragoman, they wanted an affidavit from the steward who had seen Mr. de Potter at the rail and the stewardess who had been with the steward. And they wanted an affidavit from the gentleman who talked with the two peddlers in Piraeus, and the statement of the peddlers, could they be found. Chorafas had referred to the peddlers and the unknown gentleman in his testimony. Why hadn't Aimée mentioned them to Bartlett? He demanded to know if she might have forgotten to tell him anything else.

In the weeks that followed, Bartlett complained that he was experiencing great difficulty in locating the steward and stewardess of the *Regele Carol*—he was as far from getting a clue of their whereabouts as he was when he'd started. The best they could hope for was that the sworn statement of the U.S. consul at Athens should be sufficient to satisfy the incredulity of Mutual Life.

Bartlett kept after Aimée, demanding endless documentation and warning her that the case was growing ever more complicated. But after months of legal haggling she received an unexpected letter from him reporting that the insurance company had agreed to pay out the indemnity. Without bothering to explain how the *delicate matter* was resolved, he enclosed a final bill, charging seventy-five hundred francs for his services.

It took months for Mutual Life to send a check, and until then Aimée struggled to meet expenses. She resolved to sell the travel business to Edmond Gastineau, and with the money she borrowed against the forthcoming sale she was able to pay Victor's tuition. She sold the pair of cane-mesh reclining chairs to Roland Berg, an American who had married a Frenchwoman and opened up a furniture store in Nice, and she was able to send Bartlett the first installment of his payment.

On the day she went to the bank to prepare a money order for Bartlett, she discovered a strange discrepancy in her account. According to her passbook, she should have had a little under twenty thousand francs, but according to the bank, a recent withdrawal had put the sum below fifteen thousand. She insisted that she hadn't made any such withdrawal. The teller provided her with the record: five thousand francs had been withdrawn on January 10, 1906.

The account had been opened jointly, and she hadn't gone

through the trouble of removing her husband's name. It was one of several accounts Armand used to draw from to pay his business expenses. But the five thousand francs had been withdrawn six months after his death.

Though Aimée was writing enormous checks almost daily, she couldn't have forgotten a withdrawal of five thousand francs. The only plausible explanation was that Edmond Gastineau had drawn from the account to cover the agency's bills. But why hadn't he written ahead of time to warn her? He probably hadn't wanted to bother her with the agency's financial troubles. He would explain it all if she asked him. She didn't want to ask him. She had no suspicions regarding Edmond Gastineau. But how to explain the five thousand francs that had gone missing from her and Armand's joint account? Five thousand francs. Maybe Edmond Gastineau had nothing to do with the withdrawal. Maybe it was a mystery Madame de Potter should avoid trying to solve.

She spent the rest of the afternoon walking. She walked beside the embankment and sat on a bench for a long while, looking out at the sea. She got up and walked along la Croisette so lost in thought that she walked right into an elderly woman, who would have fallen flat on her back if her husband hadn't been holding her arm.

Pardon, madame.

She wanted to ask the old woman if she had spent her years so devoted to her husband that she'd had practically no life of her own. Was this what people thought when they saw Armand de Potter's widow? The prospect filled her with bitterness.

She walked up the hill of the avenue de Vallauris in a daze. Back at Grand Bois, she went straight up to her room. She had no one she could confide in, so she confided in her diary: "5,000 missing from account at SG. Could it mean that he—" She refrained from expressing the whole of her suspicion and instead wrote in code:

". . . . —.—— ... . .." It was a mad idea, one that should only have come to her in the delirium of a fever. Five thousand francs were missing from their joint account. Five thousand francs.

She spoke the rebuttal aloud. "Impossible!" Her husband wouldn't have played such a terrible trick on his wife and son. She would mourn him, but she refused to accuse him of such an outrageous deceit. He had boarded the *Regele Carol* with the intention of throwing himself overboard, and that's what he'd done. The stewardess had even said something about seeing Professor de Potter on top of the rail. On top! A man last seen on top of the rail of a ship does not climb down and walk away.

She couldn't keep herself from imagining the terror of his final moments. Walking along la Croisette in the rain, she looked out at the swells of the sea and thought of Armand's body thrown about by the waves.

She often wondered what he would want to say to her. One night that spring she dreamed once more of her husband. He was sitting beside her on the stone bench in the garden and began whispering to her, his voice barely audible as he explained why he hadn't come home. When she woke, she was disappointed to find that she couldn't recall his words. She would spend the rest of her life trying to remember what, for a moment in a dream, she had understood.

The Columbian Exposition

ADIES AND GENTLEMEN," he said in his introductory presentation on the first day of the Columbian Exposition in the spring of 1893, "I am honored to have this opportunity to present to you my little monuments, relics of the oldest known civilization. I trust you will agree with me," he said, gesturing to the display, "that the figures in De Potter's Egyptian Pantheon are as beautiful as they are rare." He held up one of the bronze statuettes mounted on a pedestal, turned it round for his audience to admire. "Let me introduce you to the majestic Osiris, frozen in his regal stance for three thousand years. During his life, Osiris spread the influence of good. He was murdered by his brother Set, the god of evil, who trapped Osiris in a coffin and drowned him in the Nile. He appears to us as a mummy, with his hands uncovered, holding a scepter and scourge, emblems of sovereignty. He wears the crown of Egypt, ornamented with ostrich feathers, which symbolize truth.

"And this sweet goddess here," he said, gesturing down the row, "is Isis, sister and wife of Osiris, the mistress of all the elements, who represents that which has been and always will be.

She is the mother of man, crowned by a vulture, the emblem of maternity.

"And here is Horus, with the head of a sparrow-hawk, holding the ankh, the emblem of life. We have Ptah-Sokar holding the tat, emblem of stability. Here is Pasht, wife of Ptah, holding a lotus blossom. You see the wise Imhotep, with an open scroll of papyrus on his knees and his eyelids encrusted in gold. And if you look at the table to your right, you will see representatives of the sacred menagerie—a hawk, a cat, a crouching ox, an asp, a crocodile, a lion with the head of a man, a serpent with the head of a woman, a necklace of gilded bees, and, last but not least, a friendly monkey named Cynocephalus, who sits on the handles of the scales during the judgment of the soul and provides equilibrium.

"As you linger over my Pantheon," he said, stepping aside to let the visitors admire the whole of the display, "I urge you to consider that these treasures have been hidden in tombs for thousands of years. These are the possessions that the dead brought with them on their journey to the afterlife. Taken together, they are the equivalent of a shriek in the night, heard from a distance impossible to traverse. They convey a love of life and a fear of death and a desperate desire to be free. They are the expressions of an impulse that is both deeply personal and shared by everyone: they were crafted and stored in defiance of death. They invite us to admire their beauty and to stand in awe before the mystery of eternity.

"Thank you, my friends," he said with a bow. "Thank you for taking the time to hear about my exhibition . . . which," he couldn't resist adding, "is the result of careful selection by an amateur archaeologist, orientalist, and traveler and made without the aid of any government or association. I hope it will prove of interest in our great Columbian Exposition."

He gave his first and only presentation in Chicago shortly after the doors of Department M in the Anthropological Building, where his Pantheon was housed, opened to the public. He was disappointed that he wasn't asked by the administrators to give a second presentation or to participate in the formal lecture series in the days that followed. And although he always woke up in his fifth-floor suite in the Lexington Hotel excited about his prospects, his conviction that he was contributing something of universal value to the fair inevitably faltered. By the time he was boarding the tram outside the hotel with Aimée and Victor, he would start wondering whether his Egyptian Pantheon would go unappreciated, whether all the effort and money he had put into it had been for naught.

His exhibit was eligible for a prize, which would certainly have helped garner interest for a sale. He wasn't planning to sell everything—only the set of gods and goddesses. His asking price of five hundred dollars would not come close to covering the amount he'd paid for them, the shipping and travel costs, and the expense of the bronze pedestals, which he'd had custom-made in Paris. But it would be enough to replenish his savings so he could keep expanding his collection, acquiring bigger and more valuable treasures.

He always headed straight to the Anthropological Building every morning, in case a medal had been attached to his card in his absence. For four days, no medal appeared.

On the fifth day, Aimée woke with a fever and stayed behind at the hotel while Armand took little Victor to the fair. Instead of going directly to the Anthropological Building, they continued on the tram to the far end of Jackson Park. He'd thought they'd start the day with a visit to the Horticultural Building, but at the last minute he changed his mind, and he decided to take Victor to see the exhibits along the narrow strip of land known as the Midway Plaisance.

Armand had been inclined to avoid the Midway Plaisance. The official guide to the fair warned that admission fees were charged at every booth along this mile-long stretch, and the exhibits there had "no connection with the Exposition proper excepting as side attractions." Its promoters claimed that the Midway Plaisance "represented all foreign nations under the sun." Its detractors called it the Church Annex and blamed it for draining visitors of time and money. It had been added as an afterthought to accommodate the "concessionaires and entertainers." But within days, it had become so popular and the crowds so thick that, as one visitor testified, you could drop a rubber ball from a window and it would bounce off hats and bonnets without ever touching the ground. All the new arrivals to Chicago asked to be taken straight to the Midway Plaisance. That morning Armand decided to join them and see what all the hoopla was about.

From all his traveling he was adept at dodging the prongs of parasols, the glowing ash of cast-off cigars underfoot. And he knew, of course, never to let go of his son in the crowd.

There at the headwaters of the Great Fair's sideshow, the mob was thick. But Armand wasn't going to let the smell of a thousand bodies sweating beneath the blazing spring sun on a humid May day in Chicago dissuade him. He lifted Victor onto his shoulders, and as soon as he saw a gap in the roiling mass, he pushed through, synchronizing his steps with the strides of the strangers on either side as he approached the entrance, where an announcer shouting through a bullhorn promised the public shows "so remarkable that one man could never hope to find them all in his lifetime were he compelled to search for them himself."

Armand stood Victor back on his feet when they reached the first exhibit—the International Dress and Costume Company, featuring forty-five lovely women, each wearing the costume of her country. Rumor had it that this was the most profitable exhibit along the Midway Plaisance. In the time that Armand and Victor were there, it also appeared to be the place where arguments broke out and friendships were lost forever simply because one man objected when another insisted that India was more beautiful than China, or that Ireland had hips promising more fecundity than Italy.

Victor thought the fistfights were part of the show and wanted to stay to find out how they ended. Armand assured him that there were better things to see, and to prove it he led the boy to the next station, where workers spun threads of colored glass as thin as gossamer for napkins and lamp shades and even dresses that crinkled and sparkled as the girls modeling them sashayed across the stage.

Victor squinted in wonder. He looked up at his father with an expression suggesting that he was trying to organize his thoughts into a question. But he gave up and just rubbed his nose vigorously and went on watching.

After a few minutes they moved on, flowing with the crowd toward the entrance of the Electric Scenic Theater. "You sure don't want to pass this one by, little mister," the announcer said directly to Victor, leaving Armand with no choice but to buy two tickets to the show.

"A Day in the Alps" had just started. Victor sat transfixed on his father's lap as the sun rose over the highest peak, illuminating scenes of sloping meadows populated by herds of sheep. When shepherd boys danced with shepherd girls, and nine electric fans positioned around the room whipped up a refreshing breeze, the whole crowd sighed, Armand included. And when they heard the first harsh boom of thunder and saw a jagged shard of light suddenly crack the wall, Armand, like everyone else present, was inclined to take cover.

Not until Victor started crying did his father consider how foolish he'd been to pay to sit in a dingy theater with three hundred people. He felt foolish for having brought his son to the Midway Plaisance at all. Yet since his goal was to show Victor as much as possible in the shortest time, he carried him from the Electric Scenic Theater and headed west toward the thatched huts and the banquet hall of Ireland, where the crowd thickened and slowed again, since everyone wanted to have a look at the stitched and embroidered underwear from the trousseau of the Duchess of Fife.

He decided that the Duchess's underwear wasn't worth the wait, so he bypassed the banquet hall and headed directly to the Japanese Bazaar. To comfort Victor, he bought a paper fan and walked on. The shopkeepers called to them and tried to lure the boy with more toys, but Armand ignored them and continued westward to the Dutch settlements of Sumatra, Borneo, and Java, where lithe young girls were twirling in their red ballet skirts made of tree bark.

When the girls stopped to rest, they left the Dutch settlements behind and went on to Germany, where a medieval castle stood at the top of a small rise. Dozens of people were waiting in a line to get inside. Victor wanted to see if there were swords on the walls—all castles should have swords on their walls! But Armand didn't want to waste time in the line and pointed to a poster for a more tempting exhibition ahead: Cairo Street, said to be the one place at the fair that every visitor must go.

He paid the two entrance fees of twenty-five cents and lifted Victor back on his shoulders, walking along in a daze. From a tower in the mosque, a muezzin called the faithful to prayer. Two obelisks were inscribed with the names of Ramses II and President Cleveland. Vendors sold candy and miniature wooden sphinxes. A belly dancer entertained a crowd outside the entrance to the bazaar, and on the steps of the Temple of Luxor a greeter called, "Come in and see the most ancient relics! Here everything is serene!"

Who cared that the building was an imperfect copy of an actual temple in Luxor, and the displays were made up of replicas? The other visitors didn't even seem to be aware that the gold wasn't real gold, the twelve mummies were wax models, and the Egyptians milling about were Sicilian immigrants. The public didn't know to be skeptical, and back on the street they were spellbound—Victor, too—when a procession passed led by a priest in a leopard-skin robe. The audience thought the whole scene dazzling and congratulated themselves on having made the effort to come to the fair. They agreed that Cairo Street on the Midway Plaisance must be as good as the real thing and maybe even better. There were no blind beggars or starving children. The walkways were swept clean multiple times a day. Germany was less than a hundred yards to the east, Algeria an equal distance to the west. A cup of tea was easily purchased, the toilets were modern, and the temple was lit with electric lights. If you stood there long enough, you would see two young lovers joined in a traditional

Egyptian wedding. And if you remained even longer, you could count on overhearing one bystander say to another, as Armand did that morning, his heart sinking, "It sure beats traveling around the world!"

When Victor pleaded to return to the Midway Plaisance, he was taken there by his mother, who felt fine after a day of rest. Armand went instead to hear a series of lectures related to the archaeology exhibits in Department M.

After the lecture by his fellow exhibitor Theodore Graf, a woman approached him. She was wearing a navy silk dress with lace trim, with a bunched waist and puffy arms that reminded him of a dress made for Aimée in a shop in Nice.

"Mr. de Potter?"

"Yes?"

"My name is Mrs. Stevenson."

"Mrs. Stevenson!"

Mrs. Stevenson of Philadelphia, one of the most famed curators in America and vice president of the jury of awards for ethnology! Armand had heard about her work in Egyptology at the University Museum, and he'd been eager to meet her since the fair opened. He'd even made the mistake after another lecture of introducing himself to a woman he thought was Mrs. Stevenson but who turned out to be a tourist from Canada.

"I am delighted to make your acquaintance, Mrs. Stevenson. I was so hoping we would have the chance to talk. I would like to tell you about some of my little monuments. If you have the time, Mrs. Stevenson, I would be honored to give you a grand tour—I mean, if I may, not a real grand tour, which is my other line of work, I'm engaged in the tourist business, you see, when I'm not borrowing around in Luxor for treasures." Had he said *borrowing*?

Good God, he'd meant *burrowing*! Should he correct himself or just continue as if nothing had happened? Either way, he felt helpless in the face of Mrs. Stevenson's judgment. Mrs. Stevenson was steadfast, even, he would have gone so far as to say, rigid in the way she held her head, as though she meant to keep her eyes locked on his face so she wouldn't miss anything and at the same time needed to hold herself level to balance her incongruously extravagant hat, which sported an arrangement of daisies and colorful feathers and some sort of furry thing—the tail of a chipmunk, or perhaps a squirrel?

What was he going to say? He was going to say, *I am an idiot*, or plead for mercy, or invite Mrs. Stevenson of Philadelphia to join him for dinner. She surveyed him as though deciding whether to make a purchase; he stuttered and coughed into his fist and finally lifted out one of the pamphlets he'd been carrying in his coat pocket. He could offer no better description of his Pantheon than what was contained in those forty-four pages. He told Mrs. Stevenson the pamphlet was intended as a catalog, and only a few brief notes on the items were given. He added that he'd also written a "few remarks on the history of Egypt, her mythology and funerary rites," which he hoped weren't out of place.

He had labored more than a month over the pamphlet in Paris, yet it felt so meager, nearly weightless, as he handed it over. And did he perceive her hesitating? Perhaps, for a moment, her hand floated above his while she assured herself that a bribe wasn't involved.

He didn't have to bribe her. Mrs. Stevenson, head curator of the Egyptian Section of the Department of Archaeology and Paleontology at the University Museum in Philadelphia and a member of the awards jury for the Columbian Exhibition, thanked Armand for the pamphlet and declared that the Egyptian Pantheon was splendid. She attached a medal to the sign and said that the collection deserved to be on permanent display. Would Professor de Potter consider a loan to her museum?

He would more than consider it—he would agree right there, on the floor of Department M, offering the loan of his entire collection to Mrs. Stevenson and her museum. His plan had been to expand the collection with new acquisitions, using the profit he made from the sale of his bronzes. Now he wasn't sure he wanted to sell them anymore. Maybe he wasn't finished adding to the group.

Cairo to Philadelphia

H E WOULD HAVE BEEN THE FIRST to admit that he was flattered by the award from Mrs. Stevenson and pleased to be affiliated with her museum. But when he had conversations with dealers behind closed doors, it wasn't simply to earn favors with a lady Egyptologist. He remained dedicated to the effort of "bringing the magnificence of the past into the light of day," as he liked to say—which was why it didn't hurt to have the influential Mrs. Stevenson as a friend. With a word, she could put him in contact with members of the world's most elite fraternities, who might someday invite Armand de Potter to join their powerful ranks.

Since his previous source of antiquities had been cut off with the arrest of Ahmed Abd-er-Rasoul and the discovery of the cache at Deir-el-Bahari back in 1881, he had had no choice but to cultivate other connections. On Mrs. Stevenson's recommendation, he wrote to Émile Brugsch, overseer of Deir-el-Bahari and conservator of the Bûlâq Museum in Cairo.

By 1894, Herr Brugsch had strict orders from the Egyptian government not to relinquish anything from the museum. Never mind that the plumbing in the building needed repair, the doors needed better locks, two of the display cases were cracked, and the guards were demanding higher pay. While Egyptian officials expected Brugsch and his colleagues to create a world-class museum, they provided insufficient financial support and were known to use the mummies for bribes and graft.

What did it matter, then, if Herr Brugsch occasionally sold a mummy before the officials could give it away? Early in 1894, he replied to Armand's letter and invited him to Cairo, to come see "a double wooden coffin from the XXI Dynasty that was covered with numerous tableaux." They met in the back room of a shop of a local dealer in Cairo. A servant offered figs and sweet coffee, interspersed with glasses of a bitter liquor Armand didn't recognize and would have preferred to decline. But out of courtesy he drank the liquor, and a single swallow sent tendrils of warmth through his body and improved his mood. A second round was offered and accepted by all, lifting Armand's spirits even higher, so when Herr Brugsch finally got around to removing the sailcloth and revealed a dusty sarcophagus covered completely in hieroglyphics and illustrations from the ancient Egyptian *Book of the Dead*, Armand was ready to be impressed.

He was impressed by the way the paints seemed to glow beneath the blanket of dust. He was impressed by the intricacy of the illustrations that communicated the entire story of Osiris—the journey from birth to death to rebirth and all the adventures of the afterlife. He was impressed with the snug fit of one box inside the other, the melancholy eyes in the portrait of the deceased on the lid, the delicate shape of the ears. And he was impressed with the price—the equivalent of a year's worth of his income.

The sarcophagus may have been a compact residence, but consider that it had lasted for three thousand years. It was by far the most masterfully illustrated sarcophagus that Armand had ever seen. Mrs. Stevenson would be proud to display it in Philadelphia.

The deal was swiftly made. Whether Herr Brugsch had offered it to other foreign collectors, he didn't reveal. He made it clear that he wanted to put it in the hands of Professor de Potter. As far as Armand was concerned, no price for such a magnificent coffin would have been too high, even if he had to sell his railway stock to pay for it.

He gave directions to have the case carefully packed in the manner of Russian dolls, one within the other, the mummy within the first case, the first case within the second, the second within a third box he ordered especially to hold it, the third box packed in a shipping crate, and he sent the sarcophagus to Mrs. Stevenson, COD, informing her in an accompanying note that it was the only one from last year's find at Deir-el-Bahari that was sold. He emphasized that he considered himself quite fortunate to find the mummy. "Decorated cases," he explained, "are very difficult to obtain."

Mrs. Stevenson was pleased to accept the sarcophagus on behalf of the University of Pennsylvania. Her letter was cordial, full of compliments and gratitude. She asked after Madame de Potter and Victor and hoped that next time Armand was in Philadelphia, he would have dinner with her.

She didn't say that a bill from the university would follow shortly, but there it was on the mail table the next week—a bill to cover all expenses associated with the sarcophagus, from full reimbursement for shipping charges to the cost for a new display case.

Armand was startled at first, then incensed. His distinct understanding was that the University Museum would cover all expenses related to his collection. He wrote back to Mrs. Stevenson, demanding an explanation. Her reply came by the end of the month—she blamed the university bursar for sending out the bill without notifying her. She apologized but did not offer to intervene, and Armand resigned himself to paying the bill in full.

He waited two months before writing to Mrs. Stevenson to implore her to compose a description of the sarcophagus for his *Old World* tourist guide. He hoped it wouldn't be a bother. Also, if the De Potter Collection received any complimentary notices, could she send him the name and date of the publication? And if it wasn't too much of an imposition, could she return the cartouches once the scarabs were taken out of the buttons?

It was no imposition at all, Mrs. Stevenson replied. She returned the cartouches, and she sent him a description of the sarcophagus she'd written for a university publication, calling it a "superb double coffin" and a "recent valuable addition" to the department. She explained that with its illustrations of the principal elements of Egyptian faith it was of special importance. She hoped that Professor de Potter would visit her in Philadelphia soon.

But the description was too lengthy to include in its entirety in Armand's *Old World Guide*. He wrote to Mrs. Stevenson, inquiring whether he could extract just a few sentences—and perhaps, if it wasn't objectionable, could he add to the sentence "Such cases are very difficult to obtain" the words "and this one is unique in this country"?

From her brief reply granting him permission, he perceived that he was trying her patience. He told himself that he mustn't bother her and didn't write again until March 16, 1896, when, in a letter posted from Jerusalem, he described several additional items he was sending to the University Museum—four canopic vases, fifteen strings of beads, sixteen small alabaster vases, a beautiful porcelain pectoral, and two wooden stelae. He apologized for not being able to procure finer canopic vases but said they were the best he could get. He didn't say that these recent acquisitions had cost him nearly a thousand francs, which he'd had to draw from his reserve fund at the Société Générale. He just added that Mrs. de Potter asked him to send her kind regards.

Sara Stevenson's reply came late but was warmer than ever. She reported that she was planning to visit Paris, where the de Potters would be living for six months, and hoped that Armand would consider giving her one of his famous tours.

Of course he would show her everything that was worth seeing. "Dear Mrs. Stevenson," he wrote, "I am at your service." But Mrs. Stevenson was inundated with work in Philadelphia and had to cancel her trip to Paris. She would miss the opportunity to explore the Louvre with Professor de Potter. She hoped he remained satisfied with the placement of his collection. "I want to assure you," she wrote, "that the De Potter Collection has no equal in this country. I plan to compose a catalog as a small token of gratitude to you for the loan of your collection. I only beg you for your patience, my friend."

Armand was pleased. A catalog of the whole De Potter Collection would be satisfying, and Sara Stevenson was the one to undertake the project. "Dear Mrs. Stevenson," he wrote in reply, "I can think of no one I would rather entrust my collection with than you." He offered several pages of comments about his treasures to help her with the catalog. He added that he was at her service and invited her to accompany him on his next trip up the Nile.

He waited eagerly for her reply. After three months he couldn't restrain himself. If Mrs. Stevenson didn't have the time to write a comprehensive catalog for him, she could at least provide him with a token of appreciation.

"My Dear Madame," he wrote to her. "In my work it would be of considerable value to me to have received some formal acknowledgment from the University of Pennsylvania." He wondered whether she would be willing to use her influence, and the probable usefulness of his little collection, to obtain for him an honorary degree. He provided a summary of his credentials, then advised Mrs. Stevenson to ignore his request if he was presuming upon her kindness. He finished by explaining that he hadn't sent the arrows and bronze statuette of Osiris, since it would have made an awkward package.

He received a cursory response from her, with only a vague promise to look into the matter. He was irritated but undaunted. He told himself that he would wait a few months and repeat his request. In the meantime, he sent her a XII Dynasty funereal bark with eight sailors, rare textiles from Akhmin, a fine set of mystic eyes, and a small urn with the gilded cartouche of Princess Ounofris, which was especially rare and valuable. And even though she turned down his second request for an honorary degree, then failed to reply to his third request the following year, he continued to send her additional treasures for display. By the spring of 1902, he had run through nearly thirty thousand francs, yet Mrs. Stevenson gave every indication that she took his investment for granted.

He longed to find the perfect treasure, something even rarer than his wooden shabty and more beautiful than his triple sarcophagus, a find so remarkable that his loaning it to the University Museum would put Mrs. Stevenson in his debt forever. In his office in New York, on a rainy morning in late March, looking out from the second floor at the umbrellas bobbing above the sidewalk, he imagined writing the brief letter that would accompany such a treasure:

My dear Mrs. Stevenson,
    The enclosed item should firmly secure your institution its place as the country's premier location for the study of antiquities. I have the honor to remain yours faithfully,
        P. L. Armand de Potter d'Elseghem

This letter, unfortunately, would have to wait. Instead, in a letter with a return address of Summit, New Jersey, Armand wrote expressing his disappointment with the University Museum. He admitted that his request to have the contents of the De Potter Collection on display together might seem an expression of vanity. "I do not pretend to be free from this universal weakness," he confessed. He said he was thinking of withdrawing his collection from the museum. He did not mention that he would be traveling to Philadelphia the following week.

On a Tuesday morning in April 1902, a man in a buttermilk dress coat, checkered trousers, and a panama hat crossed the rotunda of the museum at the University of Pennsylvania. Near one of the doorways a painted sarcophagus was set on a glass table, and he walked a full circle around it, examining all sides, even crouching to peer from below, before continuing into the Egyptian gallery.

He was surprised to have the room to himself, since he assumed that ancient Egypt was a popular subject among the American public. Likely the crowds would show up in the afternoon. But where was the gallery's head curator? He'd been told by the receptionist at the front desk that he would find her there. Perhaps she was still at lunch. He was willing to wait.

He walked along the center aisle, taking in the room as a whole, noting the arrangement of the artifacts on display. His walking stick clicked decisively on the wood, in concert with his footsteps.

The room, full of possessions that were meant to accompany the deceased to the afterlife, was like a tomb itself. The air was stale, with dust floating in the sunlight filtered through the upper window. The walls were lined with cases displaying the smaller artifacts; square pedestals supporting stone busts, vases, and sun disks were tucked in corners. Except for two freestanding cases beneath the stairs, the main area of the room was oddly empty. Even the giant statue of a pharaoh was positioned close to the back wall, as if in an attempt to conceal it in the shadows.

The door opened, and a museum attendant appeared and observed him for a minute before leaving him alone again. The visitor continued his survey of the room. He stopped at one of the freestanding cases, counted the pieces of jewelry inside, and examined the name inscribed on the side panel. He moved on to the cabinet projecting at an angle from the left wall. He was disappointed not to find a name written on either the sides or the bottom panel of the cabinet. The only information offered by the museum were labels with approximate dates for each of the bronzes on display.

He checked his pocket watch frequently. He had been in the room for nearly an hour when a student entered and went directly to the case beneath the stairs. He'd come to take notes about one of the objects, though he must already have had some knowledge of the display, given that there was no accompanying brochure or even a curator's note to help him out.

The student was still writing in his notebook when the door opened once again, and in swept a man and a woman in conversation. The visitor didn't recognize the gentleman accompanying the woman. The woman, known for her extravagant hats, was bareheaded. It was Mrs. Stevenson, head curator of the Egyptian Section, and though the visitor hadn't seen her since they'd met nine years earlier at the Chicago Exhibition and she'd grown stouter and grayer, he recognized her immediately. Mrs. Stevenson, however, was not prepared to recognize Armand de Potter.

". . . saw in my life such intrigue," she was saying as she came through the door. "Politics, science, personal rancor—it's all mixed up over there. I'd sit on the terrace of Shepheard's sipping my lemon squash and listen to Brugsch and Petrie go at each other. I truly considered bypassing them and trying bribery with the Egyptian officials, but then thought better of it." She gave a gentle laugh.

"Isn't this from Petrie?" her associate asked, pointing in the direction of a tablet mounted on the wall.

"Oh, that? Rosher brought that back from his visit to Dendera. Now, what is it you wanted to show me, Professor Randall-MacIver?"

The man nodded toward the student. "Mrs. Stevenson, this is one of my research assistants, Walter Morley. You'll recall, madame, that my colleagues and I have had some difficulty verifying the information accompanying these items. I've asked Mr. Morley to look into the matter."

"And what have you discovered, young man?" Mrs. Stevenson asked.

The student gestured toward the case. "The scarab ring . . . the given date is incorrect. The craftsmanship is more typical of the Twenty-second Dynasty. You see the design—"

"Very fine detective work," Mrs. Stevenson said, cutting him off, probably because she was aware that the visitor standing nearby was listening. "I look forward to reading your report."

"If you don't mind my saying, Mrs. Stevenson, I told you so," Professor Randall-MacIver announced triumphantly.

"You did, you did indeed," she said with a smile that was obviously contrived to flatter. "Your attention to the matter is admirable. How may I thank you?"

The professor was set on undermining Armand's careful work, and Mrs. Stevenson wanted to thank him for it! So the date for the ring was off by a century or two—what of it? Armand had done his best to match his treasures to their provenance. But with more than three hundred items to consider, there were bound to be mistakes. Perhaps the mistake was Mrs. Stevenson's—maybe she transcribed the information incorrectly. Certainly she'd made a mistake splitting up the De Potter Collection between the free-standing case and the cabinet. The De Potter Collection was supposed to be displayed together. And why was the name De Potter written on the side of the case, and not on the front? Nothing at all by the items in the cabinet, or by the sarcophagus in the rotunda, indicated that they were on loan from Armand de Potter. What had happened to the plaques he'd made for the bronzes? And what about the catalog Mrs. Stevenson had promised to write?

Oh, she'd promised a lot of things. Looking at her from across the room, Armand thought she had a sneaky, feline air about her. He imagined her purring as she smiled at Professor Randall-MacIver. She clearly wanted something from the man, and she'd get it because he was too stupid to see through her. This professor was an idiot, yet Mrs. Stevenson was bothering to consult with him about the provenance of a scarab ring, all the while ignoring Armand de Potter.

Of course she couldn't have known he was there. She must have thought him an ordinary tourist. He'd been planning to greet her, but had by then heard enough to change his mind. He left the room in a hurry and strode toward the rotunda, holding his walking stick upright, resisting the urge to knock it against the sarcophagus to show the world that it still belonged to him.

He wrote again to Mrs. Stevenson from Geneva, Switzerland, on September 20, 1902. He expressed his frustration at the way his collection was displayed without revealing that he'd been to

the museum. "In all events," he concluded, "I will leave the Collection in the Museum for the present."

He wrote the following year with a return address of the Villa du Grand Bois, and once more in the fall of 1904. He asked for more prominent display space for his collection. Though he avoided repeating his request for an honorary degree, he reminded her of her promise to write a comprehensive catalog of the De Potter Collection. Mrs. Stevenson wrote back with infuriating brevity to say that she did not have time to write a catalog.

She didn't have time to write a catalog describing the significance of the collection, but she had time to accept anything he cared to send? He swore to himself that he would take his treasures elsewhere. But still he kept sending Mrs. Stevenson additional pieces. Sooner or later she would agree that the De Potter Collection had no equal in America.

He sent his last shipment on a damp February day in 1905, four months before he disappeared from the *Regele Carol*. He carefully arranged a group of basalt scarabaei on tissue in a small wooden box, which he set on the bottom of the shipping crate. Beside this smaller box he laid a long, rectangular box that contained miscellaneous pieces—amulets, strings of porcelain and carnelian beads, and a small lapis-lazuli frog. He padded the crate with crumpled newspaper and then laid on top of the smaller boxes a row of alabaster vases, each thickly wrapped in sailcloth. After adding another layer of newspaper, he wrapped sailcloth around the last object, a sepulchral figurine of a small faience man, with an illegible inscription. He hesitated, wondering if he should keep the faience man for himself, then decided against it. He tucked the bundle into the nest and nailed the crate shut.

PART FIVE

At Sea

HE IS AS BLANDLY INOFFENSIVE as the pea soup at dinner. He agrees with the vicar's wife that the beef is overdone, the wine is too sweet, the silverware needs polishing. He is cordial to the banker and doesn't correct him when he attributes the *Theogony* to Pindar. When the stewardess wheels over the dessert cart, Armand pretends to be interested in the lemon cake. After the meal he refolds his napkin beside his plate and follows the vicar out on deck for a smoke.

The challenge for him now is to convey a mood of serene confidence. If he has failed so far in his interactions with others on board, at least he has resisted revealing his true feelings. It is safe to assume that no one has any inkling of his troubles. He must maintain the façade right up to the end, until he is alone, if his plan is to succeed. Once there is no one to watch him, he may do as he pleases.

But his patience has been tested through the day—first with the steward and stewardess, who took his money as if it were dirty laundry, and then with the banker, who wouldn't accept a gift at all. Now the vicar is beside him looking utterly absorbed in his own satisfaction as he pats his ample belly.

Armand is prepared to entertain the vicar with small talk, but the vicar preempts him. Wasn't the dinner splendid, he says, and isn't it a comfortable ship? And could he beg a pinch from Armand to fill his pipe, since the Turks confiscated his own bag of tobacco when he passed through customs on his arrival in Constantinople?

"Why, of course," Armand replies, adding, as he shakes out the tobacco from his pouch, "There's a trick to it, you know."

"A trick?" The vicar has a round and ruddy face, his bowler is perched on his bald head, his mustache is curled in round tips, and the stem of his neck pokes up from the circle of his collar. His spectacles are round, and behind them his eyes widen, as if he doesn't understand the meaning of anything that involves deceit.

"I mean the trick to passing through customs. The technique varies widely from country to country. Sometimes baksheesh is expected. Other times you need to keep certain items on your person."

"You sound like an experienced traveler, sir."

"I should be. It has been my profession for more than twenty years." Armand hands the vicar his business card.

"'De Potter Tours,'" the vicar reads aloud. He squints at the figure of Puck standing on a jumble of luggage in the advertising emblem. He reads the slogan: "'I'll put a girdle round the earth.'" He starts to return the card, but Armand invites him to keep it. "I once played Oberon in an amateur production," the vicar says as he fishes a matchbook from his pocket. He strikes a match, offering the light to Armand before lighting his own pipe. He continues studying Armand's card as he coughs with the first puff of smoke. He clears his throat and recites:

Fetch me that flower, the herb I showed thee once:
The juice of it on sleeping eyelids laid

Will make a man or woman madly dote
Upon the next live creature that it sees.

Armand doesn't know how to respond to the vicar's recitation. What else is there to do but say "Bravo!"—a ridiculous response for such a minor feat, but still the vicar's round pillow of a face crinkles with his smile. How easily pleased with himself he is. He looks as proud as a young boy praised for drawing in the sand with a stick. Armand wants to admire the vicar for his good nature. Instead he is beginning to understand why the vicar's wife is perpetually annoyed. What a trial it must be for her to be stuck with a husband who is always content. The vicar meanders happily through life, as ignorant as a fattened lamb munching in a pasture on a lovely summer day.

But Armand is a gentleman, and a gentleman does not stand on the deck of a ship thinking ill of a vicar with whom he is sharing a smoke. He returns the vicar's smile with his own, sucks on his pipe, and gestures toward the sunset. He is about to say *Che bellisima*, but instead says simply, "How beautiful."

"Ah, yes," the vicar murmurs. "It reminds me of the bloom of shepherd's purse."

"God the artist," Armand says in an effort to impress this man of the church with his piety.

"Indeed," replies the vicar mildly. After a moment he asks, "Did you know that the lowest blossoms on a sprig of shepherd's purse always open first?"

Armand says, "Of course," though in truth he's never thought about it.

"And the order of blossoming is always ascending, from bottom to top?"

The questions are beginning to confuse Armand, and the confusion makes him wary.

"And shepherd's purse can keep producing lateral flowers one after another the whole summer long?"

"You don't say . . ." He swallows loudly. The vicar looks at him with a new expression of understanding, as if he's figured out the purpose of that "trick" Armand referred to a moment ago.

Still the vicar presses on: "There is no terminal flower if the stem continues to grow, which means that the summit can never be reached, at least not until the frost."

Could the vicar know what Armand is intending? Has he guessed his secrets? Is he cannier than he pretends?

The sky is darkening. The two men stand at the rail, smoking their pipes. Armand waits tensely for the vicar to speak. What is he going to say?

He's going to say that if Professor de Potter is ever escorting a party through the Cotswolds, he must come visit him in Swindon. Then he is going to yawn. And then he is going to find his wife, who will be eager to begin their nightly game of pinochle.

Grand Bois

AMID ALL THE BUSINESS Aimée had to attend to in the aftermath of her husband's disappearance at sea, there was Gertrude, dear, sweet Gertrude, who had more needs than poor Victor did. At the beginning of the new year, Victor announced that he wanted to return to school to be with his friends. He stayed there for the rest of the term, while Gertrude gave up her French lessons altogether. She had no scruples about borrowing money from her aunt to pay for things she couldn't afford—a new bathing costume, a dress for spring, new shoes. When the lace maker from Alençon was going door-to-door in the neighborhood and arrived at Grand Bois, Gertrude wanted to buy every tray cloth and handkerchief she was selling. During tea at Gallia's, she started talking too loudly while the orchestra was playing the "Ode to St. Cecilia" and needed to be hushed. She needed social engagements where she could meet young men. She wouldn't wear mourning, yet she needed comfort nearly every evening, when she'd drink too much wine with dinner and begin weeping over her uncle's death.

One springlike day in February, Aimée and Gertrude took the train to Vallauris and walked the full ten miles back to Cannes along the canal. The air was delicious with the sweet fragrances of heather and pine, and the sun was warm. While Gertrude chattered about a hat she'd seen in a shop window in Nice, Aimée could think of nothing but her accumulating expenses. Lawyers representing the travelers affected by the Jaffa accident were hounding her. Bartlett was demanding the next installment of his payment.

As she walked along, she hardly listened to Gertrude, who rambled on about the hat in Nice and plucked tufts of the wild grass growing along the sides of the path. Aimée was paying so little attention that she didn't hear when Gertrude changed the subject from the hat to her uncle. She didn't know what caused the girl to stop in her tracks all of a sudden, leading Aimée to think that she'd dropped something behind her on the path, until Gertrude finished the sentence she'd begun: ". . . and when Robert said that about Uncle Armand, I didn't believe him. I didn't want to believe him."

"Said what?"

"I told him he was out of line. I told him he was cruel and rude and I never wanted to see him again. And I *haven't* seen him, it's been three weeks and I haven't answered his—"

"Gertrude, please, what did Robert say to you?"

"I told you, Auntie."

"Tell me again."

"I don't know why you want me to repeat it. It's too awful. By the way, did you hear that the Drexils have left for Tunis? I wonder if we'll ever be invited to join them on their yacht? What if they asked us to sail to Tunis with them? Would we do it, Auntie? But I'd rather go to Venice. I still haven't been to Venice, you know."

What a vexing, rattlebrained girl she was, yet Aimée could tell that Gertrude was trying to change the subject. What did Robert say? Aimée had to ask, though she could make an educated guess. Somehow the truth had gotten out among the high society of the Côte d'Azur, and Robert was just repeating what he'd been told about Armand de Potter's *supposedly* accidental death at sea.

"Tell me what Robert said," Aimée insisted, though she was thinking, Don't tell me.

"Auntie . . ."

"I want to know what people are saying about Armand." They were saying that he killed himself so his wife could cash in on the indemnity from Mutual Life. Somehow they knew about the last two letters from him that she'd burned in Toblach.

"They are saying that he didn't really come from Belgian nobility. There are people out there who say Uncle made it all up and he was really a peasant. Oh, I'm sorry, please forgive me for telling you!" Gertrude hadn't had a single sip of wine that day, and still she shook with sobs and buried her face against her aunt's shoulder as she begged for forgiveness.

At one time in her life Aimée would have been insulted. Now, though, she was relieved that people weren't whispering about her husband's suicide. She linked arms with Gertrude, who dabbed at her eyes with the handkerchief from the Alençon lace maker. "It's just stupid gossip, saying Uncle Armand was a peasant!"

Aimée said firmly, "Nothing could be further from the truth."

As she understood it, Louis de Potter was to blame for denying his heirs the status that should have been their due. She knew from reading about him that he'd been rebellious as a young man and had refused to assume his inherited title. But Aimée could prove that Armand was indeed his grandson, for she had at least a dozen books with Louis de Potter's handwritten notes in the margins.

A few of the books dated back to the fifteenth century, and though they were worm-eaten, a book dealer took an interest in them. She made arrangements to meet with him on March 12, a gray day with wind and intermittent drizzle. But just as she was heading out the door, Gertrude appeared and asked if she could come along and then took so long to get ready that they missed the ten o'clock train and had to wait for the later one. By the time they arrived at the bookshop in Nice, the owner had already closed for lunch.

They had half an hour before they were supposed to meet their friends the Manques and Durands at the Cosmopolitan. The rain had let up, and they decided to stroll along the promenade des Anglais.

As they walked, Gertrude commented on everyone they passed. She approved of a woman's blue jacket with black velvet buttons. And wasn't that yellow dress cinched at the waist with a wide red ribbon lovely! Wherever did that woman find such a purse, covered with the hide of a giraffe? Was it real giraffe? she wondered aloud. And look at the heels on those boots! And the ivory handle of that gentleman's umbrella, carved in the shape of a mermaid— wasn't it something!

Aimée murmured in agreement without giving the umbrella a glance. She was asking herself if they had time for a short walk through the public garden behind the Hôtel de France. She decided that a ten-minute detour wouldn't make them late.

As she steered Gertrude toward the gates of the garden, she heard a man calling, "Madame de Potter, bonjour, hello!"

Roland Berg hurried in an effort to catch up with them. He was the American with the furniture shop in Nice. Armand knew him through his affiliation with the French Oriental Society. Aimée had sold him the Stevens chairs earlier in the year, using the pretense that Grand Bois was too cluttered and she had no room for them. "I thought it was you," he said. He had his coat slung over his arm and his hat in his hand. "And this lovely lady is . . ."

"My niece, Gertrude. Gertrude, this is Mr. Berg."

"Mademoiselle."

"A pleasure, Mr. Berg."

"Mr. Berg has a shop in the rue Droite. Have you sold the Stevens chairs, Mr. Berg?"

Either he didn't hear or he didn't care to answer the question. "I'm glad I ran into you, madame. There's a matter concerning your late husband . . ." He glanced nervously at Gertrude. Aimée invited him to continue. "I thought you should know. Gelat has been talking. . . ." He hesitated. Aimée wished he'd do more than hesitate and leave her alone. Why was everyone always talking? "I'm just back from Jerusalem, where I met Gelat—you know Mr. Gelat, who works at the embassy—"

A pony pulling a cart full of flowers trotted out through the gates of the garden, clip-clop, clip-clop. Aimée felt a drop on her cheek—it was drizzling again. She considered opening her umbrella but decided she wanted only to hear what Mr. Berg had to tell her and continue on her way.

"Gelat says . . ." Mr. Berg paused to wait for a tram to clatter past along the boulevard.

Gelat had been Armand's dragoman on tours through the Holy Land. The last time Aimée had seen him was in a hotel in Jerusalem. She remembered that Gelat had been trying to drum up investors for a new venture to export water from the river Jordan to America, and Armand had declined. The next time De Potter Tours needed a dragoman in Jerusalem, Gelat made himself unavailable, leaving the party's guide, the inexperienced Turgel, to manage on his own. And then the boat capsized at Jaffa.

Gelat had been set against Armand ever since he refused to invest in the river Jordan venture. Now he was probably telling people that Armand de Potter was a poor businessman who was being pursued by his creditors. He was saying that Madame de Potter would have to sell everything to pay her late husband's debts, and Mr. Berg, recalling his purchase of the Stevens chairs, was going to concur.

No, he wasn't. He was going to say that Gelat was telling people that De Potter Tours was in the habit of overcrowding boats and carriages for the sake of convenience. "Gelat blames the accident at Jaffa on your husband."

"Why, that's ridiculous!"

"Of course it's ridiculous! To hold a man responsible after his death—pardon my directness, Madame de Potter—for an accident that occurred in his absence."

"Gelat was upset because my husband wanted nothing to do with that silly river Jordan business."

"I've never trusted Gelat, and I can only hope that others share my view. But I thought you should know that he's set on damaging the reputation of your husband's agency. You might want to inform the office in Paris."

"I appreciate your candor, Mr. Berg. And, yes, I'll let Edmond Gastineau know what Gelat is saying. He'll come up with a good counteroffensive, I guarantee." She began unfolding her umbrella. "My husband always spoke your name with admiration, Mr. Berg."

"Let me add that your husband was much missed at last week's meeting of the Oriental Society."

Aimée made a show of stepping away from him to make room for the umbrella. "We must run now. Come along, Gertrude. Au revoir, Mr. Berg."

Off they went in the direction of the Cosmopolitan. "We don't have time for the garden," she said, grabbing Gertrude's arm and tugging her along. She thought the girl would be full of questions and was preparing to answer them. She would want to hear all about the accident at Jaffa. She would ask whether it had upset her uncle. She might begin to put the pieces together and understand better her uncle's state of mind when he left on his last tour.

In fact, Gertrude didn't speak at all the whole way to the Cosmopolitan. Only when she followed her niece through the revolving door to the restaurant did Aimée notice through the glass divider how pale her niece was. She must have been troubled by the conversation with Mr. Berg, but they couldn't speak of it then, since the Durands were already waiting to greet them. And after Gertrude perked up during lunch, Aimée didn't bother to return to the subject later.

For the next few weeks she was able to avoid speaking with Gertrude about Jaffa. The girl grew steadily more cheerful and spent most of her time with her friends. She still became sentimental from the wine at dinner, but she no longer cried over her uncle's death. When Sara Wilberry asked her at the last minute to join her on a day trip to the beach at Agay, she was quick to accept.

Victor was home from school for the weekend and helped his mother sort books in the library all afternoon. At nine in the evening, Mrs. Wilberry came by car from her hotel in the center of town to tell Aimée that the girls had telephoned the hotel—they had missed their train and would be home late.

Aimée was still awake in her room when she heard Gertrude return shortly after midnight. She heard the noise as the girl bumped against the mail table in the front hall. She heard her walking up and down the cellar steps and poking about in a cupboard in the kitchen. When she heard the pop of a cork, she went downstairs to order Gertrude to bed.

But Gertrude didn't want to go to bed. Gertrude was holding

a glass she'd filled with champagne, and she was enjoying her solitary party, standing in the kitchen with her back to the door as she swayed to a silent tune, holding the glass in one hand and the bottle in the other. She didn't notice when her aunt appeared in the doorway. She didn't guess that as she took a gulp of champagne, her aunt was trying to come up with the appropriate words to express her fury.

"How dare you!" Aimée blurted, lunging for the glass in Gertrude's hand. Gertrude drew backward, splashing champagne on the floor. "That's Armand's Montagland champagne. You're not to help yourself!"

Instead of responding with the appropriate contriteness, Gertrude raised the glass in a toast and took another gulp. "Might as well finish it off." Her voice was husky, her words slurred. "Uncle wouldn't mind. He always said, live, live as if it's your last day on earth. Live, Gertie, make every second count. So why would a man who loved life as much as Uncle Armand did want to do himself in?"

Aimée stood stunned, speechless.

"Oh, yes, I know what you think." Gertrude caught the sound of a burp in her cupped hand. "You think Uncle Armand jumped off a ship."

"I never said—"

"I'm a terrible girl, a terra-terra-terrible girl, Auntie. When you were at breakfast early this morning, I went to your room to borrow your pretty scarab necklace—you said I may borrow it whenever I liked—and there was a book on the table. Except it wasn't really a book. Oh, dear, I'm just awww-ful. It was your diary, and I read it. Auntie, I am guilty, off with my head!"

"Gertrude, please stop, I won't listen to this. You don't know what you're saying."

"I do know, Auntie. *Room 17—he is dead. I understand my beloved's nervous condition. A moment of insanity.* You wrote that. *A moment of insanity!* That's what you think—you say it was an accident, but you secretly believe that Uncle went insane and killed himself. Oh, Auntie, he couldn't have killed himself. It makes no sense. He was too in love with life. He loved everything about it. He loved the world, he loved Victor, he loved me, he loved you most of all."

"You are drunk, Gertrude."

"How do you explain the money that disappeared from your account? Come, come, Auntie, I know all about it. Dot dot dot dash. That's your secret code, Auntie. Well, I've guessed your secret!"

"You don't know what you're talking about."

"I know Uncle Armand isn't dead because I saw him last month with my own eyes."

The silence was heavy, oppressive, almost suffocating. Aimée felt a sharp pain in her chest as she breathed.

"Last month in Nice, when we were outside the public garden at the Hôtel de France and you were talking with Mr. Berg, I saw him. He was in a tram that passed us on the promenade. He didn't see me, but I saw him."

"That's a lie!"

"It's the truth."

"This is absurd, Gertrude! You spin a drunken fantasy to entertain yourself and then decide to try it out on me! Pretending that you saw my husband . . . why? To make me suspicious? To give me hope? To destroy me?" Aimée pressed her hand against the wall to steady herself. She felt faint, her head throbbed, she wanted to collapse. She flinched when she felt the gentle pressure of a small bird alighting on her wrist. Except it wasn't a bird—it was Victor, who had come up quietly behind her and was reaching for his mother. How long had he been standing there? How much of his cousin's treacherous performance had he witnessed?

"Gertrude has been drinking, Victor," Aimée said desperately. "She doesn't know what she's saying. Go back to your room, that's a good boy. Gertrude, you need to come upstairs with me. I'm putting you to bed."

Victor ran up ahead to his own room. Gertrude let herself be led up the stairs by her aunt. She let her aunt help her into her nightgown. She gave her aunt a sweet, drowsy smile before drifting off to sleep. By the next day, she'd forgotten everything she'd said the night before. Obtuse as she was, she managed to understand without being told that she should never again mention reading her aunt's diary, or seeing the man on the tram in Nice who looked like Uncle Armand.

Grand Bois

O N THE MORNING of what would be his last full day at Grand Bois, Armand stood at his window and drew in a deep lungful of the fresh Riviera air. The day was new; it was spring in Cannes; the sea glittered in the distance. He waved to François, who'd been clipping the box hedge that bordered the rose bed and had paused to wipe his brow. François waved back at his employer.

Oh, François, do you envy the man standing at the window? Do you dream about trading places with him? If you only knew the truth: Armand de Potter is not to be envied. He may put on a convincing show, but he has been accumulating debt for years and received the news just yesterday that Brown Brothers had closed his line of credit.

The telegram had come from his assistant director, Edmond Gastineau, while Aimée was out shopping for a new purse. Armand made up his mind not to tell her. What was there to say? That their happiness was an illusion? That he was a charlatan who only pretended to be successful? Some men gambled away their fortune. Some squandered their wealth on selfish pleasures. He, the esteemed Armand de Potter, had sunk so much money into his collection of antiquities that he could no longer afford to pay his bills.

—*You vain idiot, you could have gotten rich off your treasures. Instead you gave them away for the price of a compliment.*

No—he hadn't given anything away. His collection was on an extended loan that was designed to increase its reputation among the public, therefore improving its value. His antiquities were his largest remaining asset. If he couldn't borrow against his tourist business, he could borrow against the worth of the De Potter Collection.

—*A collection so haphazardly displayed that it can hardly be said to exist as a whole . . . a collection left to gather dust in a room few people ever enter . . . a collection that continues to be neglected by its guardian, Mrs. Stevenson, yet still you keep sending her more treasures, at your own expense—only a fool would hope to use such a collection as collateral.*

But what about the rare wooden shabty? The silver Ptolemaic parrot? The necklace of gold bees? Weren't these worth something? His Pantheon of bronzes had won an award at the Chicago Exposition. And, of course, there was the decorated coffin that was said by Mrs. Stevenson herself to be one of the finest examples of its kind.

—*For which you cashed in your railroad stocks. And then a boat dumps your party into the harbor of Jaffa, and you have nothing to offer them in restitution.*

He wanted to insist that he was ordinarily a careful man, with an eye on the future. He had invested in treasures that had been produced to last forever. He had planned ahead. Of course, he couldn't foresee all contingencies. But at least he had paid his life insurance policy in full.

—*And how will your paid-up life insurance policy help you with the Jaffa claims, your son's tuition, and the expenses of Grand Bois? It won't do much good as long as you're here taking credit for it. What will you do, monsieur? How will you manage?*

He'd figure it out, but in his own time, thank you, and in his own way. Until then he would ignore the goading voice inside him and would instead turn to the door as it was flung open and welcome his wife in his arms.

She kissed his nose—one; his ear—two; his lips and bearded chin and the top of his head—three, four, five; the tip of each finger—plus ten; the flesh of his chest that was exposed between the V of his nightshirt. She kept kissing him up one arm and down the other. She kissed him as if they were discovering each other for the first time. She kissed him with such force that he fell beneath her onto the bed, and they rolled together from one side to the other, both of them as in love as they were when they were newlyweds.

"What's this all about?"

"It's your birthday, darling!"

"My birthday is next month."

"But you won't be here next month, so I'm giving you your birthday kisses today."

Once a year on her husband's birthday, she came to him instead of waiting for him to slip into her bed. Once a year, she managed to surprise him when she threw open the door. Once a year, she gave him a set number of kisses, no more and no less.

He would be fifty-three on the fourth of June. He was on the verge of ruin, but right then, after Aimée extracted herself from his embrace and got up to pull the shutters closed, sealing the room in that familiar darkness that never failed to arouse him, he had to laugh aloud with the sheer delight of being healthy and in love with his wife. Deaf to the demon inside him, he stripped off his nightshirt, and the de Potters shared one last experience of happiness.

It was a cool day, partly cloudy, with the mistral blowing down from the mountains. While Aimée took Gertrude to church and then to climb the clock tower at the Villa Fiorentina, Armand stayed behind at Grand Bois to prepare for his trip.

He spent the morning poring over his passbooks and calculating the expenses ahead. He was so absorbed that he didn't notice how much time had passed until he checked his watch and saw it was already noon. He hurriedly stacked the loose papers on his desk and was about to discard a pile of old magazines when he noticed a month-old copy of *The School Journal*, which he'd never got around to reading. He paged through to make sure he hadn't missed anything of interest, then stopped when he came across an article announcing changes at the University Museum in Philadelphia.

He read with surprise that Mrs. Sara Yorke Stevenson, "well-known for her learned patronage of exploration in the East," had resigned from her position at the University Museum and withdrawn "her financial support from Dr. Hilprecht's exploration expeditions." Hilprecht was identified as the chair of Assyriology at the University of Pennsylvania. Armand had never met him, but he had heard about him at meetings of the French Oriental Society, where Hilprecht was spoken of with great admiration. It was even rumored that he would be assuming the directorship of the whole University Museum. Yet here was news that he was involved in a controversy, and Mrs. Stevenson had resigned because of him.

Armand was stunned but didn't have time to reread the article, for he heard the front door open. Aimée and Gertrude were back, and Miss Plympton was with them. Felicie had a *déjeuner* of herbed omelets and boiled greens ready to serve. Aimée was at the door of the study, asking Armand to come along to the dining room.

He brought up a bottle of his cherished Montagland champagne from the cellar. Between gulps, Gertrude told him all about the bright-eyed birds-of-paradise that were blooming in the garden of the Villa Fiorentina. Miss Plympton asked for his advice on sights they must visit while he was away. Their conversation became more animated, and Gertrude and Miss Plympton began trading gibes about women's suffrage, which they both supported, but for different reasons, Gertrude because the vote would give American women independence, Miss Plympton because it would give them a deeper sense of responsibility. Aimée weighed in with the practical observation that independence and responsibility were entirely compatible, as long as a proper education was provided for all citizens. Inevitably, they asked Armand for his opinion. He announced that he would prefer to live in a world ruled by women, since they would settle their disputes with words rather than weapons. *Hear, hear*, Gertrude agreed, raising a toast to Uncle Armand, to his health, to a safe, fulfilling journey, then holding out her empty glass to be refilled.

Armand checked his watch and was about to excuse himself to finish packing, but just then their friends the Manques arrived to wish Armand bon voyage and give Aimée a long-spurred orchid seedling they'd bought at the market in Toulon. She offered them champagne before Armand could whisper a reminder that he had to get ready for his trip.

He opened another bottle, and the group sat in the salon that had been decorated by Aimée the previous day with bouquets of pink and white carnations. There must have been five dozen carnations in vases around the room, and together with the artwork on display they prompted from Monsieur Manques, who liked to prove he had a philosophical disposition, a question about the nature of beauty. He asked the others to consider: Is material beauty, as Plotinus suggested, nothing more than a distraction from the inner beauty of the Good? Was Plotinus right to compare the effect of beauty to the effect of light playing on the surface of a river, beckoning us to reach for it? And then, don't you know, we fall in and are swept away to nothingness. . . .

Armand was dismayed that he couldn't remember the relevant passage from Plotinus. The best he could offer to prove he was learned was a comment drawn from Plato on divine art versus human art. He addressed his wife and guests as if they were his students: "You will recall that in *The Sophist*, the Stranger urges Theaetetus to agree that nature is produced by divine creation—the work of God. Art—'What shall we say of human art?' he asks. 'Art is a sort of dream created by man for those who are awake.' Look around you, and you'll see in this salon many dreams. There are my little curiosities in the cabinet, gathered from around the world. And the paintings, each one illustrating how beauty is produced with the tip of a brush. And we must include Aimée's own creation, the arrangement of flowers, in itself a work of artistry. We judge talent not by the artist's ability to persuade us that the false thing is real, but by her ability to persuade us to forget reality altogether, just as we forget it in a dream."

He reached for his wife's hand as she was lowering her glass, inadvertently jostling her. She used her napkin to dab at the drops that had spilled on the floor. Though he was vaguely aware that he'd already drunk too much champagne, he took another sip.

"Last night I dreamt . . ." He paused, as if trying to recall. "I was alone in a little boat, rowing myself across the ocean. As I rowed, a storm blew in, and my boat was tossed about by monstrous waves. In my dream, I forgot to pray to God for help. I ask you, what would God have done, if he'd heard me praying in a dream?" Aimée gave him a smile designed to remind him that they had guests and her dearest mustn't let his nerves get the better of him. But this had nothing to do with nerves—he was talking about art, and the dream of art, and the charge that it was pointless.

"It was just a dream, and I was safe in my bed and did not need the Almighty to rescue me. Which might lead us to conclude that it's all a lot of hogwash, as my friend Judge Griswold likes to say, hogwash, the dream of art in all its infinite variety, because it is unreal. But don't you see"—he shook his hand free and stood, striding toward the mantel, where the black Grecian clock was displayed—"don't you see that our very sense of reality is determined by our dream of it, and if we represent the hours of a day divided as symmetrically as the columns of a temple, then that is the way we understand time, not because we know the truth of time but because some influential artist has given us a dream of it!"

He recognized that he had surprised his guests by working himself into a passion—but didn't the subject demand it? He waited to hear Monsieur Manques concede that nothing was more important than art, or what Plotinus had so crassly described as "material beauty." Instead, Madame Manques murmured gently, "Dear Prof. de Potter, forgive me, but I'm not sure what you're talking about."

That's because she thinks you are a lunatic came the verdict within him, and in this case, the judgment might seem deserved when he was measured against the elderly bourgeoisie of the Alpes-Maritimes. Consider his liabilities: He had gone into debt to collect antiquities so that others might appreciate them. He was tired of life, exhausted by his efforts to convince others to share his amazement. The demon inside him was insisting that his mistakes were too immense to be corrected.

He looked to his wife, hoping she would explain to Madame Manques. Usually she was ready to help him out when he lost track of his meaning. But on this occasion, his wife looked right past him. If she knew that her husband needed her right then, if she recognized that his fate depended upon her willingness to offer some small gesture of solace or even just a flicker of recognition in her eyes to show him that she understood what he was going through, she didn't care. She intended to ensure that her guests would think fondly of their visit to Grand Bois, and she was already rising from her chair, preparing to usher the group into the garden to see the wisteria in an effort to make them forget Armand's confusing rant.

And so the day progressed. The Manques left, and Aimée took Gertrude into town. Alone in the house, Armand opened the gilt cabinet and removed a small figurine, a flat-headed male figure with pierced ears and a stylized body that ended in a tang. He had paid twenty francs for it in a shop in Damascus, but he thought it must be worth at least twice that, even though it was broken at the shaft.

Tucking the little statue in his pocket, he went into his study to write three last letters.

His first letter was to Hermann Hilprecht, chair of Assyriology at the University of Pennsylvania:

Dear Professor Hilprecht,

As an amateur Orientalist with a collection of Egyptian antiquities on loan to the University Museum in Philadelphia, I have read with great interest about your explorations at Nippur. I continue to acquire antiquities and now and then purchase fine pieces that interest me but have no place in my own collection. Since you, sir, are a collector as well as a renowned archaeologist, I would like to offer you an item in my possession that comes from Babylonia. It is a male figure, solid cast, with prominent brow ridges and a dark brown patina. The shaft is broken, revealing an iron core.

As it happens, I will be leading a tourist party to Constantinople in early June, and it would give me immense pleasure to meet with you. I will be arriving on Wednesday the 7th and can be contacted at the Pera Palace Hotel. I look forward to your reply.

Yours sincerely, P. L. Armand de Potter.

His second letter was to Edmond Gastineau at the agency office in Paris, on the rue des Pyramides:

Dear Edmond,

I assume you haven't had any word from our New York party and they are having an uneventful passage. By my calculations, they will call at Gibraltar tomorrow. As arranged, I will arrive in Naples ahead of time and will meet the ship on the 11th. I trust that the Hotel Santa Lucia has received the full deposit and they will have our rooms prepared. I am writing now to request that you refrain from any communication with Brown Brothers regarding credit. I plan to arrive in Paris on the afternoon of June 29 and will come directly to the office. We will discuss the matter then.

Yours very truly, Armand de Potter.

His third letter was to Mrs. Stevenson of Philadelphia:

My dear Madame,

The news of your resignation recently came to my attention. I confess that it was an unpleasant shock to hear of it secondhand. I ask you, Mrs. Stevenson, didn't you think that as the one in charge of my invaluable collection, you had a responsibility to inform me of your decision? You must realize that I could have deposited my collection at any of our country's foremost institutions. My friends often ask me why my collection is in Philadelphia, and I don't know what to tell them. A gesture of recognition from the Museum trustees similar to what you secured for Mr. Osman Hamdi Bey, esteemed director of the Ottoman Imperial Museum, would have attached me more securely to the University of Pennsylvania. Of course, I am in no position to offer the kind of thanks Mr. Hamdi Bey did when he gave permission to your own Professor Hilprecht to excavate an ancient site as promising as Nippur. But you withdrew your support from Professor Hilprecht when you resigned from your post at the Museum. I can only assume that you have resigned from the stewardship of the De Potter Collection, as well.

In the event that the new trustees decide that my collection is cluttering their shelves, they should inform me promptly, and I will cover the expense of having it removed from the Museum. And do you want to know what I will do then? I will gather my little treasures into a heap and set them aflame, and I will invite the poor of the world to come and warm their hands at the bonfire. And then I will sweep the shards and ashes into the fine double coffin that I bought at your recommendation and drop it into the ocean somewhere between Sandy Hook and the Maldives. And you, dear Madame, will hear of it and know that you are to blame.

For now, I am yours sincerely, Armand de Potter.

He put stamps on the envelopes addressed to Professor Hilprecht and Edmond Gastineau and left them on the mail tray in the hall. Then he folded the letter to Mrs. Stevenson into quarters before ripping it into pieces and throwing it in the wastebasket.

He spent some time organizing his papers, writing in page numbers on his essays, putting documents into appropriate folders. As he always did in preparation for a trip, he covered his desk with an embroidered satin runner, placed a bronze pedestal bowl on top, and arranged the drapery over the fireplace.

As he stood in the doorway and surveyed the room one last time, the effect struck him as funereal. *How terribly appropriate!* murmured the demon who had taken up residence inside his mind, as if to suggest that Armand de Potter would never come home. But of course he was planning to return; he would be back in his beautiful home by August, God willing, and, with his family, he would stay there.

He knew exactly what he had to do to protect Grand Bois and the remainder of his fortune. He was through with Sara Stevenson. Now that she was out of the picture, Armand needed someone of Hilprecht's caliber to confirm the value of the De Potter Collection. He had no intention of waiting to hear what the new set of trustees thought of it. With Hilprecht's help, he was going to put the entire collection on the auction block and earn back every penny he had spent on it—and then some.

Upstairs in his bedroom, he finished preparing for his trip, packing in the usual fashion, putting into his trunk:

> One summer suit, bought in Paris in 1901 on the rue de Rivoli
> One extra suit, broadcloth, bought last year in Nice
> One pair long johns

One undershirt

Linen for two weeks

A black overcoat

A toiletry bag with his shaving supplies, soap, and a tooth-
brush

An extra pair of reading glasses

A magnifying glass

A leatherbound notebook containing his lectures

The two pieces of his detachable walking stick

One pair of kidskin gloves lined with silk

His pipe and a pouch containing three ounces of tobacco

Another pouch containing gold cuff links in the shape of the
masks of comedy and tragedy

A brown cardboard folder containing the appropriate maps

The metal figurine with the broken shaft, bought in
Damascus

As he closed the lid and snapped the locks in place, he hummed a few measures of the first song that came to mind, "Aux armes, citoyens . . . Marchons! Marchons," in an attempt to block the kind of thoughts that weren't worth thinking. He carefully un-folded his leather Saint-Lanne money belt on top, exposing the side with his moniker in gold:

ARMAND DE POTTER
CANNES (A.M.)

He tucked four hundred francs into the billfold. In an adjacent pocket he put his passport, folded into quarters. In another pocket he found a card for Valentin's Parfumerie on the avenue de la Gare in Nice, where he had bought Aimée a present last Christmas. He tucked the card back into its slot in case he needed the address when he passed through Nice on his way home in July, and he inserted a recent photograph of Aimée and Victor. Finally, he filled the small pocket on the inside flap with a dozen copies of his calling card: Mr. P. L. Armand de Potter.

The name on the card struck him as strangely inaccurate, as did the name embossed on his belt. Measuring the two names against each other, he had the distinct impression that he wasn't fully known, even by his wife. Especially by his wife. No doubt that she loved him, and he loved her. But he had secrets: secret debts, secret ambitions, secret strategies for getting what he wanted.

He was an expert at giving the impression that he was never disappointed and had grown so used to affecting an impenetrable superficiality that he'd forgotten there was more to him. His short-lived fits of anxiety were easily cured with a week of fresh air and water cures at a spa. His wife couldn't be blamed for assuming that he was generally happy, since he had believed it for years, more than ever since they'd moved to Cannes. How could he not be happy here in their luxurious villa? They'd found a home at Grand Bois that suited them perfectly. It could only seem right that after wandering the world for twenty-five years, they had finally arrived in paradise.

There was nothing to do but finish putting his things in order for the trip. The tour would do him good, he told himself. The scenery of Sicily and Greece would offer a soothing beauty. Most of all, he was eager to meet Hilprecht in Constantinople and persuade him to provide a comment that Armand might put in print when he was ready to sell his collection.

He took a penknife to deepen the lettering of his name on the front plate of the trunk, a third variation: *Pierre Louis Armand de*

Potter. He studied it for a moment, thinking how easy it was to substitute letters in a name, or to change it altogether. He scratched into the little space left at the edge of the plate, *d'Elseghem*. On one of the blank tags he kept in his bureau he wrote *WANTED* to indicate that the trunk should be delivered to his stateroom. And then he went to say good-night to his wife.

❧ PART SIX ❧

At Sea

I<small>T IS CLOSE TO MIDNIGHT</small> on the *Regele Carol*. The last of the passengers have finally returned to their rooms, the stewards have stacked the deck chairs, and Armand is alone at the rail, searching the darkness in an effort to make out the coast of the nearest island. By his calculations, Lemnos should be a half mile off their starboard side, close enough to swim to if the steamer foundered. But he isn't worried that the steamer will founder, not tonight, not with the sea perfectly calm, the sky starlit, the breeze barely strong enough to disperse the smoke from his pipe.

He pictures his wife bundled in blankets in her hotel room in Lausanne, the window open a crack to let in the cool night air. In the morning she'll ring for room service and enjoy her tea and brioche in bed. Later she will walk into town to shop with Victor, or maybe they'll take a stroll along the Esplanade de Montbenon and have lunch on the terrace at La Grotte.

If he'd had the foresight to recognize in the midst of his foolishness that his actions would lead him here, to the rail of the *Regele Carol*, he would have attempted to design a different outcome, including joining his wife and son tomorrow for lunch at La Grotte before boarding the train to return to Cannes. Instead he is compelled to stick to the original plan, to keep on leaning against the rail, to lean a little more and a little more, not far enough to fall, but far enough for his pencil to slip from his breast pocket and plummet into the boiling foam below.

He feels a momentary pang but then reminds himself that he won't be needing his pencil anymore. He won't be needing much of anything where he's going. He won't need his pipe. He won't need his buttermilk dress coat trimmed with silk lapels. He won't even need his hat.

He's not sure which his wife will receive first: his last two letters or the official notice that he is missing at sea. He expects that she will weep for the appropriate period, perhaps even longer. But she is a resourceful woman, and sooner or later she will dry her eyes. After taking stock of her new circumstances, she will rebuild her life and watch over her son at Grand Bois.

In the shorter of his last two letters to her, he included instructions on how to handle the estate. He couldn't bring himself to warn her, however, that when she attempts to withdraw money from the Crédit Lyonnais she will find the account has been closed, and then when she continues to the Société Générale, she will discover that their joint account contains far less than she thought and their fortune has shrunk to almost nothing. Divesting all their remaining assets won't satisfy the creditors clamoring for payment. Only the sale of the De Potter Collection at its full value, along with the ample indemnity from his paid-up life insurance policy, will enable his wife and son to remain in their beloved home.

He'd tucked the photograph of them into his pocket, and he takes it out now to examine it. Aimée with her funny topknot the size of an acorn. Victor with his melancholy eyes. Is it possible that he would never see them again? Why, it's very possible! See how possible it is?

He glances over his shoulder to check that the deck behind him is still empty. He looks toward the wall that hides the bridge from view to confirm once more that the quartermaster on watch can't see him. Shadows moving below the light on the front deck catch his attention; he traces them up a pole to a pair of flags fluttering in the light wind. This, he tells himself, is as good a time as any to make his exit, and he would, he will . . . except that right then he hears a quick, muted thud that could have come from the interior of the ship or might signify that somewhere nearby a door has been opened and swung shut again.

He looks around to see if he has company. A moment later he thinks he hears the same thud again, but it is fainter this time, and he wonders if he'd been mistaken. No one is in sight. Still, he is flustered.

He takes a puff from his pipe to steady his nerves and looks down at the water. As he watches the white froth roll away from the hull into the night, breaking into patches and dissolving into the same wine-dark sea that the ancients sailed, the bitter thought comes to him that they might be passing over a sunken galley full of looted treasures.

He is sorry to have created such a mess for his dear wife to clean up. That it has come to this and he must cause his family such anguish in order to protect their happiness is a reality as absurd as it is unavoidable. He is teetering above the ocean, about to fly away from his life on the presumption that he must take responsibility, he must make sure his creditors are paid, he must remove himself as the target of his enemies and keep his family from being turned out of their home—he can accomplish all this with one simple action, shattering the surface that hides death from human consciousness, subjecting himself to the cruelest agony because he must, he must . . . good God, he must pull himself together!

He reaches for his pocket watch before remembering that he left it in the trunk in his room. He turns to see if the clock on the wooden pedestal inside the unlit dining room is visible through the window behind him. He can't see the clock, but he does notice the steward and stewardess embracing near the funnel on the upper deck, locked in a kiss.

When did they arrive? Everybody is supposed to be in bed by now. It is essential that his last act go unwitnessed. If the couple looks up just as he is throwing himself overboard, they will alert the crew and try to save him. Imagine being reeled back onto the ship, flopping and sputtering while passengers and crew gather round! Even if they don't succeed in saving him, they will be asked for a full report of the incident, and their testimony would be enough proof that Armand de Potter's death at sea wasn't accidental.

He wouldn't have predicted that love would get in the way— love, with its impractical hope. Love is the reason he is standing here. How he loves his wife and son and wants only to protect them. How jealous he is of the young couple kissing on the upper deck.

He could go to the back of the boat, where the couple wouldn't be able to see him. But in truth he is relieved that they have intruded into the scene he has so carefully arranged. He is reassured by the evidence that the two young people are persisting in their devotion, despite all the obstacles the world has thrown in their way, and he doesn't mind if he has to wait for them to get their fill of each other before he proceeds with his plan. On this journey he won't miss a connection just because he is a little late. Keep kissing, he would like to urge the couple, kiss for as long as it pleases you. Though it's unusual for him, the gentleman leaning against the rail of the *Regele Carol* is not in any hurry.

Cannes to Boulogne

THINGS ARE BECAUSE WE SAY THEY ARE. They were once or will turn out to have been. What might be this becomes that when expressed through a reasonably coherent sequence of words. Yet you can't just declare that the moon has dropped from the sky into the pond and expect to be believed—or to believe everything that others tell you. By the time you're fourteen, you should know better than to go running for your pitchfork in hopes of lifting the soggy moon from the water. Add to the normal eight years of formal education a record of travel unmatched by other boys your age, and you can be expected to demonstrate an advanced level of sophistication.

Je ne veux pas décevoir.

The challenge was to prove mastery by excelling in grammar and vocabulary and at the same time to develop an agile sense of skepticism, enabling him to differentiate between a true story and a false one.

True: Thucydides wrote the *History of the Peloponnesian War.*

False: Your science teacher is a werewolf.

True: Five times five is twenty-five.

False: Your name is George.

Skepticism, Victor had come to understand, is like a muscle—it needs to be exercised, tested, pushed beyond its limits with impossible affirmations so cleverly expressed they make it easy to forget they are lies. A boy must learn to stay alert and recognize a deception when he sees one. *Proof* is the key element in verifying any claim, and its absence is a sure signal to be suspicious. The world is in itself proof that God created it, as his Latin teacher, Father Roland, liked to remind him. But there is no proof that the world was created in seven days, according to Monsieur Pirette, his science teacher.

Proof isn't always easy to discern, and sometimes it could be contradictory—a lesson he remembered learning when they were visiting his mother's family at the farmhouse in Tivoli, and they all piled into a wagon and rode to a cemetery, where, in the high grass at the top of the hill, they found the Beckwith family gravestones. One stone was lying flat, he remembered, but when his uncles tried to make it stand upright, it toppled right over again. Victor could read the name on the stone. He was told it marked the grave of his mother's grandmother, but the name was the same as Maman's name before she married Papa: AMY SUTHERLAND BECKWITH. By then he was old enough to understand that gravestones were proof that someone was dead. Why, then, was his mother's name carved on a gravestone lying in the grass? Riding in the wagon away from the cemetery, he was quiet and didn't tell anyone how he had the same feeling inside that he'd had when he'd sat on the rim of a bottomless well in the city of Carthage. The tombstone and the bottomless well were forms of proof that didn't make sense, and he wanted to forget them but couldn't.

Victor craved proof in the months following his father's disappearance: proof in the form of a bloated corpse found on a beach somewhere along the coast of Greece, proof in the form of a coffin. There wasn't even a funeral to confirm that his father was dead. He could go into his mother's bedroom on any given evening and find her crying—wasn't this a form of proof? But then he remembered the rhyme he'd learned from his mother about *little King Boggen who built a fine hall, pie crust and pastry crust, that was the wall*. Wasn't that just made up? Mothers especially were prone to be too trusting, and sometimes it took their skeptical sons to remind them that they shouldn't believe everything they were told.

That Papa would willingly leave his enviable life made no more sense than the overturned gravestone inscribed with his mother's former name. And then Cousin Gertie saw Papa on the tram. Maman said it couldn't have been Papa because if he was in Nice, he would have come to Cannes. Cousin Gertie was mistaken. Still, when the evidence was carefully examined, he had to agree with Gertie that his father was very much alive. If he wasn't on the tram in Nice, then he was somewhere else.

"Maman, there's someone in the garden! There he goes behind the shed—quick, tell François!"

"Maman, look," he said as they strolled along la Croisette, "doesn't the man there look just like Papa? Could it be . . . ?"

Victor thought he saw Papa dressed in a sailor's suit, smoking a cigarette at a café on the boulevard du Midi. He thought a Gypsy playing the accordion was Papa. Could that be Papa in the back pew at St. John's? Or standing outside the gate of his school? There he was, with his back to Victor in the public urinal at the beach. Or there, at Victor's bedroom window, with one eye swollen shut and the other like a cat's eye in the dark, the gold iris nearly covered by the black disk of the pupil.

"No, no, no! Make him go away!"

Aimée did what she could to persuade Victor that his father was gone forever. She read him comforting letters from family members and friends, she bought him a black mourning suit, she took him to church. But still the boy kept seeing his father everywhere, whether he wanted to or not.

She was furious with Gertrude for infecting Victor's imagination with her story about seeing her uncle on the tram in Nice. She decided it was time for Gertrude to return to her mother in Poughkeepsie. Gertrude pleaded to stay, but Aimée presented her with her steamer ticket the following week. "Now head upstairs and pack," she said with a decisiveness that cowed her niece into obeying. And since she couldn't make Armand go away, she decided that she and Victor would go away instead.

On a long walk into the hills above the spa at Vittel, with the sun shining and the skylarks singing, Aimée made up her own story about Victor's father. She said that after Papa died, his wallet was never found. She reminded Victor that Papa always kept lots of money in his wallet.

"What do you think happened to his wallet?" Victor couldn't guess, so Aimée helped him out. "Maybe Papa didn't fall overboard. Maybe he was robbed. There were no witnesses. Maybe he was robbed and—" She left the possibility unspoken.

She said they couldn't be sure about what happened that night. It was awful not knowing, but she didn't want Victor thinking either that his father had chosen to end his own life or that he was still alive.

Victor wanted to hear exactly what had been in Papa's wallet. He asked how much money had been lost. He wanted to know how God would punish the thief in hell. When his mother said weakly, "It's all a mystery," he wept so hard that he exhausted himself. They'd arranged their picnic of cheese and bread on a blanket, and he fell asleep across her lap. As she watched him sleep, Aimée regretted her white lie. But it seemed to have the desired effect. After Victor woke, he was resigned to his father's death. He asked no more questions about the wallet, and in the days that followed, he was cured of his visions.

How guilty she felt then—not because she'd deceived her son but because she missed having reason to comfort him. Even though she was convinced that her husband was gone from the world forever, she missed the moment of her own heartaching credulity when she'd look in the direction that Victor was pointing, half-expecting to see what he saw.

Aimée thought endlessly about Armand, imagining the sequence of his last days, hour by hour. She pictured him riding in his carriage from the top of Pera to the customhouse, then waiting on the bench until it was time to board the *Regele Carol*. She followed him onto the ship, into his stateroom, and back out on deck. She imagined him in conversation with strangers at his table in the dining room. She hoped he'd helped himself to an extra brandy. The thought that he might have been thoroughly drunk occurred to her for the first time. She tried and failed to imagine the storm of his thoughts as he stood at the rail.

She decided she didn't want to stay in Vittel any longer and led Victor to Lausanne and up to Geneva. As they traveled, Aimée regularly received the letters and bills that had been forwarded from Cannes. A letter from Mrs. Stevenson arrived for her at the hotel in Geneva. She'd written to Mrs. Stevenson to tell her of the death of her husband and to offer the De Potter Collection for sale to the University Museum. Mrs. Stevenson wrote to extend her sympathies and explain that she was no longer affiliated with the museum. A few days later Aimée was shocked when another letter arrived from Professor Randall-MacIver, who, on behalf of the Board of Trustees, was writing to inform Mrs. de Potter that the University of Pennsylvania was not interested in buying the De Potter Collection. She had expected the sale to go swiftly. Instead, Professor Randall-MacIver asked her kindly to remove the items from the building at her convenience.

One night in a little hotel in the Alps she had a dream that she was sitting on a seaside bench in Cannes and two policemen appeared and announced that they were arresting her for vagrant lunacy. She woke wondering how she could have remained oblivious to her husband's growing debts. She wished they had never left their first apartment in Albany.

The next day she and Victor climbed up the path behind the hotel and had a picnic in the mountains, surrounded by snow peaks and the slope of the glacier. The sun warmed their backs even as they dipped their bare feet into the ice-cold stream. Victor told a joke about the glass ears of the Swiss. Aimée was puzzled. "Glass ears are the glaciers, Maman." She heard herself laugh for the first time in weeks.

In mid-August they traveled to Brussels and took the local train to the town of Melle, where they were met at the station by Armand's brother, Victor, and his wife, Leonie. It was the first time they had seen one another since 1898, when Armand and Aimée had brought their son to meet the uncle he'd been named after. The boy hardly remembered that meeting. Now their greeting was stiff, and when they stopped for tea at a café near the station, their conversation about the weather led to an awkward silence that was broken only when Leonie began testing her young nephew on his French, challenging him to conjugate a series of irregular verbs, clucking playfully when he made a mistake.

No one spoke of Armand. The elder Victor did not speak at all, though Aimée could see that he had something he wanted to tell her. She was sure it was unpleasant and hoped he would keep it to himself.

His silence lasted until the next morning, when he was preparing to take his sister-in-law and nephew back to the station and they were waiting outside on the road for the hackney cab. He presented young Victor with a wooden flintlock dueling pistol, one of a pair, he said, that had belonged to Louis de Potter. The boy whooped as he took the pistol from its case. He tested its weight and pointed it at the sky. "Bang!" he shouted.

The elder Victor said that he had once watched his grandfather Louis shoot a weather vane on a barn roof with this pistol. The weather vane, in the shape of a rooster, had spun round and round—he whirled his hand to imitate the motion. They laughed at the story, all except the storyteller.

"You know the truth about Louis de Potter, I assume," he said when they'd stopped laughing.

Aimée said, "Of course," though she had no idea what he was talking about.

"You know, then, that our grandmother was not the wife of the great Louis. She was his mistress, employed by the family as a cook. A cook! Do you understand what I am telling you! You did not know, did you? You are surprised!"

Leonie warned him that he must get control of himself, that she feared for his weak heart. Victor was desperate to have the fact acknowledged. He had kept the secret for too long and wanted someone else to guard it. Aimée lied and assured him that this wasn't a secret—Armand had been forthright about the family history, she said. She pretended to be bored, even annoyed at having to return to a subject that was so tiresome. She told her son to thank his uncle for the gift of the pistol and then said that they'd better hurry—they didn't want to miss their train.

Her husband's father was a bastard. Armand had left that detail out of his family history. She might once have resented him for the omission, but now she understood that it fit his ambition to present a front of civility that would be pleasing to all. Anyway, as she pointed out to her son, Louis de Potter must have loved his illegitimate child as much as the children of his legal wife. He had given him a fine dueling pistol, after all. And now that pistol belonged to his great-grandson.

Aimée began to feel renewed again by their week in Paris. But after they returned to Cannes at the beginning of September, she was forced to confront the reality of her debts. They were in the midst of a stretch of stifling, dry weather, and she felt weak, helpless, weary. She longed for rain. She was oppressed by the present and dreaded the future. Walking along the boulevard de la Croisette, she looked out at the sunset, golden red over the sea, and thought it cruel that the glorious light was reflected in the same sea that had stolen her husband from her. She kept thinking about Gertrude's vision of Armand on the tram in Nice. She began to wake in the night soaked in sweat.

One Sunday night in late October, a light rain fell. Aimée reported in her diary that she spent the entire day reading and then in the evening took a short walk up to the observatory. The next morning she had her first Italian lesson and declared that she enjoyed it greatly. After tea she called on her neighbors the Tamours and surprised herself by announcing that she wished to sell Grand Bois.

Did she mean it? they asked.

No, she thought. "Yes," she said.

She told herself that she had no choice—the upkeep was too much, she couldn't afford to pay all the servants and still pay for

Victor's education. That she missed her family and friends back in America was not a factor. She would have stayed in Grand Bois if she could have afforded to. She imagined her husband insisting that he'd left her sufficient resources; he hadn't foreseen the complexity of the expenses she was facing. She'd come to recognize that his courtly manner hid more than a little naïveté. The money from Mutual Life may have been enough to pay off his debts, but was not enough to sustain the luxurious life they'd grown used to in Cannes. And now she didn't know if she'd be able to sell the De Potter Collection at all.

She couldn't sleep that night, and she finally gave up and went down to the kitchen to make herself a cup of tea. While she waited for the water to boil, she stood in the doorway. The weather had cleared, and the terrace was lit with an icy glow from the full moon. As she listened to the water trickling in the fountain, she remembered the day she and Armand had come to see Grand Bois for the first time. Before even entering the house, they'd walked into the overgrown garden and seen the stone nymph lying on the ground. Armand had peeled back the tangled ivy from the figure, revealing the empty almond eyes, the fine sculpted wedge of her nose, her lips parted in a smile. "Bonjour, mademoiselle!" he'd said with a laugh, and as Aimée looked on, she'd felt a pleasant awareness of a new task ahead, as if the nymph were a living thing that needed to be cared for. And they had cared for her, at great expense—cleaned and repaired and returned her to her pedestal, where she gave the impression that she stood there pouring water back into the basin, backlit by the moon, just so her beauty could be admired, too pleased with herself ever to consider that one day she would be abandoned.

Through the next six months, Aimée slowly packed up the contents of the house. She hired a photographer to take pictures of the villa and grounds. Working with Ernestine, she prepared the linens for storage, boxed up the books and papers, and wrapped the collection of magic-lantern slides in newspaper. With François's help, she took down the paintings. On her own, she carefully emptied the gilt cabinet and packed the curios in shipping crates. She worked slowly, pausing to examine each piece. She rubbed her thumb along the edge of the pair of tear catchers before realizing that the dusty streaks were on the inside of the alabaster tubes. Wrapping the ivory elephant from the chess set, she saw that the tower on its back was chipped. As she was finishing, she suddenly worried that the strange metal figure with the broken shaft was missing. She told herself that she must already have packed it and forgotten.

On June 16, 1907, a close, hot day, their final full day in the villa, Aimée and Victor finished packing their trunks in the morning and then went to say goodbye to the neighbors. The next day they had their last tea in the garden, and Aimée went upstairs

one last time. "Took leave of our rooms & <u>my bed</u>," she wrote in her diary that night, scratching a thick line, as if she could force herself to accept her loneliness once and for all.

The servants lined up at the door to say goodbye. François promised to take good care of the garden. Young Ernestine cried loudly and periodically blew her nose with a great snort. Felicie looked on grimly. Aimée stayed cheerful, determined not to give away her feelings. She picked a big bouquet of carnations to carry away with her, and she and Victor left Cannes on the 6:00 p.m. train bound for Boulogne.

Constantinople

GIVEN ALL THAT ARMAND WANTED to communicate to his wife in his last two letters to her, it was understandable that he made just a brief reference to the disagreeable business that had occurred in Constantinople. He didn't have the desire to elaborate, especially since his hope was that the threats directed at him would be forgotten in his absence.

Aimée never knew that two influential men affiliated with the University of Pennsylvania were in Constantinople, both of them involved with excavations at the ancient Sumerian city of Nippur. She never learned about the controversy surrounding the discoveries at Nippur. And she couldn't have known that her husband had set up a meeting with the hope of winning an endorsement for the De Potter Collection.

Osman Hamdi Bey studied law in Paris but went on to devote himself to art and archaeology. He became director of the Ottoman Imperial Museum in 1881 and undertook important excavations at Nemrut Dayu. In 1884 he rewrote the laws to prohibit the export of ancient artifacts, and his permission was required for anyone seeking to excavate in the Ottoman Empire. He received an honorary degree from the University of Pennsylvania, presented to him personally by Professor Hermann Hilprecht in 1894. As a writer in *The Athenaeum* put it, "Now that the oversight of all the antiquities found in Turkey is in the hands of Hamdi Bey, he is the object of great attention from those who wish to share in their enjoyment."

Hermann Volrath Hilprecht was an archaeologist and specialist in Assyriology. Hired as a professor at the University of Pennsylvania in 1886, he oversaw the Nippur excavations from a hotel room in Constantinople. Hilprecht claimed personal credit for discovering thirty thousand cuneiform tablets that had, in reality, been discovered by an American, John Henry Haynes. Professor Hilprecht, the absentee director of the excavations at Nippur, discredited Haynes's work. According to gossip at the time, Haynes suffered a mental breakdown and returned to live in seclusion in the United States. But questions arose about Hilprecht's honesty. In 1904, the curator of General Ethnology at the University of Pennsylvania revealed that Hilprecht had appropriated a bronze goat's head from Nippur for his private collection. And early in 1905, Canon Peters, the original director of the Nippur explorations, charged Hilprecht with deliberately misrepresenting the evidence of the discoveries at Nippur.

By early June, Hilprecht was back in Constantinople. Armand arrived in the city with his touring party on Wednesday, June 7. All he knew about the dispute involving Hilprecht was that Mrs. Stevenson disapproved of his methods and had cut off all ties with the University Museum. Hilprecht, Armand believed, had successfully defended himself against allegations of misconduct. From the bits of news that reached Armand in Cannes, he assumed that Mrs. Stevenson had resigned under pressure from the trustees, and Hilprecht had emerged as an even more respected expert than he'd been prior to the dispute. He didn't know that Hilprecht had cheated and connived his way to the top of his field.

And it didn't occur to Armand that he might have judged Mrs. Stevenson too harshly, or that after she resigned there would be no one left at the University of Pennsylvania who recognized the value of his collection.

Armand wasn't entirely new to the field of Assyrian antiquities. Back in 1898 he had written to Mrs. Stevenson, "My Dear Madame: I have just closed up my house in New York and in packing away some of my collections, I came across three tablets which I have had for a number of years and which were formerly in the possession of Clot Bey, in Cairo. When I purchased them, I was told by his son that they were acquired by him somewhere in Asia Minor, and no doubt they represent some period of Assyrian art. They would probably not go with my Egyptian Collection, but I thought you might be glad to have them on deposit in the Museum of the University."

When Armand sent the tablets to Mrs. Stevenson, he didn't specify their exact provenance or date, and his tone was unconcerned. If she wanted them on deposit, she could have them. She accepted them, and they joined the De Potter Collection in Philadelphia, where eventually they were examined by the University of Pennsylvania's own Assyriologist, Professor Hermann Volrath Hilprecht—the same man Armand had arranged to meet on June 8, 1905, at a café in Constantinople.

Armand led his small party to the Seven Towers, where they were met by two carriages he had hired to drive them along the land walls to the Adrianople Gate. From there, the group proceeded on foot. They walked through the narrow streets to the old Forum Constantini, continuing on past the mausoleum of Sultan Mahmud II, and then skirted the north end of Maïdany, arriving at the Hagia Sofia. After trooping from the crypt to the dome and even putting their fingers in the notch inside the famous weeping column, they stopped for a lunch of mutton pilaf and compote for dessert. Then they strolled through the market behind the Parmak Kapoossy gate.

Leaving the Americans to shop for talismans and pipes and ebony spoons, Armand went straight to the café at the end of the alley. He was a few minutes early, but Professor Hilprecht was already there.

"Professor Hilprecht?" Armand asked, removing his hat as he approached the man.

"I have something for you, Mr. de Potter," Hilprecht said, ignoring his greeting, "but first you have to tell me what he is meant to hold." He gestured to the bronze on the table in front of him. Armand saw it was a plump figure, about four inches high, with an expressive face crowned by a copper wreath of ivy leaves and berries. The eyes and lips were enamel. In the left hand it held a staff, ornamented with a pinecone. The right arm was raised, as though in the midst of lifting something, but was broken off at the wrist. Except for this, the figure was intact.

"Why, it's a fine little statue—Greek, is it?" Armand said evasively. "I see there's a staff in one hand." He had been expecting to give Hilprecht the iron figurine from the gilt cabinet as a gift. But it seemed Hilprecht had brought along a trinket from his own collection to exchange.

"He has a staff, yes. But what is he supposed to be holding with his other hand?"

"Perhaps a shield?" Armand proposed. Though he felt wary, conscious of being tested, he was prepared to show Hilprecht the greatest respect. Mrs. Stevenson had given up her authority at the University Museum because of some dispute about Hilprecht's credibility. But Hilprecht, not Mrs. Stevenson, was the expert who had been invited to advise the Ottoman Imperial Museum. And, like Armand, he was a collector himself. Armand had thought they would feel at ease with each other.

"Why would Bacchus hold a shield, Mr. de Potter?" Hilprecht asked with obvious impatience.

It made sense, once Professor Hilprecht pointed it out, that the figure was Roman. Armand, caught off guard, had failed the test. He had come to talk with Hilprecht about the De Potter Collection. But Hilprecht didn't want to hear about the collection. He wanted to expose Armand as a man so ignorant of the art of the ancients that he couldn't tell the difference between a Roman imitation and a Greek original. The meeting suddenly seemed like a trap, and it was too late to escape.

"Maybe he is supposed to be holding a plate of fruit?" Armand suggested. "An apple? A bunch of grapes?"

"Oh, come now, Mr. de Potter, use your eyes for God's sake! He's thirsty. Does he look thirsty?"

"I suppose so."

"Why do you think he looks thirsty? What evidence do you have? If you don't mind my saying, I have the distinct impression that you see only what you want to see."

This last comment was delivered dismissively, and Armand understood the insult's broad implications. Had Hilprecht heard about the incident at Jaffa? Did he know that Armand was on the verge of insolvency and desperate to sell his collection at a profit, thus making him more dependent on Hilprecht for an endorsement? Maybe Hilprecht didn't want to give an endorsement. Maybe he saw Armand as a competitor and a threat to his own dealings.

Armand wasn't in the café with Hilprecht for long, since he had to return to his group and lead them to the sultan's palace. But he had enough time to order a coffee, which he then ignored. He had enough time to accept Hilprecht's Roman Bacchus in exchange for Armand's iron figurine with the broken shaft—a piece Hilprecht thought "very peculiar," though he evidently considered it valuable enough for him to go through with the trade. Hilprecht didn't need more than a minute or two to wrap up the figurine in a sheet of newspaper and to mention, by the way, that he'd finally gotten around to examining the three Assyrian tablets in the De Potter Collection. He hoped Armand hadn't gone into debt over them. They were lovely tablets, weren't they? Unfortunately, it was Professor Hilprecht's responsibility to tell Armand that all three tablets were forgeries. It should have been obvious, since the forgers used alabaster in two of the reliefs, while Iranian sculptors would have used limestone. The third tablet was indeed limestone, but it was light gray limestone, stained to imitate the dark tone of the ancient limestone. Once the staining was removed, it became clear that the relief was copied from the ruins of Persepolis. All three tablets were modern copies. Hilprecht had been intending to write up an appraisal for Mrs. Stevenson, but then Mrs. Stevenson had resigned and withdrawn her financial support for the fifth expedition to Nippur. There would be no fifth expedition because of the petty controversy arising from his having dared to pocket a bronze goat's head for his own collection. Mrs. Stevenson had resigned over a goat's head! Hilprecht didn't bother to admit that he had stepped down from the chairmanship of his department. That was beside the point. At issue were the three fraudulent tablets that Armand had tried to pass off as authentic to the University Museum. Maybe he had made an honest mistake. But if he'd made the mistake with the tablets, what other mistakes had he made? Wasn't there something about a scarab ring that had been misdated? Don't fret over the scarab ring, Mr. de Potter—that was a minor error compared with the three forged tablets. Were there other forgeries in the collection? Was the remarkable illustrated sarcophagus authentic?

Could Mr. de Potter be certain? If the sarcophagus was a fake, God forbid, the implications were dire. How about the bronze figure of Osiris? How about the little iron statue with the broken shaft that he just traded for Bacchus? Professor Hilprecht regretted that he would have to send a report to the museum trustees. In the meantime, he had consulted with the estimable Hamdi Bey, who pointed out that in Cairo, where Armand claimed to have bought the tablets, forgers were everywhere, waiting to take advantage of unsuspecting tourists who saw only what they wanted to see. Hadn't Armand purchased most of his antiquities in Cairo? There's food for thought . . . and on that note, Professor Hilprecht had to hurry and carry his package back to his hotel, for he was due at the Imperial Museum to consult with Hamdi Bey himself about an urn found during the last Nippur expedition. *Elveda, Mr. de Potter, guten Tag, gloria Deo optimo maximo, my brother.*

Oh, one last thing: the little bronze Bacchus once held a drinking bowl, just like the original in Ikaria. Of course he was thirsty, for he'd been standing there for nearly two thousand years! Yes, he'd been standing there for a long, long while . . . which meant that this piece, though a Roman copy, was an authentic antiquity, worth a little something after all. Maybe it would be useful to Mr. de Potter, who might want to get rid of his collection of forgeries and start a new collection from scratch.

After Hilprecht left the café, Armand wrapped up the bronze Bacchus, which was certain to be the last antiquity he would ever collect. He hurried to meet his group and lead them to the next stop on their itinerary, the palace of the Seraglio. He had written in advance, as he always did, to Sultan Abdul Hamid requesting permission to take his party to see the treasury in the palace.

Entrance into the palace's second court was forbidden without a special visitor's permit from the sultan himself. And everyone knew that the sultan granted permits only to select parties—parties such as the one led by Prof. de Potter.

On the day the *Regele Carol* arrived in Piraeus, June 11, 1905, the *Chicago Tribune* ran an article about Sultan Abdul Hamid. According to the writer, the sultan had feared for his life ever since King Alexander of Serbia was assassinated. He mistrusted his relatives, his courtiers and servants. He issued a proclamation prohibiting Turkish army officers from visiting restaurants and cafés frequented by Europeans, to prevent the officers from being corrupted by European ideas. "He smells poison in every dish, regards every group of persons engaged in conversations as conspirators against his power, and sees an assassin in his own shadow." He was convinced that his brother was plotting to assassinate him, so Abdul Hamid had his brother assassinated first. Prince Ahmed Kemal Eddin was strangled in his bedroom by three Armenian soldiers and then buried in one of the courtyards in the palace.

By June 8, the day Armand met Hilprecht, the news about the assassination of the sultan's brother was just beginning to filter out to the public. But Armand was unaware of it when he took his party to visit the palace. He led them through the gardens of the palace and to the entrance of the second courtyard, where he presented the guardsman with the permit from the sultan. When the guardsman took the permit and handed it to an officer, and when the officer, after quickly studying the permit, ripped it to pieces in front of the horrified Americans, Armand had no idea that the palace was closed because Prince Ahmed Kemal Eddin had been murdered. He could only assume that the sultan had denied the party entrance to the second courtyard because he had heard from Hamdi Bey, who had heard from Hilprecht, that Armand de Potter was a fraud.

Somehow he managed to lead the Americans to the carriages waiting at the Adrianople Gate. Back in Pera, he succeeded in directing them to their reserved table at the Splendide, where they were treated to sweet tea and Turkish delight. Then, because they had a schedule to keep, he ushered the party out of the café. But where were they supposed to go? Left, no, right, around the corner. Oh, how his head was throbbing, but he dared not admit it. He had to give the impression that others could count on him to make things right.

Come along, this way, if only, I thought, but where—

Are we lost, Professor?

How could they be lost when there was a mosaic to be seen on the side of that building? And look there on the terrace: three Turks sharing a narghile. Consider the clouds. Let's talk about the weather. Let's talk about Jaffa, Hilprecht, the sultan, and the tricks of a clever counterfeiter.

We are . . . perhaps . . . or else . . .

Why, they were on the Grande Rue according to the sign, and up ahead at the convent a sheikh had just concluded his hymn to the glory of God and the trumpeter was calling the dervishes to whirl.

What a relief. Here was something reliable, a spectacle De Potter parties had been treated to dozens of times before. It wasn't on the schedule for the day, but it was a sight worth seeing, everyone would have to agree.

Gather round, friends, and watch as the dervishes rise from their sheepskin mats, balance on the bare heels of their right feet, and commence to revolve. See how the right arm of each extends toward the sky, palm raised, the left hand tilts toward the earth, they narrow their eyes and spin, slowly at first, then faster and faster to the beat of the tambourines, turning circles inside circles, their long, white skirts billowing but never tangling, never even grazing.

You always give us a memory to cherish, Professor de Potter. How happy you've made us.

Was it possible to be too happy? his wife had asked him not long ago. He couldn't remember what he'd said in response and wouldn't know what to say now. He didn't know much about anything. At least he could tell you the value of his paid-up life insurance policy. Also, he knew about the dervishes. Turning and turning. Vanishing into a blur of white. Where did they go? Perhaps the molten silver dripping on his brain had blinded him. Oh, they made him dizzy, these dervishes. Yet from start to finish they never tripped over their robes or bumped into one another, for in their apparent abandon they were governed by the strictest precision.

Will they whirl again? It must be tiring, what they do. They need a rest, surely. And us? Where to next, Professor? What does

it say on the itinerary? Such a disappointment back at the palace. But the dervishes more than made up for it. Shall we move on? You do have a plan in mind, don't you?

Of course he has a plan. He wouldn't be without one. There he goes, with a deliberate click of his walking stick. We'd better hurry if we're going to keep up with him.

❧ PART SEVEN ❧

At Sea

ACROSS THE CLEAR NIGHT SKY over the *Regele Carol* he draws the line from star to star to define the curved tail of the Scorpion. He traces the legs of Hercules and locates the glittering cluster that makes up the heads of Cerberus. Sending a puff of pipe smoke toward the darkness, he pictures it re-forming into a new shape. He imagines following the smoke into the sky and taking his place among the constellations—a fate that would be far more welcome than the one he has devised for himself.

The lovers on the upper deck go on kissing; Armand continues to wait. His thoughts wander to a story he heard years ago, about an English architect who designed a factory that collapsed, killing six workers. Soon afterward, the architect took a trip to France and went missing from a Channel ferry en route to Calais. Everyone concluded he had committed suicide.

Armand has taken measures to ensure that the same will not be said of him. He can't help but worry, though, that they are insufficient. He glances at the upper deck and realizes that he might do more. He could let the steward and the stewardess notice him standing at the rail. He could nod to them. He could even tip his hat in a friendly greeting before they go back to their berths. Then after Professor de Potter is discovered to be missing at sea, his two witnesses would be compelled to reveal that they'd seen him on deck, and he had seemed entirely at ease. Their testimony would be all the evidence Aimée would need to contradict the suspicion that her husband had gone overboard on purpose. A man seen tipping his hat was not the sort to throw himself into the sea that same evening. The likeliest explanation for his disappearance would be that he'd suffered a dizzy spell because of the silver plate in his head. The insurance company would have no basis to contest the claim, and the indemnity would be paid in full. And with Armand taken so tragically, Hilprecht would have to find another target for his malice.

It is an excellent revision to his plan. Armand has only to make sure that he catches the attention of the lovers when they finally stop kissing and come up for air.

He is not unfamiliar with the need for patience. A professional traveler has to get used to waiting. He must wait for his luggage to be delivered, shows to begin, members of his touring party to assemble in hotel lobbies. He must wait in long lines to buy tickets. He must wait for prospective customers to send their deposits. He must wait for ships to set sail and meals to be served. He must wait at countless stations for a train to transport him to his next destination.

He closes his eyes and imagines he is far away. He pictures himself at some provincial train station, say in Italy or Dalmatia. In the scene that he imagines, a pigeon pecks at crumbs outside the station bar, and a cat sleeps on the windowsill. The platform is deserted. He checks his watch and takes a seat on the bench. How often has it happened that he rushes to a station only to discover that the train is late? Trains are late more often than not.

He knows to expect it. He can expect as well that, after realizing he'd been hurrying unnecessarily, he will be bothered by a sensation that is as inevitable as it is inconvenient and that tends to be especially urgent when he is waiting for a regional clunker that will not have a toilet on board.

The same unwelcome sensation comes to him now, on the deck of the *Regele Carol*. He tells himself that he has better things to think about. He always has better things to think about than the petty demands his body makes at the most inappropriate times. Is this why he was born? To eat and drink and then to relieve himself so he can eat and drink again? Put a God-fearing soul inside a skeleton, add blood and flesh, and this is all you get? He may be a knight of the Order of Melusine, he may have friends all over the world, some of whom have sent inquiries to him and are impatiently waiting for his reply. He may be tumbling from the peak of his success and on the verge of suffering the most dramatic disruption he could contrive for himself. But right now he is a man defined only by the basest need. Any minute, the stationmaster will ring the bell to announce the approach of a dingy little train that has no toilet.

At least he has the advantage of being skilled at certain strategies of deception. Like his noble ancestors, he is used to pretending that nature never calls him. He can slip quietly away from the foredeck to the public toilet, and before you can say *Jack, Jack, give in!*, he is back at the rail, breathing in the good smell of the sea, breathing it out again, staring into the dark.

All is as it was, except, as he discovers with a glance, the upper deck is empty. In the few minutes he was away from his post, the steward and the stewardess have gone back to their berths. He had hoped that they would keep on kissing for a long while. Now he's not sure whether they noticed him at all.

There's nothing to do but to pick up where he left off. There are no more changes to make in his plan. The end will follow as inevitably as if it had already occurred, with or without witnesses. So he begins to climb over the rail, lifting himself as he used to do long ago in the days when he was a gymnast, swinging onto the parallel bars, turning a somersault, kicking his feet over his head and then falling backward through the air after he'd overestimated his strength and lost his grip, watching the stars rise away from him, feeling his helplessness, like this, like this . . .

"Monsieur?"

Who is there?

"May I assist you, monsieur?"

The steward, the same one who had just been embracing his girl on the upper deck, is standing a short distance away, thrusting his hand out to grab Armand before he leaps and then stopping, evidently forcing himself to refrain from making any movement that might startle. Behind the steward, the stewardess, invisible in the shadows, catches a sob in her throat.

"Monsieur?" the steward says again, with urgency and yet infinite gentleness in his voice.

Earlier, the steward had struck Armand as shifty, but now he seems to have been put on this steamship to make an appearance at this crucial moment. Perhaps he is compelled to return the kindness Armand showed him earlier in the day, or maybe he is just doing his duty. Whatever his motive, his presence in the scene has the potential to change everything—or nothing. He could save Armand—or he could watch him drown. Has he arrived on the scene too late or too soon? Will he sound the alarm? Or might he be persuaded to refrain from interfering? He has offered Armand assistance. Does this mean that he might go on to testify that he'd seen him calmly smoking his pipe? Would he lie and say that Professor de Potter had even doffed his hat to him? And would the girl be willing to concur? All at once, there are too many unknowns—the black depths of the sea, the blank page of the future, the potential willingness of the steward and the stewardess to make up a story on his behalf.

Marseille to Red Hook

"Life is a book of which man has read only one page if he has seen only his native country" was the heading Armand had used to introduce his *Old World Guide*, and now his widow used the motto to define her purpose. Without a permanent home of her own and still unsure where she wanted to settle, she could think of nothing else to do but to keep reading the Book of Life straight through.

She settled her husband's debts with the payment from the insurance company and bought two first-class passages to New York on the SS *Kroonland*. After selling Armand's tourist business to Edmond Gastineau, she sold the Villa du Grand Bois and paid off the property loan. Later that same week she sold the De Potter Collection to the Brooklyn Museum for $2,500, a fraction of the money that had gone into it, but she was relieved to have found it a home—and in the very place where Armand had discovered his passion for collecting as a member of the Dredging Club. When the income was added together, Aimée had enough money to keep an apartment in New York and to send Victor to finish his secondary education at the Asheville School in North Carolina. And she could travel whenever she pleased.

She began by repeating the same itineraries she'd followed with her husband—the Annual Vacation Tour through Italy and the Long Spring Tour across Germany and the Tyrol. When Victor was in school, she would invite one of her nieces or a friend to accompany her, and she would take charge of all the arrangements. In summer she traveled with Victor. Occasionally on shorter trips she traveled alone. Wherever she went, she tried to keep an extensive record in her diary, packing as much as possible into each entry. She wanted to be sure she included information she'd missed in the hurried entries she'd made when she was younger.

She traveled confidently, her Baedeker in hand and her diary in her purse. She recorded, "Wyndcliffe outside of Wye is 970 ft-high," the roses in Blenheim were arranged "in segments of colors, surrounded by arbor," the tapestry in St. Michael's Cathedral in Coventry "represents King Henry VI kneeling, courtiers behind." Her lettering grew minute as she tried to squeeze in more on each page. She doubled the number of words she fit on a line, but her chronicle increasingly struck her as inadequate. Each day she added to her experiences, and each evening she added to her diary, but somehow the two diverged.

Recognizing that she'd fallen out of the habit of saying anything about her emotions, she tried to write about her grief, but the familiar words were losing their meaning—she'd written the same thing too many times. She didn't attempt to describe what she felt when she entered a hotel where she used to stay with her husband or looked at a painting they'd admired together. Instead she expressed disgust at herself for spending so much in stores. "I ought to reform," she wrote, then went on to insist that she did not regret buying new boots and a fur coat. She expressed nervousness about traveling to Holland, which was in the midst of a cholera outbreak, but then didn't mention cholera again. On her return to New York from a trip to Europe in 1909, she referred to "an

undercurrent of thought, anguish, almost despair," but in the same entry she expressed delight at the ease of the trip and described it as "perfect" and "most comfortable."

Inevitably, as she began to unpack her trunk in whatever apartment in New York she'd rented for the season and unwrapped the souvenirs she'd purchased—a silver crucifix from Rome, a handkerchief box from Palma de Majorca, a set of albumen prints from Tunisia—she'd feel a bitter disappointment, as if she'd spent the three months trying to reach a place that turned out to be a chimera. Yet she could be sure that just as inevitably her disappointment would pass with a good night's rest, and by the next morning she was already paging through travel brochures and thinking about where she wanted to go next.

In March 1909 she took her first trip to Bermuda, sailing with a friend from her childhood, Mary Rowley, on the SS *Mohke*. She wrote to Victor in Asheville that the roads in Bermuda were a slippery macadam, and she'd nearly fallen more than once. She told him that they must return together someday so he could see the rock formation that had been shaped by the wind and the sea to resemble a grand cathedral.

By the time he'd graduated from the Asheville School, Victor's confidence as a traveler began to take a different shape from his mother's. Where Aimée always stuck to the itinerary she'd carefully planned before leaving the United States, Victor liked the freedom to extend a stay when he was enjoying himself, to cut it short when he was bored, or to take a side trip on the spur of the moment. For a period of several weeks in 1911, his mother lost track of him while they were traveling in Europe. He'd gone off to explore the Dalmatian coast on his own and was supposed to meet his mother at the station in Brussels, but he didn't appear. Over the next few weeks she received scattered messages from him at her hotel. She grew so anxious that the entries in her diary began to echo the entries from the period following Armand's disappearance: "Am almost frantic 'tho outwardly calm. I fear great trouble." On the sixteenth of September, she went to Melle to visit her sister-in-law Leonie and visit the grave of Armand's brother, who had died from a stroke the previous year. She found her son sitting in Leonie's kitchen sipping tea. He said he'd met some boys on a train and they'd gone on a whim to Dunkirk. He apologized for worrying his mother and presented her with a lace shawl he'd bought in Brussels. He promised never to go off like that again.

She attributed her son's erratic behavior to his "nervous condition," assuming that he'd inherited a minor version of the same ailment that had destroyed his father. Yet the difference was that Victor acted irrationally without provocation. She wrote in the secrecy of her diary that she wished he could have been "a more normal creature" and put on "a better front." She called him her "poor lad" and a "strange compound," wondering if she'd ever understand him.

They had planned to spend the winter of 1911–12 in Europe, but Victor decided one day that he had to return to the United States, for reasons he wouldn't explain. They sailed from Antwerp for New York on September 30, setting out on a night with high winds and rain. "So ends my trip," Aimée wrote in her diary, "charming at first; terrible anxieties at last."

She complained about her rheumatism and gout. Even though her savings were considerable enough that she and Victor could live off the interest, she worried about paying her bills. But still she pressed on with her travels the following year, from Lisbon to Biarritz, from Biarritz up into the Pyrenees, then to Grenoble, Geneva, Venice, Montenegro, and Trieste, where, on a November day in 1913, she awaited the arrival of Victor, who had gone off to Berlin.

Alone in her hotel room, she was packing her trunk and came across a cloth pouch containing a perfectly formed conch she'd found on the beach in Biarritz. She held it up to her ear to hear the rush of the surf. Then she opened her diary and wrote, "Fine warm day." She paused, reflecting on the sights she'd seen, but when she failed to remember the name of the chapel in the cathedral in Trieste, she wrote instead, "Slept after lunch & watched beautiful sunset sea rosy & horizon shading into pale blue." She stopped to open and close her stiff fingers for a moment, then added, "My heart is full of gratitude for all I have and for all I am allowed to see of this beautiful world."

Aimée had an intrepid determination to see as much of *this beautiful world* as she could, though as time went on she worried that she was only drifting and longed for a permanent home. At the Hôtel d'Angleterre in Paris in the fall of 1914, she wrote that she would always be in love with France and was almost ready to settle there again. But by then France was at war.

The war, in Aimée's words, "poisoned all existence." About the German occupation of Belgium, she would say, "It almost reconciles me to Armand's death—for he would have been so furious and heartbroken over this war and the fate of his country." Instead of taking long walks through the countryside, she spent her days working at a Red Cross station in Paris and her evenings talking with other English and American tourists, all of them "waiting here for some decisive event, as it is very uncomfortable now to go home."

But Aimée and Victor did manage to make it back to America. In early May 1915, they traveled by train from France to Italy, and one week after the sinking of the *Lusitania*, they boarded the *Principe di Udine* in Genoa, sailing first to Naples before heading for New York.

At sea, the Marconi telegraph delivered a report about fighting in Trieste. When the news was conveyed to the passengers, an Italian woman seated at the next table burst into tears. On May 24, the ship started pitching unexpectedly and struck a wave, and Aimée jumped from her chair with a shout. That same day she recorded in her diary that the Marconi was reporting disturbances on the Austrian front. The next day the captain announced that war had formally been declared against Austria. Airplanes were over Venice, and the Austrian fleet was bombarding the Italian navy on the Adriatic.

The *Principe di Udine* reached the Jersey City dock safely, and Aimée and Victor booked rooms at the Murray Hill Hotel. Through the months that followed, Aimée tried to make a home for herself in a series of rented rooms. She went regularly to the opera, to the Cathedral of St. John the Divine for Sunday service, to art galleries, and lectures at the Brooklyn Women's Luncheon. She complained about gray old age and her gouty fingers. She worried about friends in Europe and reported on the deaths of an entire family she'd met through Leonie—the parents and two children had been killed by chlorine gas the wind carried through the open windows of their home in Ypres.

Victor spent several months in Florida, where he bought land and then sold it at a loss. He tried to enlist in the army but was rejected for poor vision. He came home to New York and announced that he was going to train to be a deacon but soon gave that idea up. He enrolled in Teachers College but never attended classes. He claimed he wasn't feeling well and needed more time to decide on a profession. Soon he really did fall ill with bronchitis and for two weeks didn't leave his mother's apartment. When he recovered, he announced that he had decided to study law and would apply to school in the fall. Until then, he would keep his mother company, he said. When she decided to move to the Beckwith family house in Tivoli, he went with her.

She missed her travels, but shortly after moving to the country, she reported proudly that she was growing stout. She spent the days stemming gooseberries for jam, canning corn and tomatoes and pears, driving around with friends and family. Though she would write about her life in America, "Certainly a lovely country full of peace. Why am I not at home in it?," and complain about "the incapables," as she called the family members she was supporting, she had no desire to return to the city.

She didn't record the date when she made the offer on the old Moore house, but on September 25, she drove to Upper Red Hook with her friend Mary Rowley and walked along the boundary of her new purchase. The daughter of the owners showed her the garden, which Aimée hoped to improve. The house, a warreny, old farmhouse with tin ceilings, stood on a hilltop, with a view of the distant Catskills. She named it the Ridge and was eager to get to work. She didn't care that Mary Rowley didn't seem to like her purchase. Aimée looked forward to making the Ridge her home. "Think it will interest me," she wrote in her diary.

By October she was setting up stakes to indicate her property and looking out at the mountains, "superb with color," from her back porch. She lived there with Victor, Leila, and Gertrude, who liked to get drunk at night and chatter about her happy memories of Cannes. Aimée would hardly listen, she was so worn-out from her work in the garden during the day. She planted bulbs, cut back the hedge, and cleared out the briar thickets that had grown up around the pond. The next spring she hired a gardener and his wife, the Donnerlys. The first thing she had Mr. Donnerly do was build a small grass terrace in back of the house. She bought clay pots to put around the perimeter of the terrace, and she filled them with hardy carnations.

Jobs were difficult to come by in the area, but Victor finally found work at National Tailor for seven dollars a week. "A rather poor result of so many years of culture & travel," Aimée complained, "but it may be a good beginning."

Meanwhile, she kept her own chronicle of the war, reporting, "The Allies are slowly gaining ground in the Somme, and Greek affairs are in chaos." She thought of the old friends who now "bedecked cemeteries in France & Italy." At the same time, she wanted it to be known that the flowers in the Shakespeare Garden in New York's Central Park were still in bloom.

Victor gave up his job at National Tailor after less than two weeks, but he reported to his mother that he was happy after his experience of manual labor. He wasn't sure he wanted to be a lawyer anymore; he said he wanted to sample different jobs before committing himself to a profession. Aimée's frustration at his aimlessness was offset by her relief that he seemed less agitated since they'd moved to the country. He'd begun courting a girl, Eleanor Meade, the daughter of Reverend Meade, and had hinted about the possibility of marriage. Later in the month he made a second attempt to enlist and proudly announced when he returned home that he'd been accepted into the ambulance corps.

The week after Victor sailed for France, Aimée tried to distract herself from her worries about him and went alone into New York to a performance of *Tosca*. On December 13, she went with a Miss Coleman to the theater to see the one-legged Sarah Bernhardt, who performed the part of Cleopatra in a chair. "Still the greatest actress living, charm radiates from her," Aimée reported.

It wasn't until nearly a year later when Aimée could write, "The armistice has been signed and Peace Conference is to meet in mid December. Wilson expects to sail Dec. 3rd. Last Thanksgiving we were so sad over the Italian retreat, and now we are so glad over the victory. . . . Germany is beaten & humiliated, after four years & four months of terrible fighting & destruction. King Albert has returned to his capital amid wild enthusiasm. Now comes the difficult task of making peace."

Through the years her garden grew lusher, her house more cluttered. She had a memorial erected for her husband in the cemetery of St. John's Church—a stone surmounted by a Celtic cross, which her friend Mr. Emerson, a member of the local Masonic lodge, had told her was fitting for a man who would have been inducted into the brotherhood if he'd lived.

Her son came home from the war and married his sweetheart, Eleanor. Soon there was a granddaughter to care for—

And then a second granddaughter—

Across the extended family, there were births and deaths and

marriages. Gertrude married Dr. Cookingham after he prescribed whiskey for her sore throat. The Cookinghams became known as the town drunks, but Aimée continued to watch over them, and over Victor and Eleanor, who brought out in each other a giddy childishness to such a degree that sometimes they forgot they had their own children to care for. It was their grandmother who made sure the girls' clothes were properly laundered and their shoes were shined for church. She shampooed and brushed their hair and tutored them in French. When they outgrew the schoolhouse down the road, she paid their tuition at boarding school. When she went abroad, she left the Ridge open for Victor and his family and paid the Donnerlys to attend to their needs.

She returned to Europe in 1920, and twice more in 1923—in April and again in October. On the second trip in 1923, she traveled with Mary Rowley, and they stopped in Cannes and stayed for three days in a small hotel on the rue de Fréjus. Since Mary complained about too much exertion, they avoided the hills and spent their time strolling along la Croisette, wandering through the flower markets and shopping for hats and gloves. On her own early one morning, Aimée walked up the avenue de Vallauris, all the way to the gate of Grand Bois.

From the street she could see the tall peaks of the cypresses François had planted in 1904. She noticed that the wisteria vine that trailed the top of the wall had died. She wondered if the house itself had been kept up, but the tall metal gate blocked her view. Though she hadn't planned to, she rang the bell.

The backfire of an auto rounding the curve up the hill startled her, and she huddled against the gate as the driver raced past. When the street was empty again, she strained to hear some sign of life coming from the yard. For no reason, she opened her purse and snapped it shut before catching sight of a gaunt black cat that walked slowly beside the wall opposite, dragging one of its hind legs. She remembered watching a black cat at the Villa Fiorentina when she'd gone with Gertrude to climb the clock tower. The idea that the old cat across the street might have been the same cat she'd seen twenty years ago suddenly made her feel that she'd been all wrong in her estimation of time, and the distant past was only as recent as yesterday. She became nervous at the thought that the servants who'd worked for her might still be at Grand Bois, employed by the current owners. How plain and worn she would look to them, an old woman in her untrimmed straw hat and brown coat.

She was relieved that no one came to the gate and she could slip away without having to explain herself. But just in case the driver who'd passed by earlier reported that he'd seen a stranger idling on the street, she dropped a calling card into the mailbox to prove that she had nothing to hide.

At times she saw men who reminded her of her husband. In 1929, she sailed with Gertrude through the Panama Canal and up to Los Angeles. Walking out from her hotel one morning before Gertrude woke, she saw a man crossing the street who not only looked like Armand but was holding the same kind of mahogany walking stick he liked to use. He was nothing like what Armand would have been by then—his hair was hardly gray, and he walked with the firm step of a younger man. Yet she had to clamp her hand over her mouth to keep from calling out to him. Then in 1930, she sailed with her niece Lilly on the RMS *Aurania* to Le Havre and spent the next four months traveling through Italy and Eastern Europe and up to England, and when they were at La Scala in Milan for a performance of *Siegfried* conducted by Wagner's son, she saw an older man in a box across the theater, with glasses identical to Armand's, and the same cut to his beard. He was with strangers, and the group left at intermission and didn't return.

Nineteen thirty was the same year that Aimée, back in America, commissioned the painter Wilfred S. Conroy to paint a portrait of her husband based on a set of photographs. She directed Conroy on all the details, from the suit Armand would be wearing to the book he would be shown holding and the map of the world behind him. For the back of the canvas, Aimée gave Conroy a biographical narrative to write out in pen.

She described Armand as the "grandson of Louis de Potter, one of the 3 regents of Belgium." She listed her husband's honors, the date of their wedding, and Victor's birthday. She said that Armand had been born in the "Château d'Elseghem" in Belgium. She called him a "World Traveler."

When Conroy delivered the painting in December, Aimée had it hung prominently above the fireplace in the dining room. She was pleased with the result and unconcerned that the biographical information on the back of the painting didn't match the facts in the obituary she'd written for her husband years ago. She could tolerate inconsistencies in the story, as long as the portrait showed Armand as he would have wanted to be remembered.

She took her last trip abroad in the spring of 1931 with Lilly. On April 21, she recorded that the Judas trees and wisteria were in bloom in Florence, and that she went to the American Church for Sunday service. Afterward, as she was holding out her glass to be filled with wine at the reception in the courtyard, she found herself standing next to the painter Wilfred Conroy. He kissed her hand, and the bristle of his silver beard against her skin left her speechless and confused. Handsome, suave Mr. Conroy, who knew how to please a patron. And she an old woman who, for an instant, was young again.

She sailed from Genoa at sunset on April 25. The next day they stopped in Marseille but had docked so far from the center of the city that Aimée and her niece decided to stay on the ship. "Left Port of M. at 5:30, alas!" she wrote in her diary. They had such a rough passage home that Aimée was forced to stay in bed for two days. It was the first time she'd ever suffered from seasickness, and she lay awake through the night listening to the crash of the surf against the ship's hull. She couldn't stop imagining the horror of being sucked below the surface of the waves. She knew she would never travel abroad again.

Back at the Ridge, she planted hyacinths and rosebushes and carnations. She had a raised porch built behind the kitchen so she could sit outside with Victor and Eleanor and watch the sunset. The granddaughters grew strong in the country air when they came home for the summer, and friends and family could always count on Aimée to provide them with a good meal. All the while, until the Ridge was sold and Aimée's belongings were carted away, Armand de Potter looked out from his portrait at the life he was missing.

She is left with the task of occupying herself in ways that won't strike her as futile when she thinks back on the day. She strives to make herself useful, and when she is satisfied that the needs of others have been met, she attends to herself. She still enjoys the thrill of the opera, the colors of a sunset, the taste of bonbons. She welcomes every opportunity to put on magic-lantern shows for her friends and lead them around the world without ever leaving her parlor. She has never lost her passion for artistic expression. And though she is too old to travel abroad, she is not too old to travel from the first page of a book to the last.

She has always found refuge in reading and has made a point of recording the title of every book she has read over the last three decades, fifty or more a year. These days she reads more avidly than ever. Having finished *Lorna Doone*, she looks around for something new. But it seems she has read all the other books in the house. Her gaze settles on the steamer trunk at the foot of her bed, where, below the piles of legal documents and loose photographs and the rest of the papers she'd brought from France, she has stored her old diaries.

It strikes her as strange that though she has chronicled her life going on fifty years, never before has she had the urge to read what she has written. She removes the stack and opens the earliest volume. Turning the brittle pages, she is surprised to see how her handwriting has changed, and that the entries grow longer with each passing year.

She brings the diary downstairs to the parlor, where the light is better, and begins with the first entry, reading through one year after another. She is fascinated but not dismayed to discover that she has forgotten so much. Is she really the same woman who celebrated Easter 1889 in Athens and walked up to the Acropolis with her husband? Who spent a "most interesting day viewing the cisterns of Carthage" with Victor and Armand in 1896? Who once wrote on her anniversary in 1900, in an apartment on 97 rue de la Pompe in Paris, "In afternoon we went to Exp. and up the Trocadéro tower, then to tea at Élysée Palace Hotel, saw King Leopold come in. In evening at dinner we ordered St. Honoré and champagne. M. Guerrier got up and improvised a poem and there was much gaiety and good humor. Armand gave me a gold watch charm"?

Ever since Gertrude read one of her diaries in the spring of 1906, Aimée has kept them hidden away. But now, so many years later, on a winter's day in Upper Red Hook, she's not afraid to page through her diary in front of the children while they play Chinese checkers on the floor at her feet. They will probably assume that she is reading a novel from her library.

It might as well be a novel. She becomes so absorbed that she goes on reading through most of the night, long after the girls have gone to bed. She nods off for a short time, but her dreams get all mixed up with the experiences she was just reading about, and she can't tell them apart. At times she isn't sure whether she's awake or asleep.

She fetches the next diary from the stack, and for the first time since she wrote the entries, she reads through the period from 1903 to 1905, after they had settled in the Villa du Grand Bois. She reads about the weather, her plans for the garden, her new dresses and hats. She reads about their walks and teas and visits with friends. She reads about the last weeks she spent with her husband.

As she reads, she thinks about how she came to know Armand

first by observing him from across a classroom, next from across a tea table, then intimately, as his wife. But she also came to know him in other ways after he was gone, by reading his last letters, then examining his papers and paying the debts he left behind. She continued to discover new things about him when she paged through the travel albums, packed up the curios in the gilt cabinet, and made a full inventory of the De Potter Collection. Which is why she can say to herself that she knows him better than he ever knew himself. She knows who he was beyond the man he pretended to be. She knows his true history and disguises, his desires, his failings. She knows him in his irrepressible potential. And after all these years she is confident that she knows him best for his capacity to love her. He was her darling, her sweetheart: *Never leave me*, she should have told him when she had a chance. Too late. He was gone, with the crash and suck of a wave, depriving her of her main purpose in life for no good reason.

The same man who had drawn from her a promise that would never be broken—to love him for the rest of her life—left behind an emptiness in his place. She has abided by her promise and continued to love him, yet to do that she has had to love an absence and so must feel the stab of loss all over again whenever she thinks of him, year after year, all the while hiding the truth of the manner of his death from the world.

June 11, 1906. Anniversary of that awful day. Damp & warm. Went to town to do errands in a.m. in p.m. worked at study. Insurance Co. refuse to pay without bond. Am almost glad as if there was still hope. Last night was troubled but today am calm as if turned to stone. Showery.

June 11, 1907. The <u>anniversary</u>. I wanted to pass the day quietly. It is after nine & the first moment to myself. Worked all day getting library in order. Was taking tea in garden when Manques arrived, stayed till 6:30. 2 years of increasing pain & regret. A perfect summer day.

June 11, 1908. In p.m. met Victor at Jersey City. Find him informed, more manly. Sent him to call on Miss C. This day finishes 3 years since my love left me & still my heart is bleeding.

If he had foreseen that thirty years later the wound of his death would be as fresh as ever, no matter if the weather was perfect or Victor was manly, he wouldn't have hurled himself into the sea. But he must have foreseen it. His love for her would have made the consequences all too available to his perception, even amid the chaos of his unreason. Then how could he have chosen the ending that would hurt her more than any other?

On the evening Armand stood at the rail of the *Regele Carol* looking out into the darkness, Aimée was absorbed by a book in her hotel room in Lausanne. She doesn't need her notes to jog her memory of that night. She remembers on her own, without the help of her diary, staying up late to follow the adventures of a man and his time machine, completely ignorant that her husband was readying himself for a fate he had decided was inevitable. At some point, perhaps as she turned a page, he must have started to climb over the rail to the outside lip of the deck. When she paused and looked up from her book to rest her eyes, he might have paused, too.

She pauses now, for an interval long enough to enable her to come up with an idea, as striking and urgent as if it had come to her thirty years ago, when she was reading her book about time travel and her darling was preparing to enact his desperate sacrifice on behalf of his wife and son. The idea is born out of her abrupt certainty that the scenario as she'd been imagining it for thirty years made no sense. Once, her drunken niece Gertrude had said just that. Aimée is ready to admit at long last that her niece had been right, and to imagine the very possibility she'd refused to credit.

Her husband was too practiced in self-invention not to have considered the obvious alternative to the fatal action he'd been planning when he boarded the *Regele Carol* in Constantinople. He would have ruled it out as a coward's choice and an untenable betrayal. He was a gentleman. Gentlemen do not run away from their loved ones and hide in a foreign land. But he also had an insatiable desire to keep seeing more of the world. *To travel is to live*—and he wasn't finished traveling. She knew that about him, and he knew that she knew it. So there must have been a moment when he thought of his wife and in that instant, with his future hanging in the balance, was able to predict what she would have said to him if she'd been given the chance.

It has taken her this long to understand what her husband needed to hear, not just the obvious protest—*Stop, do not throw yourself into the sea!*—but the permission that would offer him the only form of release he would have been able to accept: *My love, there is another way to disappear.* . . . As he conjured her in the midst of his misguided effort to protect her, she conjures him now to communicate to him that she would be willing to tolerate a magnificent deception devised for the sake of a new beginning, opening up the possibility, however faint, of his return.

She pictures him perched on the rail of the *Regele Carol*, his head cocked as he listens, her voice reaching him with such magical clarity that she might as well be standing beside him, speaking across the warp of space and time, insisting, *Life is the more daring option*, giving him leave to start over again. After having spent decades studying the rules of courtesy as they'd been formulated in civilizations around the world, he will have to agree that a gentleman is never less than daring.

When she finally looks up from the diary, the room is full of sunlight. She can't find her watch and isn't sure of the time, but she estimates from the shadows crisscrossing the floor and the misty clouds of melted frost on the windows that it is already midmorning.

Down in the yard, the Donnerlys' dog, General Grant, is barking with the steady rhythm of a church bell, as though it is his job to wake her. She is awake, thank you, and what a splendid day it is, Christmas Day in Upper Red Hook! She can smell the grease from the bacon and eggs Mrs. Donnerly fried earlier for the children, who probably were awake before dawn. They will be mad with impatience, waiting for their grandmother to appear so they can open their presents.

But first there is church to attend, then telephone calls to make. She remembers that her brother Tom is coming over—with Victor and Eleanor and the children, that will make six at the table. Mrs. Donnerly will serve dinner before she leaves to have dinner with her own family. Aimée will wash the dishes herself after Tom leaves. She'll take a long bath before she opens her diary, the clothbound one she bought in Paris after discovering that the leather diaries she'd used for years were no longer being manufactured.

She'll write, "Sunny. I went to church with Eleanor & Victor as Mr. Huntington stopped for us. On return opened parlor door & lit up glittering Christmas tree. Lots of presents for children & several for self. My family & Tom were only ones at dinner of goose and mince pie. Children very excited."

Then, because she suspects she won't have time to fill in the entries for the remainder of the month, she will decide that the volume is complete, and she'll add it to the stack of the earlier diaries. Since no secret is worth the effort of keeping it if it isn't eventually revealed, she won't return the diaries to the bottom of the trunk, hiding them beneath the papers. She'll nestle them on top, where they are sure to be found if anyone ever bothers to look.

❧ PART EIGHT ❧

Somewhere in Greece

THE REPRIEVE, he'd thought at the time, was entirely unexpected. He was committed to his fate. Yet it seems to him now that he'd been prepared for his plan to take a different turn, as if he'd somehow foreseen from the start that he would be granted permission to save himself. He can't even summon a clear memory of the fear he must have felt as he straddled the rail of the *Regele Carol*. He doesn't remember what the steward said to him, or what he said in reply. All he remembers is that his mind filled completely with the thought of the one who knows him best in the world. For her sake, he was compelled to climb down from the rail.

Newly beardless, in a black jacket with his fedora pulled low, he melts away from the gangway in the direction of the chain-link fence that separates the customs area from the wharf, aiming for an opening he'd taken note of when he'd traveled through Piraeus earlier in the week. He tucks his walking stick under his arm and keeps his eyes averted, pretending to be fascinated by something on the ground ahead of him. As officials call out orders in Greek, causing packs of baffled tourists to scramble toward the right, then left, then right again, he makes his way along the fence line until he comes to the opening. With a glance behind him to confirm that he hasn't been followed, he slips through and continues hurriedly down the wharf away from the ship.

After having spent twenty-five years corralling tourists into the appropriate lines in ports around the world, earning favors with baksheesh and smooth talk, he is amazed at how easy it is to avoid the customs officials, as easy as it is to walk from one life into another. All he has to do is continue along the unmarked gravel path into the hills. No one tries to stop him. Two boys unknotting a fishing net don't even look up when his shadow passes over them.

He walks through the barren fields and abandoned olive groves on the outskirts of the port, traverses a deserted churchyard, and continues for a mile along the path above the sea before circling back in the direction of Piraeus. He walks for hours. In mid-afternoon he finally reaches the Central Station, where, after helping himself to a long drink from the public fountain, he boards the third-class compartment of the electric train leaving for Athens. He sits as far to the rear as possible to be sure that the conductor won't reach his seat, if he bothers to collect any tickets at all.

He disembarks as soon as the doors open, ahead of the other passengers, emerging like a puff from a smokestack onto the platform and a moment later reappearing across the busy street. He walks diagonally across the intersection and heads quickly down the avenue, as if to an appointment.

Farther along he passes a line of kiosks, and the smell of roasted nuts reminds him that he is hungry. This is one of the many problems he did not anticipate. Unused to traveling in such haphazard a fashion, he acts on impulse, reaching discreetly for a peach as he passes the bins of a grocer.

To think that he used to go to great lengths to warn others against the clever tricks of petty thieves and pickpockets, and now he has joined their ranks. He can't believe he has come to this. He feels as if he were stuck in the romance he'd penned long ago, the one about the nobleman who flees from disgrace, dons a disguise, and lives out his years in exile. He would have expected the shame of it all to stun him into inertia. But there is one crucial difference: unlike his fictional counterpart, he intends to go home one day. He hasn't abandoned Grand Bois forever; rather, he has taken the necessary action to preserve it for his wife and son, and his intention to join them there propels him forward. With every step he takes and every piece of fruit he steals, he is demonstrating a tenacity that would please his dear wife. He will be crafty and unscrupulous, never wandering from the route, however circuitous, that will lead back to the avenue de Vallauris in Cannes.

He is fortunate that no one sees him slip the peach into his hand. No one calls *Stop, thief!* as he walks briskly up the boulevard. Unnoticed, he stops to eat his peach in a little park, in the shade of a monument to the Sacred Band. He watches the people wandering by—clerks coming from their offices at the National Bank, women wearing black mourning cloaks despite the heat, workmen pushing carts of gravel, and a pair of peddlers, who accost a party of British tourists, shaking ostrich feathers and strings of bells in their faces, offering them crucifixes and miniature clay models of the Parthenon.

He looks on as the tourists exchange money for trinkets, and the trades remind him of the one item he has kept from his previous life that he wishes to be rid of—the small bronze figure in the shape of Bacchus. He takes the piece from his pocket and approaches the peddlers. Only when both men turn their heads in his direction and he looks straight into their watery, red-rimmed eyes does he realize that he doesn't register in their assessment. To them, he is not even another careless tourist they will use to their advantage. He is invisible. All they see is the treasure in his hand.

He trades the bronze for a silver spoon with a picture of the Acropolis on the finial—a crude souvenir, worth a fraction of the bronze, but he isn't in the mood to bargain. At least it's a start, he thinks to himself as he walks away.

He continues down to the rue Constantin. In the crowd outside the Peloponnesus railway station, he is singled out by a German couple asking for directions to their hotel. After showing them the route on their map, he sells them the souvenir spoon. He uses the money to buy himself a ticket, then boards the first train that is about to depart. He finds a seat in an otherwise empty compartment and closes his eyes.

Sometime later he is jostled when the train grinds to a halt. He tucks the burlap curtain around the hook and sees that they have stopped between stations and a solitary soldier is standing beside the tracks. Worrying that the soldier has been stationed there to search for the passenger who disappeared from the *Regele Carol*, he closes the curtains and waits. The compartment is airless, stifling. A few minutes later he hears the murmuring of men in the corridor and the squeaking of their boots as they pass along to the next car.

He is relieved when the train begins moving again. He pulls the curtain aside and peeks out at the soldier, who stands in the same place as before and is studying a document he has been handed.

The train picks up speed. As they pass between piles of rubble and rocky outcrops, he wonders whether he should get off at the next station. He hasn't decided on any particular destination. He hasn't decided on much of anything yet. He is as unformed and unknown as when he first arrived in America, full of potential that mustn't be squandered, given its terrible cost.

Most of all, he yearns to go home. He will wait for as long as it takes before he can stroll along the streets of Cannes unrecognized, but he *will go home* one day, he is determined. He will let himself in through the gate at night and slip unseen into Grand Bois, surprising his wife. They will fall in love all over again.

But what of his son? How will he ever persuade Victor that his desertion was contrived to protect the perfect world he'd worked so hard to create?

He thinks about carrying the boy on his shoulders along the Midway Plaisance at the Chicago fair. He pictures Victor wearing a crown of daisies on his fifth birthday. He remembers one of their voyages to Liverpool when Victor discovered a litter of kittens on board the ship. This boy who once appeared in the stateroom with kittens tucked in all of his pockets—what will he say when his father returns from the dead?

He is lost in thought, past and future blending in confusion, when, to his dismay, the door to the compartment opens and a man about his age enters and takes a seat on the bench opposite. He is not ready for company. He wishes he had pretended to be sleeping, but it is too late for that now.

The man, he assumes, is French, or at least he is fluent in the language, for he has a French newspaper tucked under his arm. He is dressed in a brown suit that is too large for him, and he has weedy, tangled hair that hangs below his ears. He makes a show of loosening his tie and brushing the soft cloth of his beret before setting it beside him. Once he is sufficiently settled, the Frenchman clears his throat, a sure indication that he is going to strike up a conversation with his fellow passenger, who, put on the spot, had better think fast if he's going to concoct a convincing new story to replace the one he can no longer tell.

The Ridge

SHE WAS HOME ALONE when the stranger knocked on the door. That's the way she began the story when she told it years later. She explained that although she had been a young girl at the time, she was used to staying alone, and she could usually guess who was at the door. She knew the difference between the sound of the mailman's knock and the woodpecker rapping of Mr. Bascomb from the farm across the street. She could judge from Cousin Gertrude's knock whether she was drunk. Her friend Mimi, who lived next to the schoolhouse, preferred to tap with her knuckles on one of the front windows. Mrs. Donnerly, who lived in the cottage across the yard, wouldn't bother to knock at all and just came into the kitchen and started cooking breakfast, while Mr. Donnerly would call upstairs, Halloo, where's our little lady?

The unfamiliar knocking she heard that day definitely meant that a stranger was at the door. She knew she was supposed to be careful with strangers. There were hoboes wandering around the town, and worse. The Donnerlys had instructed her never to open the door if a stranger looked suspicious. But how could she tell if a stranger looked suspicious if she didn't open the door?

It was a warm day, she recalled, muggy and still, with the

locusts buzzing at full throttle—the kind of peaceful, ordinary day designed for a girl to spend reading about a family shipwrecked on a deserted island. She didn't want to have to predict the intentions of a stranger, but there he was, knocking on the door. From the upstairs window of the bedroom, she saw a car parked out front, with a driver inside. He had turned the motor off, indicating that he expected to be kept waiting. The stranger, then, had come on business that would take some time. What a bother.

She was only thirteen, and everyone said she was very brave to stay in the big house alone. Rumor had it that the Ridge was haunted. That same morning, little Irene Donnerly, five years her junior, had popped out from behind a door and scared her senseless: *BOO!*

Yet as she remembered it, she lived like royalty. Though her father had died when she was eight, and shortly after her father's death her grandmother had died, and then her mother had moved to Queens, she had more money than she knew what to do with. When she and her sister came of age, they would officially inherit the estate. Until then, they were free to stay there when they weren't at boarding school. She could have spent the summer dodging bees and blackflies with her sister at a camp in Maine, or suffocating in her mother's small apartment, but she preferred the comforts of the Ridge, even if it was haunted. The Donnerlys continued to be paid through a trust fund her grandmother had set up. They cooked for her, did her laundry, kept the garden in order and the house clean. She had Mimi nearby when she wanted a friend. And she never ran out of rooms to explore.

There were so many hidden treasures to discover, she remembered wistfully. Up in the attic there was a tent her grandmother said had been used by bedouins in the Sahara. One day she propped up the tent on boxes and laid a feather quilt over the floor and pretended she was lost in the desert. Another day she buttoned herself in a military coat and strapped on one of the heavy swords in a metal scabbard and pretended to shoot a bear with an old wooden pistol.

In her grandmother's bedroom, she liked running her fingers through the straw basket full of foreign coins and examining each medal in the cigar box. Once she put on the scarab necklace set in gold that her grandmother used to say was as old as Methuselah. She remembered finding a pearl brooch and a velvet bag of iris powder, a sandalwood handkerchief box, a set of white vest buttons, and a cameo of her grandfather. Inside a patent-leather hatbox was a silver-fox fur. In a mahogany box was a gold wreath that had crowned the head of a Roman general. Photograph albums and scrapbooks filled a whole shelf of the bookcase. And stacked on top of papers and photographs in the steamer trunk at the foot of Grammy's bed were all her leather diaries plus a cloth one.

She had found it too difficult to read her grandmother's handwriting and closed the diaries back inside the trunk. But other trunks were in other bedrooms, and these were stuffed with crisp linens—embroidered sheets and curtains, bedspreads and tablecloths, cretonne doilies, tea cloths, and pillow scarves. Every wall was covered with paintings. On every floor were Oriental rugs with pretty patterns of whirligigs and curlicues for her to try to copy in a sketchbook.

Sometimes she would set the table for a feast, with the silver-plated soup tureen and the chocolate pot, the champagne glasses, the bread-and-butter plates from Ovington's, the china fruit bowls, the Turkish coffee cups, the cut-glass saltcellars. She would pretend that a king and queen were seated at opposite ends of the table, and she would pour water from the blue glass pitcher shaped like a bird.

But what she liked to do best of all, she said, was to go into the parlor and open the gilt cabinet that contained the treasures collected by her grandfather. Grammy always called him the Professor and said he was distinguished. In the portrait hanging in the dining room he looked like a professor, with his book in his hand and a map of the world behind him. He must certainly have been a distinguished man to have died in such a mysterious way. The official explanation was that he accidentally fell off a boat and drowned, though her daddy believed he'd been pushed into the sea by a thief. His body was never recovered, and no one could say with certainty what had happened to him. Once Cousin Gertrude whispered to her that maybe he hadn't died at all but had instead disguised himself and snuck away so Grammy could collect the money from his life insurance policy.

The contents of the gilt cabinet were all the family had left of his legacy, to be admired through the beveled glass but never touched, never handled, except by Grammy herself—that was her most important rule at the Ridge. Grammy regretted that once an iron statue from the cabinet had been lost, maybe even stolen, and she didn't want anyone opening the door of the gilt cabinet and mixing things up. But then the day came when Grammy wasn't around anymore.

There were buttons and coins, jars and little figurines that were even older than Methuselah, Grammy used to say. Some of the pieces had been purchased by Granddaddy, some he'd dug out of the earth himself. Granddaddy had bought the handsome cabinet to display the collection, and Grammy had kept the key hidden in her bedside drawer. But the girl found the key, and she was free to play with all the treasures as if they were toys.

They were *her* toys, and the Ridge was *her* home. Though she liked to have the big house to herself when her sister was at camp, she wasn't entirely alone. She had the Donnerlys' dog, General Grant, for company. A fat, drooling, curly-haired Airedale, he smelled like dirty laundry and lived only to eat everybody's leftovers and then collapse. He didn't give the impression that he'd ever be roused by an emergency. Still, she was glad to have him around, and she always made sure he was in the room with her when she was alone in the house.

He'd been sprawled like a rag rug beside her bed the day the stranger knocked at the door, but by the time she thought to give him a good shove to rouse him, he was already gone. He had probably squeezed his fat, quaking body beneath the bed in another room and intended to hide there until the danger was past. As usual, he was ashamed to be revealed as a coward.

As she remembered it, she resolved to ignore the knocking and pretend no one was home. But after a minute, the stranger knocked again, more boldly this time, signifying that he was growing impatient. What did he want? If a bill needed to be paid, he could have dropped it in the mail slot. If he had come to sell something, he might as well give up. The girl went to the window, hoping she'd see him returning to his car. But he remained on the porch.

Why didn't he just go away? And why, oh, why, was he turning the front knob and opening the door on his own?

Irene Donnerly, who liked to pretend to be a ghost, had a thing or two to learn. Ghosts were nothing compared to evil men who let themselves into a house without an invitation. Ghosts could be willed away by common sense.

She remembered rising on leaden legs and walking out of the guest room. If nothing else, she said, she had to see the stranger first, before he could surprise her. She had to brace herself against something Irene Donnerly wouldn't have known to imagine, something so awful that down at the bottom of the stairs that sloth of a guard dog General Grant was planted in rigid attention, his fur rising along his spine, a growl coming from deep within his fat body, a rattling growl expressing a murderous ferocity as he confronted the stranger in the hall.

She felt some measure of curiosity as she looked down at the scene, though as she recounted the story so many years later, she couldn't help but worry that she was mixing up the memory of that day with dreams she'd gone on to have.

Did she really call from the top of the stairs, What do you want?

Did the stranger answer, Bonjour, mademoiselle, and then ask, Is this your dog?

He was an old man, she recalled, with gray, wrinkled skin like a newborn mouse and tufts of white hair poking out from beneath his fedora. When she noticed that his bow tie was crooked, she had to clamp her lips closed to keep from laughing aloud.

I said, What do you want?

I am looking for Madame de Potter . . . your grandmama, I assume.

She's dead.

She . . . ?

She's buried in the cemetery behind St. John's.

And Victor?

She was offended to hear him speak of her father. If he'd

known him, he should have known that he had died of pneumonia five years earlier.

He's there, too. Go see for yourself.

From that point, she said, she had no doubt about what happened next. The man raised his cane as if preparing to plant it in a new position and rebalance himself, but the dog took the gesture as a sign that the stranger was preparing to attack. Baring his teeth, General Grant chomped at the air and started barking in a murderous rage.

That's all: an old man came to the Ridge one day looking for Grammy and Dad, and he went away when the Donnerlys' dog started barking. He certainly wouldn't be returning anytime soon. See, look at her, she was perfectly fine!

When she reached the bottom of the stairs, she opened the door wider, and the dog rushed out. Mr. Donnerly came hurrying across the side yard from his cottage, still dressed in his pajamas from his afternoon nap. From the safety of the porch, the dog barked furiously as the stranger, whoever he was, climbed into the backseat and the getaway car disappeared down the street.

At first she agreed with Mr. Donnerly's theory that the old man must have belonged to a gang responsible for recent burglaries in the area, and he'd been sent to case the house. But by the next day she would insist that he'd seemed harmless, and she hadn't been scared at all. Many years later, when she was a gray-haired woman with a grown daughter of her own and the two of them had opened the old steamer trunk in her basement to see what it contained, she would tell the whole story and then, at the end, offer another possibility: perhaps the stranger had been her grandfather. Oh, sure, it was hardly likely, she'd say as they looked inside the trunk. Still, she couldn't help but wonder. Wasn't it too bad that the dog had scared him away before she could ask him his name.

Acknowledgments

A story titled "De Potter's Grand Tour Around the World" appeared in *Conjunctions*, Volume 56 (Spring 2011). It is not included in the final version of *De Potter's Grand Tour*. A section from this novel appeared in *Conjunctions*, Volume 60 (Spring 2013), under the title "A Collector's Beginning."

I'd like to thank the following people who helped make this book possible: My mother, who gave me the key to the gilt cabinet when I was a young girl, thus igniting my interest in the dusty treasures left behind by lost stories; the librarians in Rochester, Brooklyn, and Philadelphia, and Nicolas de Potter of Belgium, who helped me ferret out revealing clues from the muddle of history; Lisa Wright at the University of Rochester, John Knight at Farrar, Straus and Giroux, and Steve Boldt, who helped put my words and pictures into print; Aimee Lykes, in memory, and Heather Partis, who gave me access to material on their side of the family; my agent, Geri Thoma, who brought me into the warmth of her office when I was twenty-two and has been giving me shelter ever since; my editor, Ileene Smith, who worked tirelessly to make this book stronger; my colleagues Kenneth Gross, Jennifer Grotz, and Stephen Schottenfeld, who, with their work and probing conversations, spark ideas; my friends and fellow artists—Maureen Howard, Mark Probst, Steve Erickson, Lori Precious, and Louise Glück—who helped me find my way through a labyrinth that at times threatened to defeat me; my daughters, Kathryn and Alice, who are my inspiration; and James Longenbach, who keeps me marveling as we travel together on this grand tour through life.